OF DARKNESS DROWNING

ASHES OF EDEN BOOK #2

HEATHER L REID

OF DARKNESS DROWNING:
Book One of the Ashes of Eden Series
Previously titled PRETTY DARK SACRIFICE
Copyright © 2014 by Heather L. Reid

All rights reserved. This book or any portion thereof may not be reproduced or used in any manner whatsoever without the express written permission of the author except for the use of brief quotations in a book review.

Second Revised Edition
Published by Snowy Wings Publishing
Turner, Oregon
www.snowywingspublishing.com

ISBN: 978-1-948661-01-0

This book is a work of fiction. Names, character, businesses, brands, places, events, and incidents are either the products of the author's imagination or used in a fictitious manner. Any resemblance to actual persons, living or dead, or actual events is purely coincidental.

Edited by Courtney Koshel
Cover Design by Cammie Larson

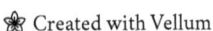 Created with Vellum

For Olivia

"Someone I loved
once gave me a box full of darkness.
It took me years to understand
that this, too, was a gift."
-The Uses of Sorrow by Mary Oliver

1

*F*lorescent lights flickered above Quinn, casting an eerie green tint on the stark white of the hospital room. A large square window next to an open door revealed the deserted corridor outside, but it wouldn't be deserted for long. Where she went, the demons followed. Already, they invaded the ever-widening cracks in her mental barrier. She could feel their insidious claws digging into her memories, searching out her pain.

A door slammed and echoed down the long hallway. Quinn held her breath. Footsteps, attached to a pair of Doc Martens with yellow stitching, grew closer and with them, the distinct smell of earth and sunshine.

She pushed back the scratchy blue blanket and wrapped her hand around the cold metal of her IV pole. Stiffness seized her muscles, bandages seized her skin, but she pulled herself up onto her unsteady bare feet. A bag of clear liquid swung above her head, pumping her body with the memory of fluids absorbed months ago.

"Aaron?"

A halo of light illuminated dark hair and a shallow

dimpled cheek as he leaned against the doorframe. It didn't matter how many times she'd dreamed this very moment, her heart still leapt. He was the light in her darkness, her safe haven.

Yet something was off.

Gray clouds rolled outward and choked the narrow corridor. Behind Aaron, a storm gathered, and with it, old remnants of fear twisted in Quinn's gut.

"Hurry. They're coming," she said, grabbing his wrist to tug him forward. Once they were both inside, she slammed the door and engaged the lock.

Aaron's green eyes danced in the moonlit rays that shone through the window overlooking the hospital garden, and she searched them in hopes of sparking a link to him, to give her a clue as to what happened to him after the storm. Of course, it wasn't really him. No spark of life, of connection, bonded her to the image in this dream. Not like the one she'd had the night after she'd been pulled from the water.

Five weeks ago, as she lay half-conscious on the muddy banks of Bluebonnet Creek, she'd felt his fear, his panic like a rising tide, if only briefly, and then everything had gone dark. Now he was nothing but an echo she chased each time she closed her eyes.

"I'm sorry. So sorry," Quinn whispered.

His shadow didn't tell her it was okay because it wasn't. Nothing would ever be okay again. Tears welled up when he drew her to him. She tried to remind herself this was nothing but a demon trick, but when his hand cupped her cheek, so real, she couldn't help herself. As always, she let the ghost of his lips find hers. Lines between dream and reality blurred as she clung to him, hands in his hair, skin on fire, and she let herself loose control, to fall into the fantasy. This was almost worth the pain that would follow, worth the risk of trying to find him night after night. This memory of his face, of his lips on hers, this moment together—it was her bliss and her penance.

Goose bumps rose where Aaron's fingers brushed her spine. She gasped as he undid the knots that held the thin cotton gown to her body and, in turn, ran her hands under his T-shirt and up his torso. Releasing her, he raised his arms and let her strip the shirt from his chest, throwing it to the floor in a wrinkled ball.

Quinn swallowed. Thick scars wound up his forearms. Tears rolled down her cheeks. This was the Aaron forever etched on her heart—beautiful, broken.

The long silver door handle turned slowly to the right, then rattled, angry, hungry. *Let us in.* A light knock grew to an angry banging. The demons' desire to suckle at the darkness living within her constantly gnawed at her soul. She had enough guilt and regrets inside to feed an army of evil, and they could smell it.

Taking his right hand in her left, Quinn slowly traced the map of his past pain upward from his wrist to just below his elbow with a finger. Pain and guilt ripped through her gut. Despair choked her lungs, squeezed her heart.

A web of fog formed over the glass partition that separated her room from the hall. Gray smoke seeped through the cracks in the door, pushed through the fissures forming on the glass as the demons ate away the last of her tattered defensive barrier and breached her mind. Hungry little leeches waiting to magnify her misery and feed on her pain.

Look what you've done to him.

She listened to the cold whispers of their influence. They seized on her thoughts, her fears, and amplified them tenfold. They loved to torture her while she slept, and a sick part of her relished the darkness they brought. *You can take whatever you want from me,* she thought, *as long as I get to see him.*

Beneath her touch, Aaron's old scars turned to rough scabs, as if fresh instead of healed only moments before. Something writhed beneath his puckered skin, and he scratched at the tainted lesions, green eyes wide. Thick, black water oozed from the edge of Aaron's wounds. He shuddered, face twisting in pain.

"Tell me where he is!" Quinn lifted her chin and screamed at the air in defiance. "What did you do with him?"

Laughter of a thousand demons echoed through her mind. *You think you have a greater purpose. You don't. You're not a savior.* She pressed her hands against her ears, but nothing could keep them out, they were inside her head, they were in control now. *You know exactly where he is because you put him there. Look at him, Quinn.*

Tossing his head back, Aaron let out a guttural scream.

Pop, pop, pop.

His scars split at the seams. Brown, brackish water leaked from his open wounds, wept down his forearms, and off the ends of his fingers. The drips grew in size and speed and bounced against the cold floor, as did her tears. Pinpricks of inky liquid pushed through every pore. Quinn gagged at the smell, all rotting flesh and soured silt as the rivulets ate through him to dissolve the soft tissue from his muscles and bones.

Your fault.

"Your fault," he parroted in the demon's voice. The words gurgled from his mouth, rough and accusing. She deserved it, every hurtful word.

Aaron's intense eyes fixed on hers. Tears formed in their corners, turning his irises muddy brown, and then to a black so deep she could see her reflection.

"I loved you," he croaked and reached for her, rotting fingers grasping at her gown, mire oozing down his chin. Sludge burst from his mouth and from where his eyes used to be, soaking her hair, drenching her gown in foul filth as he liquefied in front of her.

Quinn knelt in front of the dark puddle in the middle of the floor. Aaron was gone. Nothing but a stain on her heart remained. Despair crushed the air from her lungs, and a pit of hopelessness opened inside like a gaping wound that would never heal.

"Aaron!"

Quinn threw back her head and screamed so loud the walls quaked in the wake of her anguish, and the foundation rocked beneath her anger.

2

From his palms to the soles of his feet, Aaron's skin burned as if dipped in molten lava. Face down, he moaned in agony. His consciousness floated in a sea of boiling blood, fever liquefying him from the inside out. Soon he would be nothing but a puddle, a dark red stain for someone to mop up. Would they use one of those spongy things with the blue head that you squeezed between two rollers to clean him up? Or would they go for the white, ropy kind that looked like an alien octopus? A laugh bubbled in his brain but never made it to his lips. Would they use water to wash him away?

Water?

His thoughts frowned. Water seemed important. He had to get out of the water, make it back to shore.

His thoughts laughed again. He was too hot to be in water. He was on fire, and fire can't survive in water. More likely he had fallen asleep in a volcano or was shoved into the oven by some evil children like the witch in Hansel and Gretel. Was he a witch in a gingerbread house like in some fairy tale? Gingerbread, his stomach rumbled.

Beneath him, he barely noticed the rough stone floor cooling his naked body. He'd never felt so weak, so empty. His insides were a melted mess, his skin a thin layer of plastic barely holding them back. Without his skin holding it all in, he would be a pond, a lake, a river.

River. Water.

If only his skin would release the raging fire and flood within, he would drink and drink and drink until there was nothing left. Nothing. Not one drop.

So thirsty.

"Shhhh." Moisture trickled into his mouth, and he stuck out his tongue to catch each drop. A cool hand stroked his cheek, nurturing, loving. His body relaxed, the water reviving a tiny piece of his sanity.

There was something important he needed to do. A girl with blond hair, he had to protect her, to warn her. Who was she? Warn her about what?

Aaron!

A hot poker lanced through the back of his skull, a fire of his psychic gifts in the back of his brain.

Tell me where he is!

Quinn. Her name thrummed through Aaron. A slim thread connected them. A familiar magnetic pull yanked him as she reached out with her mind. The river, he had jumped in to save her. Panic filled him. He had to get back to her, save himself, but his body had no fight left.

"Sleep now, and forget about her," a woman's voice cooed. His mother's maybe, its soft, familiar cadence lulling him like a drug. Gentle fingers ran through his hair. "You must forget to remember."

Quinn's energy ebbed, and he felt her moving farther away, her voice in his mind growing fainter. As quickly as it came, his shimmer of clarity faded, the girl with the blond hair nothing but a ghost in his unconscious.

"Shhhh. That's right."

His breath slowed along with his heartbeat, and within seconds, he found himself in a raging river. Relentless tides dragged at his limbs, forcing him down, down, down beneath the surface. He fought his body's need to breathe as pressure squeezed against his chest, a thousand ropes pulling tighter and tighter. The more he struggled, the tighter the ropes pulled. Left, right, down, up? No matter which way he turned, nothing but brackish water surrounded him. Ate his strength. Crushed his resistance. Then the currents dragged him deeper.

As Aaron slipped farther and farther beneath the inky waves, a girl's hand appeared. Small and pale, it reached out to him. Tendrils of red hair glowed in a shaft of moonlight, floating like a luminescent halo around her smooth, heart-shaped face. Ruth. She was the only bright spot in the rolling dark. Fitting that his baby sister would come to take him home. They should have drowned together long ago. Fate had finally gotten around to correcting its mistake.

Ruth smiled, suspended above him like a water angel.

He smiled and tried to take her hand, but it remained just out of reach.

The box. What did you do with it?

What box? What was she talking about?

I need it. Please, it's important. Aaron frowned. Something wasn't right. Ruth's lips spoke with someone else's voice. The vision of her rippled, red hair turned to black, green eyes to silver. Ruth but not Ruth.

Aaron felt a tug at his leg and looked down to see a swirling vortex open beneath him. The current sucked at his limbs, trapping him in its grip as Ruth floated away, her face twisting in anger before disappearing all together.

A maniacal laugh bubbled to Aaron's lips. *You're dying. Can't you feel it? Your organs are shutting down, your neurotrans-*

mitters going on the blink as your brain turns off. Soon there won't be anything left of you but a lifeless body. Aaron's mind laughed at him again. *You're literally circling the drain, dude.*

No use fighting anymore, Ruth was gone, and he was alone. Sinking, sinking, sinking, his heart a weight dragging him into an abyss of hopelessness. Hope was nothing more than a lie. Ruth couldn't save him. Nobody could. He was already dead.

3

"Quinn! Wake up!" Azrael's stern voice pierced through the dream, his face swimming before her as the nightmare faded. She was home, safe in her own bed, her two-week recovery in the hospital nothing but an extracted memory used to torture her. The sulfurous fragrance of dead demon permeated the room, clung to her hair and pajamas. Azrael's handy work, no doubt. He had dispatched the demons feeding off her while she slept. No matter, there were plenty more where they came from.

"Quinn." Light spilled across her bedroom floor. Her Sentinel burned brighter than any sun, and she wished she could turn him off. "How many times must I tell you? Keep your shield up at all times, even when you sleep." Azrael's steely tone matched the look on his face. If frowns could kill, she would be dead.

A curved, runed sword hung on each hip—one blade etched with electric blue symbols, the Qeres blade, poison to any immortal soul; the other etched by golden sun, a blade with the power to separate an essence from a mortal body. Black leather vambraces protected his forearms and a red sash adorned the waist of his loose-fitting pants, carefully tucked into a pair of knee-high, black combat boots. "It is a dangerous game you play, Quinn, and I am not always around to clean up your messes."

"Go away, Azrael." She pulled the covers over her head. "I command you."

Muscles tensed as the mattress squeaked beneath the weight of her guardian angel.

"Why are you still here? I commanded you to leave. You said my powers would compel you to obey."

Azrael pulled the duvet from her face and sighed. Quinn still didn't understand how an ethereal being, which moved between dimensions and was invisible to everyone but her, could interact with everyday objects.

"Your power does not lie within a word itself. Words are like the wind, ever changing and unpredictable." Quinn rolled her eyes with the start of yet another of Azrael's lectures. "It stems from the core of your essence, from your thought. Be clear and true in your intent and confident in your execution. It must be felt as well as spoken. Know what you want and command it to happen."

"I really wanted you to leave, believe me."

Azrael shrugged. "You will get the hang of it soon, I'm sure."

"Soon? You said I would have all this power when I turned eighteen, that I would be able to banish them or whatever. That was weeks ago, and I can barely block them, let alone kill them. Teach me. Show me what to do."

"It is your gift, not mine. Only you know how to use it."

Azrael claimed she was the reincarnation of Eve, Keeper of the Garden of Eden, born to be some sort of savior and restore the balance of good and evil in the human realm. But how could she be expected to save humanity when her own life was such a mess? Or maybe she wasn't really the essence of Eve. Maybe Azrael made a mistake.

"Eve's blood does indeed flow through you. No mistake."

"I told you to stay out of my thoughts." Quinn loathed the idea of Azrael tapping into every secret tucked away inside her.

"That's rather hard to do when your mind is nothing but chaos, and your thoughts are spewing out like bits of shrapnel, hitting anyone passing by. You lack focus, even after all these weeks. Even now, the demons confuse and distract you with thoughts of that boy."

"Aaron. His name is Aaron." Quinn stared at her hands.

Azrael's voice softened. "It was Aaron's destiny to die as it is yours to live. Nothing could have changed that path. It was chosen with every minute decision you both made throughout the span of your lifetimes, as was mine. It would be easier to untangle a million knots soaked in glue than to try to change your fate. Don't throw away Aaron's sacrifice by playing Russian roulette with those beasts. They do not hold the answers you seek."

"Then who does? You?"

Azrael crossed his arms over his chest. "You know the answer as well as I. He is gone. The sooner you accept it, the sooner you can fulfil your duty."

"He's missing, not dead," Quinn mumbled.

Azrael shook his head but didn't argue. She was sick of all this talk of duty. Why wouldn't he leave her alone?

"Because my job is to protect and guide you." He gripped the pommels of his swords, muscles rippling beneath flawless flesh.

Annoying as his personality was, he was glorious to behold. A fire burned beneath his olive skin and behind his marbled, amber eyes. Dark hair hung around his face, framing a square jaw and perfectly symmetrical features. It didn't matter how often she'd seen him standing before her, his ageless beauty went beyond human words, awe forcing her jaw to her chin. Although she guessed he was thousands of years old, his looks were deceiving. Except for the onyx wings that spilled from his back to brush the floor, in a modern outfit, he could have passed for another high school student.

"Darkness approaches, and my task is to prepare you for battle. Your task is to let me. I can't do that when you're letting yourself get eaten up by guilt. Now, stop sulking and get out of bed. You must be able to guard yourself and not rely on me for everything."

Goose bumps rose on her arms as the chilled air met bare flesh. Quinn glared at Azrael, who held the duvet in his fist.

"I'm tired." She crossed her arms and pushed her lip out.

"All the better. Demons don't care if you're tired." He took a step back and drew a sword with his free hand. "They eat tired for lunch. Even now, I see at least a dozen holes in your barrier." He flourished the golden blade. "Have you learned nothing?"

"Perhaps there is a problem with your teaching methods." She snatched at the duvet, but Azrael was quicker.

A blur of black wings and golden light flashed past her as Azrael darted to the far corner and took his battle stance. "I assure you my teaching methods are sound. It's your attitude that's the problem." With his other hand, he dangled the duvet in challenge. "You want it? Come and get it." Dropping the cover to the ground, he unsheathed the other sword hanging from his right hip. The markings etched on its metal blazed as it cleared the scabbard. A whirlwind of blue and gold flared as Azrael advanced, swords twisting and spinning in a bright flourish around him.

Quinn scrambled away until her back pressed against the headboard. Azrael slashed the golden blade down across her shoulder. Sweat beaded on her forehead as she threw an invisible barrier up with her mind, deflecting the attack, but not before the sword's tip grazed the fabric of her T-shirt, ripping a small hole in the sleeve. Her favorite Skipping Zombies band T-shirt, ruined.

"Hey! You could have cut me!"

"But I didn't."

The barrier of light surrounding her quivered as Azrael's essence bumped against her protective wall, testing, looking for a way in.

"You must not hesitate. Once they breach your protective barrier, it will crumble and leave you defenseless." The pressure grew as he pushed harder, his intent clear. Her palms were slick with sweat as she resisted, willing him, commanding him to stay out of her thoughts. The sound of her ragged breath overtook her rapid heartbeat. He was strong, but she was determined.

"Better." The pressure eased, and he grinned. "You must be strong of mind. That is the most important." He circled the bed, one sword poised above his head, the other in front of his chest in a defensive posture. "Add that to a strong body, and you'll be twice as deadly."

Lunging forward, he slashed low at her leg. Quinn jumped from the bed and rolled out of his reach and crouched behind him. Years of cheerleading were coming in handy. Azrael turned for another attack, but Quinn was ready.

Focusing all her energy into the command, she directed it in the form of a telepathic dart straight at Azrael. He stopped, left arm frozen above his head, swords poised to strike. She sensed his resistance as he fought against her command. His whole body vibrated with frustration, but he couldn't break free.

Azrael's chest heaved as he pushed against her control

one last time. She held firm, and finally, sensing his compliance, released him. The lighted blades dimmed as he slammed them back into their scabbards. "It seems you've been practicing."

"Don't look so annoyed." Quinn smiled wryly.

"I am not annoyed. I am surprised." Azrael smiled back at her, and she thought she saw pride behind his eyes. "I still say you're too lazy when it comes to your defenses."

Quinn's phone vibrated somewhere beneath the pile of bedding on the floor. She pressed a finger to her lips to shush her Sentinel. An amused look played across Azrael's face. He was so real to her that she sometimes forgot nobody else could hear or see him.

Rolling her eyes, she dug for the phone. It buzzed again, urgent and angry as a hive of bees. Reese's name flashed across the screen.

"Hey," Quinn answered.

"Hey. Sorry, I know it's early. Did I wake you?"

Quinn looked at Azrael. "No, not really."

"My dad just got home. He's been over at the Colliers' most of the night." Reese's voice was thick and hollow on the other end.

Quinn held her breath and chewed on her thumbnail, afraid to ask. "Did they find something?"

Azrael shook his head and crossed his arms over his chest, as if he knew what Reese was about to say. Quinn glared at him, pointed to the ceiling, and mouthed the word "go," her intent perfectly clear. Azrael bowed low. His dark wings filled the room as he launched into the air and ghosted through the roof of her bedroom.

"I don't know how to tell you this." Reese went silent, and she could hear her swallowing on the other end.

"Just say it." Quinn's heart sank.

"They're calling it off."

Another round of silence.

"Did you hear me, Quinn?"

Quinn nodded to the phone in response. Her voice had drifted away, and she wasn't sure how to retrieve it. Quinn stared at the map of Westland pinned to her closet door. Bluebonnet Creek ran through the center. A grid separated the map into tiny squares, and red X's marked the spots that had already been searched. She ripped the map from the wall, wadded it into a ball, and squeezed, her fist tightening around the paper like Reese's words had squeezed her heart.

"Volunteers finished searching late yesterday." Reese sighed. "There's nothing left to do. They're going to drag the river one last time this afternoon."

Quinn's hands shook, while Reese sounded miles away. Five weeks, two days, eight hours. The only proof he might still be out there was a fading dream, and the echo of an electric connection that no longer existed. Nobody else truly believed he might still be alive.

Quinn pressed her fists to her eyes to stop the flow of tears. Hollowness seeped into her.

"I want to watch them," she blurted.

"Watch what?"

"Them drag." All anyone was likely to find was the bloated, white flesh of a boy she used to know, but her heart couldn't let it go. Not yet. If Aaron was dead, why did she have such a gnawing feeling that he needed her?

"I don't think..."

"For closure. What time are they starting?" Quinn tucked the phone between her shoulder and cheek and grabbed a pair of yoga pants from the pile of clean clothes stacked on her dresser.

Reese sighed deep and long before replying. "Sometime around noon."

"Okay. That gives me time to get to the gym before I swing by and pick you up."

"What? No. You need to go to school. With me. You remember school, don't you? That place where all your friends go every day? Come with me, and we'll go together after."

It was the same thing every day. Reese insisted she come back to school, and Quinn refused. Guilt stabbed at her gut, but she couldn't face the crowded halls and sidelong looks, not yet. "I'm not ready."

"Yeah. That's what I thought." Reese hung up before Quinn could even inhale for a response. *Crap.* Alienating everyone she loved and making things worse, that was Quinn's true gift. A few minutes ago, she had wanted nothing more than to be alone, to think through everything that had happened, but now all she wanted was her best friend. Angry tears slid down her cheeks. If she could have punched herself in the face, she would.

You can't have it both ways, Quinn.

QUINN: I'M SORRY.

Her fingers typed and hovered over the Send button. Two words never looked so hollow, so inadequate. Each letter disappeared with the press of the back button.

QUINN: I KNOW, I SUCK. I'LL TRY TO SUCK LESS, I PROMISE. PLEASE MEET ME THERE AT FOUR. I CAN'T DO THIS WITHOUT YOU.

Send.

4

Quinn wiped sweat from her brow, hung the jump rope back on the hook, and dropped to the floor. "Eye of the Tiger" blared from the gym speakers as she counted off a hundred push-ups. She loved how quiet the gym was between the pre-work crowd and those who spent their lunch hour on the long line of treadmills. Nobody to stare at her or to whisper and point at the one who'd caused Aaron Collier to jump in to save her only to lose his own life. The whole town praised Marcus and Aaron as heroes and looked at her with downcast eyes. What do you say to the girl whose death was traded for another's?

Rolling on her back, she crunched her way through her usual twenty-minute ab workout. Preparing for the final part of her torture, an hour of kickboxing, she pulled a pair of gloves over her hands and faced her target. The heavy bag, covered in red vinyl, hung from a chain in the ceiling. Here it was just her, her grief, and the waiting shadows. That's the way she liked it.

Gritting her teeth, she dropped her protective barrier and slammed a fist into the bag, basking in the pain.

Aaron kissing her beneath the stars.

Two more jabs in quick succession.

The look on his face when he found her with Jeff.

Another hard roundhouse left her ankle aching and probably bruised. *Good.*

Singing songs he'd written just for her.

Left hook.

Something moved in the corner of the gym, and the temperature dropped.

Right cross.

Regret and anger drew the demons out of hiding like mosquitoes looking for blood. Their dark essences reminded her of the moment before a storm, electric and dangerous.

Jab, jab, jab.

Tendrils of familiar fog coiled around the bag, swathing it in thick, gray strands. A side kick with the heel of her foot sent the heavy bag swinging in a wide arch, the smoke twisting and writing around it like a web struck by a broom.

Three dark shapes inched closer, materializing from the dissipating fog. Six pairs of orange eyes glowed in their small, feline-like bodies. Saliva dripped from their fangs; air rushed around their wings. *Let them come*, she thought, not even trying to keep them out.

Quinn dodged to the right and came at the bag from behind, landing another hard blow with her fist.

Killer. One demon materialized on her shoulder and hissed against her ear; its sulphur-laced breath so strong she gagged. It understood her secret, her shame. With it, she didn't need to hide.

Azrael would not approve. How long would it take before their bond alerted him to her danger? One minute? Ten? He'd been called away on some secret mission to the angelic city of Arcadia, and she'd promised to lay low. If he even got a whiff of what she was up to, he would drop everything and return to her side.

One monster dug its claws into the red vinyl and hung upside-down, its forked tongue licked at the air to slurp at the negative emotion pouring from her.

Screw Azrael. This was her life, her powers. She could use them any way she wanted. Quinn aimed a right cross for the center of its body, but the demon blinked out before she made contact.

Another beast flew in.

That's right, you bastards. Come on. Anger, regret, shame, she gave it all to them as they crawled inside her mind and magnified the bleakness living inside.

Left hook.

It disappeared in a puff of smoke before she could hit it.

So guilty. So much pain. We want it all. Give us more.

Two more roundhouse kicks, an uppercut, four jabs.

Another echo of laughter.

You never loved him.

Quinn slammed another fist into the bag. That was a lie. She had loved him, enough to let him go, to keep him from the demons, from her crazy.

You were a coward. You took the easy road and look where that led.

The demons blinked and spiraled around the heavy bag, leaving long trails of gray wisps behind them. Each dodging her blows, magnifying her frustrations, and growing fat from her pain. Hungry, so hungry. They would never get enough.

He's dead, and you're alive. It should have been you at the bottom of that river. If it weren't for you, if you hadn't jumped, he wouldn't have been in the water that night. You should have died, yet you live, and he's gone.

All three converged in the center of her line of sight, a dark triangle of evil hanging in mid-air. Demons like these had urged her into the water, pecked at her hands, and forced her under the waves. They had pushed her into Jeff's arms, made her believe that letting Aaron go would keep him safe, that choosing Jeff would make them go away. If she had listened to her heart instead of their lies, if she had been stronger, maybe Aaron would still be here. Azrael was right; they didn't have any answers. She was guilty, but so were they, and she would make them pay.

Quinn pulled her arm back and slammed her fist through them. It hit the bag with a sickening crunch. Pain flooded her hand. The demons laughed and danced while Quinn gritted her teeth and ignored the numbness spreading down her fingers. Right cross, front kick, side, kick, dodge left, punch left. Her breaths grew ragged, the room swam, but she kept lashing out, pouring her whole self into more punishing blows. The demons dodged and weaved between impacts, gorging on her frustrations. Sweat dripped into her eyes; she wiped it away with a gloved hand.

"Hey, Blondie, I think that bag has had enough punishment for today." Two strong hands attached to a Mr. Tall, Dark, and Annoying grabbed the bag and stopped it swinging. She'd seen him before at the reception desk, cleaning equipment, and occasionally training a girl with short brown hair whose outfits got skimpier every workout.

"I'll say when it's had enough. And don't call me 'Blondie.'" Quinn tried to ignore him and took another swing, landing one just shy of one of his fingers.

"Well, you are blond, aren't you, Blondie? Or is that from a bottle?"

The demons laughed. If they thought this creep was funny, she didn't. She lashed out at a demon hovering over the Everlast logo embossed on the red vinyl, but as always, it was too quick. Not that her fist could do any real damage to dark spirits from the Underworld. They weren't even corporeal. But it felt good to try, to kick the crap out of something.

"That was seriously poor form."

Quinn's jaw tightened, and a ball of fury burned in her belly. If this guy wasn't careful, she might "accidentally" miss the target and sweep his leg instead.

"Your hips are out of line, and your stance is all wrong." Mr. Arrogant circled her, studying her every move. His toffee-colored eyes raked across her body, and she suddenly wished she'd worn more than just yoga pants and a sports bra.

"Nobody asked you." Quinn glanced at the nametag attached to the almost-too-tight red 4 Ever Fit T-shirt. Caleb. Well, she would be sure to complain about Caleb's rudeness to the manager.

"I could show you some moves, if you want. If you're going to keep skipping school to come here and punish your body, you should at least do it correctly. I won't even charge you. What do you say, Blondie?"

"No thanks, I don't need any help from a meathead who didn't get good enough grades to go to college." Quinn glared at him. "Besides, don't you have some stay-at-home-mom to whip into shape?"

"Looks like your bark is just as fierce as your bite. Just so happens those stay-at-home moms are paying for my biochemistry degree. Some of us don't have rich parents who let us skip school to sulk every day."

"You don't know anything about me." Sick of the demon game, she pictured a bubble of light surrounding her, cutting them off from their meal. They hissed and backed into the corner, and Quinn smiled. She was in full control.

"Despite my meathead status, I read quite well. And even if I didn't, you look exactly like your picture, Quinn."

"I think I preferred it when you called me 'Blondie.'" She

turned away, yanked a glove from her hand, and winced. Her knuckles had split. Blood dripped from the tips of her fingers.

"That's what happens when you don't wrap your hands before you start wailing. Plus, those gloves are too thin for heavy bag work."

"It's fine. Just a little cut."

"It will get infected if you aren't careful."

"What's it to you?"

"Just trying to do my job. How can we continue to take your money if you injure yourself and cancel your membership?" Caleb pulled a small tube from the pocket of his sweatpants and threw it at her. "Use this at least."

Quinn mumbled her thanks and made her escape to the locker room.

"What was that?" Caleb called to her before she opened the door.

"Thank you, Meathead," she replied over her shoulder, putting all the sarcasm she could behind her words.

"You're welcome, Blondie."

The heavy wooden door to the women's changing room swung closed. Leaning against the wall, she rolled the tube of antibacterial ointment between her fingers then tossed it into the trash.

Quinn half-smiled and nodded at the dark-haired woman changing into tight-fitting spandex shorts and made her way to her locker to retrieve her towel. Caleb's next victim. Good luck to her.

Quinn checked her phone. Still no reply from Reese. Her best friend would be sitting in homeroom right now, probably flirting with Marcus and sharing the latest gossip with Ami. A pang of jealousy pinched at her heart. If only it were that easy for her to go back to being normal. What was normal? She couldn't remember.

Quinn wrapped the white cotton towel tight around her chest, tucking one end snugly against the other to hold it in place, and slipped on her flip-flops. No matter how clean the gym might look, who knew what kind of fungus lurked on the wet floor. Water dripped in the empty shower stall. She reached in, set the handle midway between hot and cold, and waited for it to warm up.

"What do you think you're doing?"

Quinn jumped and whirled around.

"You can't be in here," she hissed and pulled her towel tighter around her. Drops of red dotted the edge, evidence of her injured hand. She looked at the ground and tried to hide it behind her back.

Azrael leaned against the tiled wall, eyes burning with unexpressed accusation. "Naked human flesh means nothing to me. Go about your business."

"I need my privacy."

The dark-haired woman glanced at her, oblivious to Azrael. Quinn smiled and turned the shower to full stream. The woman grabbed her water bottle, raised an eyebrow at Quinn, and left.

"You have now lost your privacy privileges." Azrael wrenched her wrist from behind her back and pulled her split knuckles to the light. Blood dripped onto the tiled floor, and he shook his head. Quinn squirmed but couldn't escape his grasp. His touch burned like too-hot tea spilled over flesh.

"I can command you away." It was an empty threat. All the fight had already drained out of her and been replaced with a light-headed wooziness that pushed her off-balance.

"You could." Azrael's voice soothed her, all low dulcet tones and soft coos, and her hand relaxed in his. "This is my fault. I have been too soft on you, cleaning up your mess for weeks now and not allowing you to suffer the consequences."

Azrael didn't need to explain what the demons could do; she had experienced it first-hand. Besides, she could handle them, cut them off anytime she wanted. Azrael caught her gaze, and his look told her that her thoughts were not her own.

"This is not just about you. Those demons you let feed on you—they're dead by my sword. If they had been allowed to live, they would have gone on to create more chaos and darkness, perhaps with an unloved and broken vagrant on the street or one of your beloved friends, Reese or Marcus. No one is immune."

Quinn broke eye contact and looked at her feet, and Azrael went back to inspecting her injuries.

"This is bigger than you. Stop being selfish. Now, I need you to take a deep breath, Quinn. No healing comes without pain."

Pulses of hot electricity coursed up her fingers, between her muscles, soaking through her bones. The bruise on her ankle turned purple, black, green, and then faded all together.

Every ache deepened and throbbed like a bitch, and she wanted to cry out, but before she could, her muscles relaxed. Pain replaced by a warm tingle.

"This one will be the worst. You have a small fracture in your finger."

Quinn bit her lip and pushed back a sob. She refused to let him know how much it hurt. Fire, the cracking of bone, and pain so intense she thought she might vomit. And then it was over, the skin over her knuckles weaved back together, leaving nothing but a smear of blood across clean skin and a light scar.

"Thank you." Quinn flexed her fist.

"You should take up that trainer's offer to help you. He is right. Your form is erroneous."

"Who, Meathead? No way!"

"I do not want to spend every day treating self-inflicted wounds. You want to punish your body, take your anger out on that bag hanging from a chain, fine, but you will learn to do it properly."

"Whatever." Quinn folded her arms over her chest and glared at Azrael. "Can I take my shower now?"

Azrael nodded and turned his back.

Quinn pulled the curtain closed and waited for him to leave. He didn't.

"Really? You're going to stand there the whole time?" Nothing but a thin sheet of plastic separated her from her Sentinel.

"You have privacy. I cannot see you."

Quinn stomped a foot in protest, turned the water up as hot as it would go, and let it pour over her head and down her body.

"You may be able to cut them off, but once they have drained you, taken all the misery you have to give, then what?"

Quinn rolled her eyes, a captive audience to more lectures.

"It comes back, does it not? The emotions, darker and deeper?"

Quinn paused, hand on her shampoo bottle.

"And the demons live to find another victim. The more pain and chaos they are allowed to create, the more demons can cross the veil. The more demons that cross the veil, the more chaos and darkness they exploit, and the weaker the veil between worlds becomes. It's a vicious cycle."

Quinn lathered and rinsed, hands yanking through the short tangles. Where was he going with all of this?

"Other humans can't see what's out there, but you can."

Ripping the towel from the hook, she covered herself up

and turned off the spray. When she yanked back the curtain, Azrael grinned at her. Did he have any idea how much she wanted to punch him?

"I'm sick of hiding."

"That's why I have, what do you humans call it—a belated birthday present for you." Azrael reached into his boot and pulled out a knife roughly eight inches long. Blue runes danced across the blade, reminiscent of Azrael's Qeres sword. "A dagger, actually, very rare and imbued with Qeres poison. I had to jump through a lot of hoops to get this for you."

So that's where he'd been all morning. Laying the blade across both his palms, he offered it to Quinn. She picked it up by the ornate hilt and spun in between her hands. It hummed in her touch, the runes burning bright. A wicked grin spread across her lips. A poisoned blade, deadly to immortal essences. Now she could kill them.

5

After two near-death experiences, Aaron thought he wouldn't fear the afterlife, but this time was different. Before, there was a tunnel of light, something tethering him to reality. Now, it was a tunnel of blackness. This time, nothing held him back as he spiralled down, down, down into oblivion, helpless and alone.

Days, months, minutes, years—time meant nothing as the swirling waters faded into a foggy cyclone. It tossed Aaron this way and that, like a limp towel in the spin cycle. This couldn't be all there was? To be lost in a dark void forever, alone, cut off from everyone and everything he ever loved.

"Why now?"

Nothing.

"Why is this time different?"

No one. No answer.

"Why?"

His voice didn't even echo. It was swallowed, choked off by the non-existent air. That was impossible. He needed air to breathe, to live. And that's when he noticed the stillness within his lungs.

OF DARKNESS DROWNING

Denial gave way to anger, and he kicked and screamed until his voice was ragged and torn. He didn't deserve this. Where was the light? His mom? Why had the image of Ruth abandoned him when he needed her most?

Because you abandoned her to the same fate, Aaron. You lived when she died in that river. It's only fitting that you would suffer the same way. Payback's a bitch.

No, that was madness talking. Ruth wasn't like that. His sister loved him. She wouldn't want him to suffer. It had been an accident, not his fault.

If only he could have one more chance. Josh needed him. Home, it was all he could think about. A warm bed, Josh and his dad arguing down the stairs, even the smell of whisky on his dad's breath, he would treasure it all.

There was no escape. Exhaustion dragged at his limbs. His soul and his body relaxed, accepting his fate, his death. Nothing left to do but succumb and hope it would all be over soon, that he would find peace at the end of this journey. Go with the flow, ever downward, ever darker.

After an immeasurable time, the funnel slowed, and he noticed spots of light within the swirling gray. Pictures flashed on the wall of the maelstrom. Is this what people meant when they said their life passed before their eyes? He expected to see Josh, his dad, but instead he saw a mirage of flashing images, doors opening to show him a brief glimpse of strange worlds beyond before closing again.

One held a million tiny bubbles with glowing fireflies blinking in and out. Another showed the image of a tree made entirely of white butterflies. Then came cities of glass, piles of bones in a desert wasteland, and fields of ice with wraiths dancing beneath a green moon. Some light, some dark, all strange and wondrous.

Next, the portal opened on a garden being swallowed by

darkness. Piercing screams tore through a swirling mist, and the smell of smoke and sulfur choked his lungs.

Sobs drew Aaron's attention. There, in the middle of the twisting fog, sat a girl. She wept, a box held tight in her hands as demons destroyed the beauty and serenity of her home. As her tears fell on the wood, a rainbow of phosphorescent runes etched themselves upon the box, fading seconds later. The writing seemed oddly familiar to Aaron, and his memory fumbled the puzzle of it over and over in his head, trying to find the answer to the curling shapes, but before he could decipher their meaning, the window slammed closed, and he was dragged down once again.

Still, he fell, the portals winking open and closed before him. When he stopped to float in front of a work of art, complete with an ornate gold frame, hope that his journey might be over surged through him.

A boy, similar to him with the same dark hair and green eyes, stood bare-chested in a field dotted with purple and white flowers. His face looked slightly more chiselled than Aaron's, and a bit older, too. His beauty stood out, unparalleled, complete with muscles, sword and a short red tunic. Instead of Aaron's pale white, the boy in the image had skin that glowed darker, as if the sun were trapped beneath the flesh. Unlike Aaron, his arms were blemish-free, no sign of his attempted suicide etched for the entire world to see. Aaron gasped as the boy in the image unfurled a set of golden-red wings that spread behind him in a twelve-foot span.

In the distance, an ivory tower sliced through the blood-orange horizon, its stained-glass windows casting three-hundred-sixty-degree rainbows across the landscape. Aaron's heart ached, and a longing he'd never felt before brought a tear to his eye. Deep down, he sensed this was his heaven, and he was ready to go. Finally, he would be home.

Are you here for me? Aaron asked the angel, reaching out a hand to see if he could step through the painting and join him in paradise. The angel nodded and reached back, but before they could touch, something sucked him farther down the vortex and away from the one place he wanted to be. Sorrow filled him. Despair and anger made their way through him like poison as the portal winked shut, and he found himself wrapped in darkness, spinning on and on with no end in sight.

6

*L*ate afternoon sunlight bleached Quinn's vision as the rays beat against piles of driftwood and debris that littered the shore of Bluebonnet Creek. She looked at her watch. Four thirty, and still no sign of Reese, no text, no phone call.

Clusters of small gnats rose from the boggy shore and swarmed Quinn's face. Waving them away, she shaded her eyes and picked her way through the piles of branches and cast-off stones until she reached the edge of a muddy cliff.

Two search and rescue boats rounded the bend, their engines chugging up the tributary from the Gulf. Grappling hooks attached to long chains dragged the bottom of the river behind them. Every few minutes a line would grow taught, and Quinn's stomach with it. The rational part of her wanted closure, for his body to be found, but her heart wanted to hang on to hope, and every time a car tire or a tree dangled from the end of one of those hooks instead of a body, she breathed a little sigh of relief.

A branch cracked beneath a footstep, and Quinn whirled

around to find Reese standing beside her, arms folded, lips turned into a frown. They didn't say anything for a long time. Both stared at the water bubbling past and watched with bated breath as the boats inspected every tiny pull on their hooks. Hard to believe this now-quiet stream had torn apart her life and changed her forever.

"You suck." Reese broke the silence first.

"I know."

"You don't deserve me."

"I know, but I'm glad you're here." Quinn took Reese's hand, and the thin layer of emotional ice that separated them started to melt.

"Have they found anything?" Reese asked.

Quinn shook her head. "But I know he's alive. Somewhere."

"I know you believe that, but he's not." Reese's words were weary, not cruel.

"Is having hope such a bad thing?"

"No, not when there's something to hope for, but Quinn, he's gone."

"If he's really dead, then why can't I shake this feeling?"

"Because you miss him, because you don't want it to be true." Reese leaned her head on Quinn's shoulder, and Quinn leaned her cheek against Reese's hair. It was the closest she'd felt to her best friend in months.

They stood like that until the sun dipped beneath the horizon, and the drag boats sped back down the river, hooks gathered high out of the water, empty.

Quinn held her breath at the buzz of Reese's phone. A rising tide of panic surged inside her. Reese chewed her bottom lip, her eyebrows knitting together. She looked up from the text and held Quinn's gaze. A single tear and a shake of the head was all it took for the dam inside to break.

Grabbing the phone from Reese, she read the message over and over. The words "officially presumed dead" pulsed in and out of focus with the beat of her heart.

"This can't be it." The trickle of tears grew to a flood. But this *was* it, the inevitable moment where everyone gave up and buried, if not his body, his memory, forever.

Reese placed a hand on her shoulder. "You knew the dragging was nothing more than a formality. It's officially over."

"Don't say that." Quinn's voice cracked. She couldn't stop herself. Everything inside her screamed that he was near. Any minute they would find him weak, hungry, shivering in a cave or a hole somewhere in the woods. "They can't give up yet, Reese." Quinn paced the shore. "What if he's washed up somewhere, starving, hurt? Something's not right. I can't explain it, but I have this feeling in my gut. Please, Reese, you have to make them keep searching. Your dad …"

"Has done everything he can, and more. It's not his fault Mother Nature decided to throw a hurricane at the Gulf a few days after the accident." Reese pushed her hands into the pockets of her jeans and kicked a loose stone. "All the flooding made it almost impossible to search right away. We all did the best we could under the circumstance." Reese's breath sounded strained. "His family already planned a memorial. At St. Angeles. Friday."

"Friday?" Quinn couldn't quite wrap her brain around it. "So, they already arranged it before they finished searching, while there was still hope?"

"Hope was lost weeks ago, Quinn, for everyone but you. Nobody could have survived out there for that long, Quinn."

"Wait. You knew? This whole time?" Nails dug into her palm; teeth ripped at her bottom lip. "And you didn't tell me?"

"You didn't want to hear it." Reese wouldn't meet her

eyes. "Aaron's gone. We need to move on. You need to move on. Please let him go." Reese pushed a strand of hair behind Quinn's ear. "I'm tired of being reminded of it day after day. I'm tired of grieving, aren't you?" Reese's tears mirrored her own. "I love you, but you have to let this go. Your obsession won't let any of us move on, to heal. The sadness is eating away at all of us, and I can't take it. We all have to face it. *You* have to face it. He's gone." Reese choked on the word "gone."

Aaron. Gone. Returning to a world where he didn't exist meant she would never be whole again. She wanted the chance to tell him the truth, to admit that the idea of loving him and him loving her back frightened her, that she was a coward.

The silence between them lasted an eternity. Reese looked frozen staring at her feet, jaw clenched.

"Please don't make this harder than it already is."

"What do you want me to say?" Quinn asked.

"I don't want you to *say* anything." Reese threw up her hands. Coal eyes full of hurt and love stared into Quinn's. Hands on her hips, Reese glared. "I want you to start acting normal again. Come back to school. Obsess about your SAT scores and what college we'll attend together. And stop chasing ghosts."

Quinn shrugged and picked imaginary lint from her shirt. "I need time to process."

Reese shook her head. "Yeah, you keep saying. The whole school misses you. I miss you." Reese touched her arm. "I want my best friend back. I want to be the friend you go to with every little secret, big and small. Remember when you used to trust me?"

Quinn stared at her hands, afraid to look her best friend, afraid her secret would explode from her lips with just one glance. She couldn't handle the look Reese would give her.

"I do trust you." Quinn rubbed the back of her neck.

"Do you? It feels as if the last few months have been nothing but secrets and lies."

Trusting Reese used to be so easy, before the demons invaded her life and changed the very core of her being. She was so far away from the popular, straight-A, carefree cheerleader she once was that she didn't even recognize herself anymore.

That Quinn drowned in the swirling flood, never to return. This new Quinn couldn't go back to normal. For good or ill, she'd accepted a destiny that would never quite fit in with Reese's future of frat parties and all-night cram sessions for finals. Quinn might not be able to live an ordinary life, but Reese could. If she brought her into this secret, that might change everything.

"You wouldn't understand." Twisting the edge of her shirt in her fist, she looked sideways at Reese. If Reese couldn't believe that Aaron was still alive, something that was plausible, how would she believe Quinn was the reincarnation of Eve sent to save the world? She barely believed it herself.

"Yeah? I'm so sick of you telling me I wouldn't understand. Try me."

"I have tried you. Aaron's not dead."

"Stop it." Reese's voice hit Quinn hard and heavy as a concrete brick to the head, cutting her off. "Just stop! You need to understand that he is not coming back." Her fists balled at her side. Tears coursed down her cheeks as she locked on Quinn. "I watched him die, not you, don't you understand? You think I don't feel the guilt, too? I know you think it's your fault, but it's not. It was an accident. You're not the only one who lost someone that day. We all loved Aaron. Me, Marcus—the pain doesn't belong to you alone." Reese folded her arms across her chest. "It was an accident, a horrible accident, and now we all have to pick up the pieces and try to move on."

True, she wasn't alone in missing Aaron, wasn't alone in losing him either, but an accident? No. She had jumped into the raging river, not fallen. A part of her sought to die that night.

"Of course, it's my fault!" Quinn snapped a twig in half with the heel of her boot. "I'm sick of everyone dancing around me as if I'm a fragile piece of porcelain. He jumped in to save *me*. He's terrified of the water, Reese, and he jumped in anyway. There's nobody to blame but me."

Pinching the bridge of her nose, Quinn swallowed the emotions that threatened to break her. *Confession is good for the soul. Spit it out. Tell her you didn't fall, that you jumped, that you put them all in jeopardy that night. You and you alone.* She squeezed her lip between her teeth until she tasted blood. Voicing the blame that was eating her alive, sharing the secret, would be a relief. But what if Reese hated her for it? What little courage Quinn had mustered left her, and she swallowed the truth that settled on the tip of her tongue.

"You want me to stop treating you like you're fragile? You want the truth?" Reese took a step forward, knuckles white, face flushed. "You want to hear how Aaron insisted Marcus take you first? How I watched Aaron let go of the branch he was holding onto while Marcus struggled to drag your lifeless body back to shore?"

Quinn turned away and covered her ears. Twin waterfalls of tears ran down her neck, soaking her T-shirt.

"How helpless I felt watching the current drag Aaron's body under? I thought I was going to lose all of you, everyone I loved, in the depths of this goddamn river." Reese picked up a giant rock and hurled it to the riverbed.

Marcus, Reese, Jenna—all had kept the gory details from her for weeks, feeding her bits and pieces but never the whole story, and part of her was glad to be spared. Now Reese granted her no reprieve.

"You weren't awake to hear Marcus screaming his name." Another rock hit the water with a smack. "You didn't hold your breath every time Marcus dived under the water, or comfort him while his heart broke into a million pieces because he had failed his best friend. I did." Reese poked her own chest with a finger. "I witnessed it all while you lay half-dead on the muddy bank. Do you have any idea how freaking scared I was?"

Each word pricked like a wasp sting. Throat tight and aching, Quinn thought of Marcus pulling her to safety as the boy she'd spurned suffered in the cold water alone.

"Aaron traded his life for yours. He knew he wouldn't make it back to shore. Don't you get that? Did you even know that Marcus won't go back into the pool because he feels so responsible? No, you wouldn't, because you haven't asked about any of it, how any of us feel. You're too wrapped up in yourself to care."

"I didn't know. I'm sorry. Why didn't you tell me?" Quinn wanted to wrap her arms around her friend, wanted to take the pain from her, but the anger in Reese's face stopped her cold. "Of course, I care. Do you really think I don't understand what he did for me that night, what you all did?"

"No, I really don't." Reese folded her arms over her chest. "You think you feel bad? What about me? And Marcus? We should be mourning together instead of pushing each other away. Stop pushing me away. You might not need me, but I sure as hell need you right now." Reese's hand trembled as she wiped the evidence of her emotions from her cheek. "You didn't die with him, Quinn, but some days it feels like you did."

Silence, awkward and oppressive filled the air. Quinn reached for her best friend, but Reese swatted her away. Without another word, she disappeared back down the path, not even turning around when Quinn called her name.

"THERE YOU ARE. I was starting to worry."

Quinn winced and turned. Her mother leaned against the kitchen doorframe. Jeans and a white T-shirt replaced her usual business suit, her blond hair tied back in a rare casual ponytail.

"I thought you had a meeting tonight."

"I've been home for hours. I sent you a text." Ever since she'd been released from the hospital, her mom had spent more nights at home and fewer at her office. A few months ago, Quinn would have relished having more time with her mother, but not now. Now, having her mother around meant more lies and more hiding.

Quinn slipped her phone from her pocket. Three texts from her mom, all unread. Oops.

"Sorry. It was on silent." Quinn hoped her mother would drop it, but no such luck.

"Where were you? I was so worried."

If her mother had known she'd been down at the river, she would flip. One more little lie wasn't going to hurt anything.

"Shopping with Reese. She wanted to buy a new outfit for her date with Marcus this weekend." Quinn pushed a smile to her lips and hoped her mom would buy it.

"I'm so glad to see you out of the house and spending time with your friends." Her mother smiled back. "Did you find anything?"

"Not really." Quinn shrugged

"Well, at least you're getting out again. Are you hungry?"

Quinn didn't have a chance to say no before her mom draped an arm around her shoulder and steered her into the kitchen.

"I ordered pizza for dinner."

Quinn sat down at the bar, and her mother slid a slice of pizza in front of her. She picked a chunk of ham from the cheese and dangled it between her fingers.

"Now that you're feeling better, getting out more, maybe we should talk about school." Quinn choked on a bit of stringy cheese and glared at her mom. Great. First Reese, now Mom, a relentless alliance forcing her back into a life she didn't want anymore.

"You've been through a lot, I get that. I've been patient, but I think it's time to start putting all this behind you and get back to normal." Her mother took a pre-made salad from the fridge and drizzled a small amount of dressing on the top. Enough for a rabbit to eat.

"I've decided to get my GED." Quinn wasn't going back, but convincing her mother wasn't going to be easy. "There are online classes I can take, and I'll be ready for the test by summer. I'll even pay for it myself."

Quinn's mom sighed and shook her head. "I know it's been hard on you, sweetie, but locking yourself away in this house isn't the answer. It's past time you got back to a routine, to friends and cheerleading. I'm sure Aaron wouldn't want you to miss your senior year. I won't agree to the GED."

"I'm not going back. I can't."

"You can, and you will. I've already made an appointment with your counselor. We have to be there at nine, sharp. I've taken the morning off."

"Cancel it."

"I could, but I won't. I'm putting my foot down on this. You'll go back to school on Monday and walk the stage in June with your class. End of discussion." Her mother put her hand on Quinn's. "Trust me, you'll thank me for it later. You can't hide from life, Quinn."

How could she explain that it wasn't life she was hiding from? It was death. His death. Quinn pulled her hand away and picked a pineapple chunk from the pizza. Her mom crunched on her lettuce. She might be able to make her go on Monday, but she wouldn't be able to watch her every day. *Play the game, Quinn, then you can do what you want when she thinks she's won and her back is turned.*

"So, your dad called again today," her mom said, changing the subject. "He's finally booked a flight and will be here Wednesday. He wants to take you out for your Eighteenth." Her voice was laced with nerves and annoyance.

"Tell him he's about four weeks too late." Quinn noticed a slight darkening of the kitchen as the dozen overhead bulbs flickered and dimmed. The Qeres dagger strapped to her leg pulsed and burned against her calf.

"Anyway, I'm sure something will come up." Quinn flexed her fist. "Like a paper cut or a flat tire or something. Anyway, I'd rather he stayed away."

"Yeah, well, he is your father whether you like him or not." Cracks in her mom's civility were starting to show. "Taking you to dinner is the least he can do since he didn't even bother to show up to see you in the hospital. He should have dropped everything and hopped a plane."

"I've learned to keep my expectations low," Quinn mumbled through a mouthful of crust. Truth was, even low expectations didn't keep her heart from breaking every time her father disappointed her. He wouldn't want to leave his new baby to visit his daughter in the hospital. No, that would be cruel. "Tell him to stay home with his real family. It's not like we aren't used to not having him around."

Two shadows slithered up and over the counter, attaching to each of her mother's arms. Quinn swallowed. Beads of sweat dotted her forehead as she flexed her fingers, unsure what to do. Bile rose in her throat, and her heartbeat like a thousand wings inside her chest.

"Tell him yourself. I'm tired of being your messenger." Her mother stabbed at the lettuce, the fork poking holes in the plastic container, scraping against the granite below.

"Mom?"

"We didn't talk for almost a year, and suddenly, he's calling me all the time." Her mother's jaw clenched. "He talks to me as if we are old friends catching up. Going on and on about the restaurant, his new baby, and his life with that woman." Bitterness hissed from her mother's mouth. "Does he really think I want to hear him call that whore he cheated on me with his wife? Where was the steady job when we were together? And a baby?" Her mother's expression hardened.

The shadows solidified into familiar forms. Two leathery beasts, a foot in length, whipped long tails from side to side, as they climbed up her mother's back to perch on each shoulder. Claws sank into flesh. Double forked tongues licked at wave after wave of secret confessions erupting from the deepest, darkest place within her mother.

Anger drew Quinn's hand to the pommel of her dagger, but she hesitated. She didn't even know what it did. What if she missed, hit her mom instead?

If she could extend her shield, maybe she could cut them off from her mother's increasing scorn. Focusing her thoughts, she ignored the stinging comments flying from her mother's mouth and imagined her light barrier expanding, encircling both of them in a giant golden ball. Nothing happened.

"He never even wanted to be a father. Maybe I should have had an abortion like he wanted." Her mother's hands flew to her mouth, and her eyes widened.

Knots tightened in Quinn's stomach, and she froze. It

might have only been a passing thought, but the demons seized on it, bringing it to light. That was their MO. Exploit negative human emotions, feed on them, magnify them, create chaos and darkness. Azrael had explained it all to Quinn, how the demons grew in power, a vicious cycle. The more pain and chaos within humanity, the more demons crossed the veil. The more demons that crossed the veil, the more negative emotions were exploited, and the weaker the veil between worlds became.

"God, Quinn! I can't believe I said that aloud. I didn't mean it. He didn't really, we didn't ..."

Placing a hand over her mother's, Quinn shushed her. She gritted her teeth and tried to calm her racing thoughts. She wouldn't let them get to her, wouldn't let them turn her mom into a sadistic picnic for them to grow fat upon.

Breathe. In, out. Focus on what you want. It's all about intent, about what you want.

Light crept from Quinn's fingers, over her mother's wrist, and inched upward. The skin of the first demon sizzled and popped as the barrier grazed its long, leathery tail. Smoke rose from its burned flesh, and it howled, taking to the air. Wings twisted into shadowy smoke and back to demon form as it flew in circles over the counter, angry at being separated from its prey.

She had done it. The bubble of light glowed and pulsed around both of them. Deprived of a meal, the demons zoomed upward and disappeared through the ceiling. The kitchen brightened, and Quinn slumped against the counter.

"What was that?" Her mother pulled her hand away from Quinn and looked around. "I thought I saw ..."

"Saw what, Mom?" Quinn held her breath.

"Nothing. I don't know. My head, it's all fuzzy." She rubbed her temple.

She didn't remember; maybe it was for the best. If only

Quinn could forget, too. "You must be tired, Mom, that's all. I know I am."

"Yes, must be all the stress." Her mother frowned but didn't argue. "I love you, Quinn." She placed her hand over Quinn's and met her gaze. "You know that, right?"

"I know."

Once Quinn left the kitchen, Azrael's familiar hum greeted her at her bedroom doorway.

"There were demons attached to my mother," Quinn accused, as if it were Azrael's fault. "Where were you?" Quinn asked.

"Close enough to step in had things gotten out of control."

"I don't like you taking chances with the people I love like that." Quinn pushed past him and into her room. "What if my powers hadn't worked?"

"But they did. You took care of them with grace and strength. Soon, you won't even need me." Was that sadness or sarcasm? Quinn wasn't sure.

"I think it's time." Azrael ruffled his feathers.

"Time for what?"

"To take you to Arcadia to claim your birthright."

"Not this again." Quinn rolled her eyes and plopped down on the end of her bed.

"Yes, this again."

"I told you, I won't leave until I know what happened to Aaron."

"Stubborn girl," Azrael mumbled. "I can tell you what happened to him. He is dead. Drowned in an attempt to save your life." Quinn stared open-mouthed at Azrael. "You chose to accept your role, and that means doing your duty. Even Eve did not whine this much. The Light did not spare you to watch you act like a spoiled child and waste your life on the memory of some boy."

"His name is Aaron, and why should I believe a word you say? All you do is talk about this great power, about me being Eol Ananael, but what does that even mean? According to you, there are thousands upon thousands of demons crossing the veil all over the human realm. There's only one of me. Banishing one demon when I'm mad doesn't make me a savior. I don't even know how to control this power. I can barely save myself. How can I save anyone else?"

"If you go to Arcadia and claim your birthright, you will have the entire heavenly host at your back."

"I'm not going. End of discussion." It surprised her how much like her mother she sounded. But this wasn't just about finding Aaron—her life was here, her friends. All of this was so new, but she refused to admit to Azrael how scared she was. "I want to be alone now, please." She forced her will upon him so there would be no doubt she meant it.

He nodded, stepped through the wall, and disappeared outside.

Exhausted, she closed the floral drapes, blocking out the rays of moonlight and blanketing herself in shadows and grief. She couldn't bear the reminder of the one moment of happiness she and Aaron had together, staring up at the harvest moon, the heat of his breath on her cheek.

Reese was right; he'd been gone for five weeks and three days. The possibility of him being alive was less than zero. She pressed her fists to her eyes to stop the flow of tears. Grabbing the crumpled map, she unfolded the edges and ironed out the wrinkles with a palm, examining the grid that marked the fifty-mile search radius.

But if Aaron was dead, why couldn't she let go? There had to be somewhere they'd missed.

"Aaron, where are you?" she whispered, turning her attention back to the map. Of course, she didn't get a response. If it were that easy, a glowing arrow would have appeared to point the way. "I should let go." Her hand shook, poised to make the final mark, but she couldn't bring herself to do it. Letting go meant accepting that he wasn't coming back. Instead, she dropped the pen on the floor and crawled under the covers and placed her hand on the map.

"Aaron, I'm sorry. I'm so sorry." She patted the paper, letting the rhythm of his name and her whispered wishes lull her to sleep.

Despair crushed the air from her lungs, and a pit of hopelessness opened inside. Tendrils of familiar fog reached for her, and she lowered her defenses, letting them suck the shame and regret from her heart until there was nothing left, and she fell, headfirst, into a dream.

꿀

IT WAS WELL PAST MIDNIGHT, and they were finally alone. This time the dream placed them in her room, not in the hospital. They sat cross-legged, knees touching beneath the floral duvet spread across their laps, Aaron's back to the door, hers leaned against the wooden headboard.

"Happy birthday." Aaron placed a small wooden box in front of her. Strange symbols had been delicately carved on its mahogany surface.

"It's beautiful, but my birthday was weeks ago." Quinn took the box in her hands and examined the etched symbols. She tried the latch, but it wouldn't open.

"It's locked." Quinn frowned. "What's in it?"

Quinn shook her head, and then jiggled the box. A tingling started in her fingers, and she gasped as the carved runes began to glow, first blue, then gold. She cocked her head. "What do they mean?"

"Don't you know?" Aaron took the box from her, and the carvings dimmed.

She wanted to examine it more, but out of nowhere, an inky wave crashed into Aaron, washing him out into a sea of darkness, the box along with him.

7

The small cemetery of St. Angeles held a handful of mourning dresses, heavy perfumes, and dark suits. Close friends and family come to pay their respects to an empty grave. Quinn squeezed a crumpled tissue in her fist. A pair of large black-rimmed sunglasses hid the deep bruises under her eyes from a restless night and dulled the bright rays that glistened off the blanket of morning dew. Birds hopped along the wrought iron finials that adorned the churchyard fence, chirping to one another, oblivious to the grief and mourning around them.

Jenna and her twin brother Cade had insisted the memorial be held here, in a place Aaron loved. They'd even convinced her dad to let them add the small, modern marker among the crumbling, moss-covered graves around it. The first in over fifty years, it looked strangely out of place, new marble shining in the morning sun.

AARON JAMES COLLIER
BELOVED SON, BROTHER, AND FRIEND.
HEAVEN HAS A NEW ANGEL.

If Aaron was dead, he wasn't an angel. According to Azrael, humans don't become Angels. Their essence merely moves to another plane of existence.

"Into your hands, O merciful God, we commend your servant."

Marcus clenched and unclenched his fists, biting back a soft sob as Jenna's dad, Pastor McClure, prayed. Reese, tall and slender in a black dress and heels, her long dark hair twisted into a knot, stood between him and Jenna. Three peas in a pod, clustered together for support, a pod Quinn had once been a part of. None of them even glanced her way as they comforted one another. Apart, separate, alone but for her invisible protector standing by her side. Her friendships were decaying like the bodies beneath her feet, and she only had herself to blame. Quinn lifted her chin and stuffed her emotions back inside.

Every other eye was closed, and every head bowed, but Quinn's faith lay at the bottom of a river, buried with the knowledge of her guilt. Instead, she kept her eyes on the gathering shadows. Tendrils of fog hung from the bare branches of the trees beyond the rusted gate, like cobwebs over bone. The Qeres dagger strapped to her calf and hidden inside her knee-high boot pulsed against her skin. Muscles tense, she longed to grab her blade and ram it down their shady throats. Her barrier thrummed and dimmed.

Sensing her unease, Azrael moved closer until his fiery shoulder touched hers, cloaking the chill that was trying to take up residence under her skin.

Do not let your emotions defile this sacrament, Quinn. His hands gripped the pommels of the two curved swords at his hips, alert and ready to protect and defend.

My presence here is enough to keep them from feeding on the grief pouring from the souls gathered here today, but I fear if you do not hide yours from them, it will tip the scale, and I will not be able to kill them all before they get their claws into your friends. Stay focused. Raise your shield, and by all that is holy, try to control your feelings.

Azrael was right; this was not the time or the place to incite a fight. His echo within her mind smoothed out the wrinkles in her thoughts. It was his job to stand vigil, and he would watch them, keep them safe, while she focused on mourning. Steadying her breathing, she closed her eyes and reinforced the all-encompassing shield against the darkness. Calm steadied her essence.

"Eternal rest grant unto them, O Lord, and let perpetual light shine upon them.

May the souls of the faithful departed, through the mercy of God, rest in peace."

"Amen," Quinn added her voice to the others.

When she opened her eyes, the shadows flickered and faded into the background as she closed off her connection to the spirits of the Underworld completely. Azrael nodded his approval. Light streamed through the trees where the shadows had been, painting the world in beautiful amber hues, buoying Quinn's own spirit.

Aaron's father and brother approached the small marble headstone. Both were tall and slender, one dark haired, the other gray and haggard. They looked as if they hadn't slept in weeks. Josh twisted a guitar pick between his fingers, reminding her of Aaron's nervous habit. His father clasped him on the shoulder and bent, stiff kneed, to place a bouquet of roses beneath Aaron's name.

Josh knelt at the headstone with his father. He pressed the tip of the plastic plectrum to his lips and placed it next to the flowers. Quinn wanted to run and throw her arms around him then and there, to apologize and beg his forgiveness. She dug a heel into the mud, twisting and grinding it deeper and deeper into the soft ground.

Her movement caught Josh's attention, and he turned his green eyes, the exact shade of emerald as Aaron's, swollen and rimmed in red, on Quinn. Her breath caught in her throat, and she gasped. His fierce glare, filled with pain and accusations, pierced her heart. Guilt etched itself on her face, and she quickly looked away. She couldn't blame him, any of them, for their sidelong looks and hushed whispers. This was her fault, after all. Soon there would be nothing left but empty grief for an empty grave.

"Receive Aaron James Collier into the arms of your mercy, into the blessed rest of everlasting peace, and into the glorious company of the saints of light. Amen."

Reese had an arm tight around Marcus, her soft sobs muffled against his heaving chest.

"Amen," they all said in unison. Once those final words were spoken, people filed past the marker, placed a flower or a trinket on the soft earth, and then scattered to the wind. Off to grab a coffee, back to work, to move on with life. Even Josh and his dad didn't stick around for hugs and condolences. Weeks of waiting and wondering must have left them drained. To them, this was the end of it, say goodbye and move on, something they'd had more experience with than most. Quinn wished they could teach her how. Together, they turned their backs and walked, stiff and halting, back to the waiting red pick-up.

"You coming?" Cade hugged his sister and she shook her head.

"I need a minute. You go on."

Cade nodded and followed their dad out of the cemetery and into the parking lot.

As the cemetery emptied, Quinn, Reese, Marcus, and Jenna gathered around the grave. Four pillars crumbling under a sky full of heartache, the last ones to see him alive.

8

*A*aron had no idea how long it had been since he'd been ripped away from his glimpse of nirvana, but the vortex slowed again, suspending him in front of a red door with a brass handle this time. He turned away. The door turned with him, placing itself directly in front of him. Closing his eyes didn't help either; the door still floated in the blackness, taunting him. He shook his head. Whatever was behind this door wasn't something he was ready to face. When the handle turned, his whole body trembled. And then the portal swung open, and Aaron's stomach rolled.

Beyond the door, Quinn, in a tight black dress, stood in the cemetery of St. Angeles. Sunglasses swallowed her face, hiding her eyes from his. Misery and remorse pulsed through her, and he could feel every tear falling from her cheek. Her emotions jumbled inside her like a box of broken glass, each one slicing into his soul as she mourned the loss of someone she loved. Aaron swallowed the boulder in his throat. Not just anybody—him. This was his funeral.

"Quinn!" His voice sounded hollow, empty. "I'm here. Look at me." She stared at the ground; he felt guilt pinch her gut as his name crossed her lips like a prayer. Could she sense him? The longing to hold her in his arms overwhelmed him, and he balled his fists at his sides. Aaron ached to run to her, but he remained trapped in the dark tunnel that held him, forced to be a voyeur to her pain. Would the torture ever end? If he could get through the portal, he would be home, with her. Closing his eyes, he focused all his thoughts on walking through the doorway and into the cemetery, but his body was stuck, suspended between life and death.

"I'm here. I'm here. I'm here." He sent out his appeal, a steady knock against the door that could bring him home. Quinn could bring him home, if she would just look at him. "Please, look at me. Please help me. I want to come home. Dammit. Look at me!" Fingers clawed at the air, and his soul begged to be released.

9

They all stared at his headstone for what seemed like a lifetime, each wrapped up in their own thoughts, none of them ready to say their goodbyes. Wind moaned and bellowed through the ruins, rattling the broken stained-glass windows of the long-forgotten chapel. It set Quinn on edge, and she shuffled her feet and stared at the ground, afraid that if she looked at anyone, she would crack into a million pieces.

Marcus was the first to break the silence. Shoulders heaving, he stiffly stepped forward to face Aaron's memorial and fell to his knees. Tremors rocked his hands; his chin trembled as he pursed his full, dark lips. Reese trembled with him, patting his shoulder, running a finger through his dark, wiry hair, whispering, soothing even as her own emotions got the best of her. Quinn bit her lip and sniffed. No crying allowed. This was a memorial and nothing more. No body, no casket, no internment.

When Jenna began singing "What If You," one of Aaron's favorite songs, in tribute, her clear, rich alto tones wrapped around Quinn's heart and tugged hard. Blood, metallic and warm on her tongue, trickled from the side of her mouth where her teeth tore at her inner cheek. Each note crumbled a little more of her resistance. Aaron should be singing with Jenna, catching the harmony and weaving through the music, perfect partners. He'd survived the car crash that killed his mother and sister, survived an attempted suicide, only to drown for the sake of saving her. An ultimate act of heroism she didn't deserve. And worse, he died not knowing how she really felt. Empty grave, empty soul.

A wail erupted from Marcus's throat that echoed through Quinn's bones. She wanted to comfort him, share his pain, but something held her back. No right to mourn with him when she was the reason for his torment.

Jenna knelt on the other side of Marcus, linking her arm with Reese's around his back, finishing the song in soft overtones into his ear, the three of them freely mourning. They didn't invite her into their grief, and she didn't intrude. Instead, she stood apart, an outsider.

"This isn't your fault." Jenna directed her statement to Marcus, but something about the way she stressed the word *your*, made Quinn squirm. Jenna didn't have to say it. Quinn knew perfectly well whose fault it was.

"Jenna's right. You did everything you could to save him." Reese stroked his back and kissed his cheek. "Quinn's here because of you. We could have lost them both. You're a hero."

Quinn wanted to say something, to agree, but every time she started to speak, her mouth turned dry as burnt toast.

Marcus shook his head and balled his fist. "I'm no hero." He pulled something shiny from his suit pocket, a round golden medal on a red ribbon. His hand shook as he rubbed his swimming champion medallion between his thumb and finger. "He's the true hero." He placed the trophy next to the guitar pick.

"You're both heroes," Jenna added, looking sidelong at Quinn through long, dark eyelashes.

Quinn didn't know what they wanted her to say, didn't even know what *she* wanted to say, so she stared at the ground instead. Words, thoughts, feelings jumbled up inside her, and she didn't know how to start piecing them together. Her head throbbed, and she rubbed the scab of her healing scalp wound.

Chaos and tragedy had engulfed her friends while she was stuck between, unconscious in this realm and listening to Azrael drone on about destiny and choice in another. Every precious second she wasted debating on that rock, Aaron struggled to keep her afloat, his energy draining away, fighting for his life while she selfishly debated if she had anything left to live for.

I'll never forget the desperation in Marcus's screams. Reese's words echoed through her soul, and she choked back a sob.

Regret flowed through her, pumping her heart full of "what if's." If she could go back and trade her life for Aaron's, she would. She should have been the one washed out to sea. It had been her death wish, her selfishness that killed him. Aaron was gone. Quinn ached at the thought. He left a gaping hole inside her that only he could fill. She loved him, and he would never know it.

"Aaron," Quinn whispered his name as benediction, tears springing unbidden and down her cheeks. All the placating words in the world couldn't bring him back now.

Clouds passed across the sun. Quinn shivered and drew her scarf tighter around her neck. Something tugged at the edge of her consciousness. The sense of Aaron's presence overwhelmed her, and she turned.

A shadow, long and dark, moved within the ruins of the old, gothic church, twisting and writhing, taking shape.

Azrael's wings unfurled, and his fingers hovered over the

grip of his swords. *What do you see?* he asked, and she sensed his confusion. It was invisible to him then. Strange. Pressing her finger to her lips, she shushed her Sentinel and crept closer.

"Quinn?" Reese and Jenna both stood, questioning. It was the first time they'd acknowledged her, but she didn't care. There was only one person in the cemetery she wanted to see right now. Walking right past them, she followed the dark mass weaving between the crumbling markers. Sweat beaded on her forehead as she fought to keep her barrier intact, but the light waxed and waned as the shadow grew closer. Something about it seemed familiar. The light barrier she'd constructed around her pulsed as the thing glided past her to stand behind Marcus.

Quinn's defenses throbbed again, and as she approached, the shape began to reinvent itself. First came two legs to stand on, then hips, torso, two arms. A long neck surged upward and bounced back like a rubber man, snapping into human shape. One she recognized. She stripped her psychic armor down to nothing. She didn't care; she had to see him, all of him.

With a flicker, the shadow changed from gray to full color, dark hair, green eyes, rugged face twisted in pain. Had he come to mock her? An angry ghost seeking revenge on her for his death? He reached for her. Ropes tightened around her chest, and she dared not breathe.

"What's going on?" Reese tapped her foot and glared at Quinn.

"I see him, Reese."

"Who?" Reese asked.

"Aaron," she whispered and reached a hand to him. "He's here."

10

Crossing the thin veil that separated them felt like being dragged over a floor of sharp daggers. It hurt, more than anything he'd ever experienced, but he kept pushing his essence forward. Every spasm of agony was worth it if only he could touch her. She stepped closer, and the smell of her shampoo, vanilla and strawberry, enveloped him.

Lightning struck when Quinn's eyes found his, and his roaming spirit solidified with the power of their connection. A connection so strong, Aaron felt the warm longing of her heartbeat. Hope surged through him, and he reached out for her.

"Quinn," Aaron begged.

She called his name and stretched a hand to him. All he wanted to do was fall into her arms and breathe her in, to feel her touch, to be alive, to be home, but a force stronger than anything he'd known before tethered him to the black hole. Even now, he could feel a cold suction at his back; he wouldn't be able to hold on much longer. Nearly there, a few more millimeters, and her skin would brush his.

"Quinn!" Too late. Every atom inside him split apart as the force of the vortex dragged him back through the veil. The red door slammed in his face, separating him from his realm forever.

Hate writhed in the pit of his stomach as he fell, fast and heavy. The pain of his skin ripping to shreds was nothing compared to the ache of being so near Quinn, yet dimensions away. Trapped in a vacuum, the pressure pulled him deeper and deeper into darkness, and Aaron had no power to stop it. Now he was nothing but a stone cast from heaven to burn up in the fire of his descent, and he wondered if he would ever hit bottom.

11

"Aaron! Wait!" Quinn stumbled forward, hands outstretched, her fingers grasping at the empty air. A trickle of tears grew to a flood. Quinn couldn't stop herself from drowning in emotion. He was physically gone, but his presence was everywhere. She could smell his damp, earthy scent on her clothes, in her hair, as if she'd been swimming in a river.

Quinn. You're losing control. Keep your barrier up, Azrael hissed, one sword coming loose from his scabbard, but it was too late. Coils of fog exploded from the graves around her, too many to count. They were surrounded. When Azrael slashed at one, two more sprang from the earth.

I can't. A million cold lances pierced through her exposed mind at once, digging deep beneath her thoughts. Quinn tried to picture a wall of light, but there were too many, and she couldn't break away. Tears stung her eyes. Iced wind and dark shadows swirled around her, catching her scarf, knotting the ends of her hair.

The Qeres dagger burned against Quinn's calf, calling to be freed. Reaching inside her boot, she slipped the blade from its sheath, but before she could use it, shadowy ropes punched through the dirt on either side, grabbed her ankles, and yanked her feet out from under her. She tumbled backward; the wind knocked from her lungs as the dagger was knocked from her hand.

Whispers, a dozen overlapping, accusing voices swarmed her ears, and her palms pushed to keep them out. Weight dragged at her limbs, and she jerked sideways, her cheek planting in the mud.

Digging deep, Quinn searched for a spark, anything she could grab onto to bring her defenses back up, but she couldn't focus. The demons were everywhere, slithering inside her mind, confusing her, distracting her.

Whips of fog twined around her body, binding her inch-by-inch with living rope, just as they had in her earliest nightmares, but this wasn't a dream. She kicked and flailed, but the fog entombed her. Tendrils of living rope coiled around her throat. She screamed, but the noose pulled tight, digging into her windpipe, cutting her cry short. Rolling on her back, she clawed at her throat as the tendrils snaked across her neck and mouth. Fingers of gray mist tied around her wrists and pulled her arms flat to the ground, binding her fast.

Marcus, Reese, and Jenna were all on their feet now, staring at Quinn, eyes wide. Quinn wanted to scream at all of them to run, but the demons reached into her mouth and stilled her tongue.

Dark shapes swarmed her, crawling over her body, sucking at her essence. Azrael's swords glowed and arched as he hacked away at them, but they kept coming, swarming him, pushing him back, and separating her from her protector one inch at a time.

Marcus rushed to her side, confused at seeing his friend flung around by an invisible force. Quinn shook her head in warning, too late. A hooded figure rose behind him and plunged a dark hand straight into this heart, stopping him cold. Black pupils ate all the white around his eyes as the demon forced its way inside, possessing him.

"I should have saved him that night, not you. You should have been left to rot at the bottom of the river." It was Marcus's voice, but with all the usual warmth and charm drained from the tone. Reese and Jenna circled in from the other side.

You are but one, we are many. Reese's lips curled into a snarl. She knelt next to Quinn; eyes full of ink. The demon had a full hold on her now. It cocked her best friend's head.

Leave her alone. Quinn squirmed and kicked against her misty bonds.

You all called us here, and we came at your invitation. Do not be a bad hostess. Let us feed. We are so hungry.

You want to feed? Take me but leave her alone. I have so much more to give than she does. Can't you feel it? Quinn stopped struggling and brought all her emotions to the surface. The pain of it was almost unbearable, but she lay perfectly still and didn't hold anything back.

Reese leaned into Quinn and sniffed her neck. *So dark, so good.*

It was working. Quinn sensed the demon's greed, and she drew on all the pain and sadness that had leaked into the cemetery's soil. So much death, so many loved ones lost. Tragedy, anger—she took it all in and fed it back to the demons. None of them could resist. Drunk on the darkness spilling from Quinn, they surrounded her on all sides to lap it up. Ink spilled from Reese's mouth, and she fell to the ground as the demon abandoned her friend's body to seize on Quinn's misery.

Distracted, the ropes holding her wrists loosened, and Quinn inched toward the glowing dagger to her right.

Fingers brushed the handle. She might be a killer, but so were they. Aaron's death was as much their fault as it was hers, and they would pay. Never again would she let them control her, let them turn her into a whining wreck of a girl. The shadows shimmered and vibrated as she harnessed the thought of Aaron sinking to his death, his sacrifice, his ultimate love.

The dagger slammed into the center of the beast that had possessed Reese. It hissed and dissipated into wisps of smoke. This woke the others from their food coma, and they started to back away from her in confusion. Azrael seized the opportunity, his sword taking down at least half a dozen beasts in seconds.

Now. While they're distracted.

Three breaths brought up her armor, and she sprang into a crouch, dagger at the ready.

The atmosphere around Quinn crackled with her one wish—to kill them all. Fixing her glare on the shadow to her right, she held it suspended with her mind. It squirmed against her power, pushing to free itself, looking for a crack in her barrier. She felt its malicious intent. Its fear tangled with loathing.

Killing us won't bring the boy back. No one is safe from his fate. He has gone to meet my maker. A soul for a soul. Yours for his. A soul for a soul. Dead is dead.

It laughed. Quinn gritted her teeth and pinned its dark essence against a crumbling headstone with nothing but a thought, its name coming to her lips as if she'd known it her whole life.

Call it by name, finish it, Azrael urged.

"Erithea." She pointed at the shadow hanging in mid-air and released her anger at the beast. "Go to hell." A beam of light exploded from the tips of Quinn's fingers, piercing Erithea and cutting his morbid life short.

Quinn's heart pounded against her ribs. The kickback of expending all that pent-up emotion rattled her. She had banished a demon. Satisfaction twisted her lips into a wicked grin as she sank to the ground, all her energy spent. So that was what she could do.

Seething hate emanated from the remaining demons as they fled in the wake of her power and the tip of Azrael's sword.

12

"Quinn," Aaron rasped her name and swallowed the bits of gravel lodged in his throat. Only the echo of water droplets hitting rock answered him. She wasn't there, never had been. The portals, his funeral, Quinn, it was nothing but a dream, a nightmare. He was back where he started.

A fever, that was all. The fire inside died, leaving nothing but a hollow husk of skin and bone lying face down and shivering, spread-eagle against the cold stone beneath him. Every inch of Aaron's body felt bruised and weak as his awareness returned, nerve-by-nerve. How long had he been lying here? Days? Minutes?

Ignoring the situation won't make it go away. If you don't try, you'll never find a way out of this mess. What did Mom always say? Seeing the problem is the first step to finding a solution. Stop being a coward.

It took all his strength to force his eyes open, his lids ripping from the tender cornea. He blinked in the moist, cool air until the irritating particles washed away in a flood of salty tears. When the streaming stopped, and he regained focus, all he saw was an endless void of darkness spinning out before him.

Oh, my God! I'm blind! I'm blind and alone and probably bleeding and broken. Shit. I knew it. His heart rattled against his chest, and his lungs constricted.

Don't panic. It's dark. That's all. It doesn't mean you're blind. You have to move, or you'll die here.

And how am I supposed to do that when I can't see a hair in front of me! His thoughts fractured into two opposing sides, the optimist and the pessimist. *Not to mention the fact that I used up all my energy opening my eyes.*

Don't panic. It's not that bad.

Not that bad? Really? How could it be worse?

You could be nothing.

At least if I were nothing, I wouldn't be so afraid.

Arguing with himself seemed crazy, but it was the only thing keeping him from falling apart. He had nobody else to rely on or to council with.

That's a laugh. Don't you remember how terrified you were the last time you died? This doesn't feel anything like that. If we're dead, where's the light?

He doubted there would be any lights in hell but pushed away the thought as soon as it reared its head. Metaphorically, hell was exactly where he was right now.

Listen. There's water dripping in the distance. The water must be getting in from somewhere. So if there was a way in, there's a way out.

Yes. Yes. His thoughts finally made sense, worked together.

Aaron shivered. Not a scrap of clothing covered his body. Whatever happened to him stripped him of every stitch, as well as his dignity. In a different situation, he might have been embarrassed, but he was too exhausted and frightened to care. He would worry about clothes later. For now, he had to get moving and get out.

His neck, stiff from lying in the same position for too long, tingled and ached as he scraped his cheek against the rough stone. A musty mix of rusted metal and salt filled his nostrils. The smell of mustiness and stale air reminded him of home, of his father lying on the couch after drinking all night, the curtains drawn tight. But he wasn't home. The stone floor beneath his naked flesh proved that. Did his dad even miss him? Did Josh? Would he ever see home again?

You won't if you don't stay focused.

Giving up wasn't an option. Panting, he struggled again to shift the lead weights of his arms splayed out over his head, but they wouldn't budge. They remained stuck to the floor, heavy and useless. He might as well try to move a mountain.

Light flickered in the distance. He could make out the halo around a flame, an orange eye staring at him from the blackness.

"Hello?" Aaron's voice was rough and low. "Is anyone there?"

Whispers hushed and shushed around him, soft and ominous, but he couldn't tell exactly where they came from.

"Please, help me. I need help."

If he didn't get their attention, they might miss him. Determined, he gritted his teeth and concentrated his efforts. He stretched the fingers of his right hand, then the left. A moan escaped his lips, and he sucked in his breath as pins and needles danced across his nerves.

Metal scraped and clanged against stone as he dragged his right arm in toward his body. Panic knotted his empty belly, and he pushed himself up to a sitting position. Something bit into his wrists, weighing him down, restricting his movement.

He scrambled backward, the clatter following him. Something cold and wet scraped against his leg, a chain. Shackles bound each wrist and ankle. He grunted and tried to tug them free, but the more he fought against them, the tighter they held him.

A scream so raw with anger and despair surged up from his gut and exploded from his throat. He screamed and clawed at the ground in a red rage until he collapsed. Exhausted and defeated, he curled into a ball and stared at the flame winking in the distance, teasing him, taunting him. His stomach clenched in spasm after spasm, and he prayed for death to take him, to save him from this misery.

"Even death can't save you now, Kaemon." Aaron flinched as a finger traced his spine, ice-cold, dangerous. "It's too late for that," a voice whispered in his ear.

He whipped his head around, his bindings a harsh clang in the gloom, but she was quick, a shadow moving in the corner of his eye.

"Your souls weren't welcome in any of the other realms, too twisted, a human-angel hybrid abomination. Where would you go?" Her voice seemed to come from everywhere and nowhere. "Even The Light wouldn't have you. But don't worry; I've made room for you here, my pet." Something rattled his chains, tugging at his wrists. "An exception for the exceptional."

"Who are you? Where am I?" Aaron demanded.

"Home, of course." A ring of fire exploded around him, and he squinted as his eyes adjusted to the sudden brightness. "Welcome to the Underworld."

Torches lined the circular platform on which he sat. Two identical skulls with curved horns and long bony snouts sat atop two ten-foot-high metal spikes. The spikes stood roughly six feet apart in the center of the circular platform. The chains binding his wrists looped through the empty eye sockets, around an iron ring attached to the nose cavity, and back out of their mouths like lolling iron tongues. Each chain coiled down to the floor, leaving him enough slack that he could pace the length and breadth of his prison and no more. The platform had no walls. Instead, three hundred and sixty degrees of edge plummeted downward into a bottomless pit. A domed cave ceiling soared three stories above in a sweeping arch, making him dizzy. The small stone island in the middle of a sea of ink and air trapped him. Deep red marks stained the floor in drips and splatters reminding him of a Jackson Pollok painting he'd once seen at the museum with his mother. Aaron shivered, wondering whose blood had been there before his own.

"Don't worry your pretty head about that just now, my pet." A woman stood before him, a dark hood obscuring her face. Shadows draped her curvy frame, knitting together to form a tight-fitting corset and long flowing skirt. The floor-length cape seemed to whisper and move like smoke. Within the fabric, faces appeared as if emerging from a murky pond. Empty sockets stared back at him, a thin layer of skin muffling their cries and moans, each face more tortured and twisted than the next.

"Don't stare too long, lest you join them, my pet." She flipped the fabric, and it rippled and stilled as if by her command, the faces dissolving back into the fabric.

"What do you want from me?" He strained against his manacles. "Who are you?"

"Don't you remember me, Kaemon? I'm hurt." She pouted.

Aaron gasped as she pushed back the hood. He'd never seen anyone more beautiful. Curly raven hair cascaded across her shoulders and past her waist. Skin so perfect and cold she could have been made of marble. Her eyes glowed as if lit from behind, slices of iced silver ringed her black pupil.

"Lilith." The name sighed from his tongue, a remnant of an ancient memory.

"See, I knew you could never forget my face, old friend. Not after everything we've been through together." She paced along the edge of the circle, extinguishing and relighting the torches with a flick of her hand. "You don't really remember though, do you? Not with that mortal soul leaching onto your essence, getting in your way, holding you back from your true self?" She stopped and studied him. "How did it feel to be tricked by one of your own? We'd heard rumors that you'd fallen, Kaemon, for the love of your ward. That's what they get for trying to tame an Elite and make him a Sentinel. I couldn't believe it when my minions brought back word that Azrael poisoned you with your own Qeres blade and trapped you inside the mortal body of a dying boy." Lilith smiled a cold, hard smile. "I didn't think he had it in him. Such treachery from one who serves The Light, don't you think?"

Aaron lunged for her, but the manacles tightened around his wrist, the slack taken up by an unseen force, pulling him back enough to keep her just out of reach. He raged and kicked until metal bit into flesh.

"Ah, there's the fight that saved you both. How else could such souls fuse together, if not for a common desire to live? Two essences, one angel, one human, sloughed off each of their afflicted parts, then fused what was left together to form a healthy hybrid essence in the body of a mortal teenager. It's quite the bedtime tale."

Aaron, Kaemon, he held a part of both of them inside. The realization sent shockwaves through him all over again, and if he'd had anything at all in his stomach, he would have vomited.

"Your thirst for survival is renowned in the realms, Kaemon. Too bad it couldn't help you in the end. Killed by the very thing you wanted to live for, love, very poetic. You had no idea what you guarded, or you would never have left her alone and vulnerable. More's the pity."

An image of Quinn falling into the river slid across his mind like a key sliding into a lock, and the door to his memories yawned open, waiting for him to step through. The realization that he'd been Quinn's Sentinel blew his world apart. He'd been sent to protect her, and he'd failed every time. It seemed to be the only thing he was good at, failing.

Kaemon had left her at the mercy of those demons, chasing a myth that he could become human when he was supposed to be protecting her. Instead, Kaemon had left her alone and vulnerable to their influence. He was the reason for her pain, the reason she'd jumped into the river in the first place. Aaron hated Kaemon, his selfish nature, his obsession with Quinn, his failure of duty.

You are Kaemon.
No. I'm Aaron.
Are you?
I didn't turn my back on her.

"Didn't you? Over petty teenage jealousy?" Lilith replied to his thoughts once again. "Oh, the drama of the modern high school. Their angst is so yummy, each mean word or whispered hateful thought can sustain my army for months. The perfect feeding ground."

Aaron covered his ears, replaying the last few minutes of Quinn's rescue over in his head. A black-winged angel, Azrael, stood over her, an evil smirk on his face. The idea of Quinn lying broken and pale on that slab of black rock ripped his heart open.

"Oh, don't worry; your precious Quinn is very much alive. Azrael saw to that. Aaron fulfilled your duty as Sentinel, and his sacrifice will not go unpunished, and neither will Kaemon's previous crimes against me." Her lips twisted into an evil grin. Anger flooded him, the metallic and bitter taste for vengeance hot on his tongue.

"Don't blame me. It was Azrael's blade across your throat that finally put an end to your mortal frame, but don't fret. The good news is that Qeres only affects immortals, not humans, and since you are both, your human side absorbed the poison, leaving your essence intact." Dragging the Qeres blade across Aaron's throat should have finished the job Azrael had failed to complete, but if Lilith were telling the truth, his human side saved the immortal but damned him to a realm-less existence.

"You should be grateful. I saved you from a life wandering in the void. There is no place in the realms for an essence like yours. Maybe not so lucky for the human side of you, though."

How had she read his mind?

"Telepathy, a gift all immortals share," she answered his thought.

An immortal's gift, Kaemon's, the reason he'd been able to read other people when he touched them. Aaron's heart hammered against his chest. Aaron's connection to Quinn wasn't chance. It was the reason he couldn't let her go, couldn't stop thinking about her. It was Kaemon all along, seeking her out. His psychic gift must be Kaemon's, too. Which part of him was human and which angel? Was there any part of him that was fully human?

"I'm sure Azrael's taking good care of her. Better than you. He's not the least bit distracted by her short cheerleading skirt. I hoped he wouldn't be so good at his job."

Aaron strained against his bindings again, the metal rattling in defiance. "Where is she?"

"Safe. For now. I can help you get back to her. All I need is for you to tell me where the box of Agathe is hidden."

"I don't know what you're talking about." Aaron's mouth felt like it was stuffed with cotton balls.

Lilith narrowed her eyes, the sides of her grimace twitching as she considered him carefully. "No. I don't believe that *you* do. Not yet, anyway. It seems that even he doesn't trust you with the whole story. Isn't that right, Kaemon? The box may be hidden to me, but not to Kaemon. I tried the easy way, to guide you there gently, but you both defy me. He knows where it is, and he's the one who took it from me. Weren't you, my sweet? I aim to get it back, Kaemon."

"Stop calling me that."

"The great warrior Kaemon, reduced to nothing but a half-mortal child squabbling with himself over his own identity. I couldn't have asked for a better gift." She lifted a finger, her long silver nail biting into the skin beneath his chin. He swallowed, standing at her command, mesmerized by her beauty until they were face to face. "I'm not talking to you, child. He's in there, though. I can see him in the depths of your green eyes.

Lilith pressed her mouth to his ear, her warm breath tickling his skin. "Come now, Kaemon," she whispered. "You used to be so fierce, full of fire and heat. Hard to believe this sniveling weak thing houses the soul of the warrior Elite who joined with Eve to destroy half my demon horde and helped her lock the rest away in that wretched box. Watching you kill was like

watching an artist at work, such power and glory, even if you fought for the wrong side. I can free you, Kaemon, put everything to rights. I'll even let you go back to your precious Quinn. Of course, you won't be able to live in the human realm, but there are plenty of other places the two of you can live happily ever after. I hear Eden is uninhabited." She laughed at some inside joke Aaron didn't understand.

"All you have to do is help me find the box. You must know."

Licking her full red lips, she pulled him closer. Desire welled up inside Aaron. He felt ashamed and humiliated, but he couldn't help himself.

"No, you aren't Kaemon anymore, are you? I would never have been able to manipulate him the way I can manipulate you." He shivered as her hands wandered across his shoulders and down his back. She ran a nail down his cheek, drawing blood. Parting her mouth ever so slightly, she moved closer until he felt the curves of her taut body against him. When she licked the blood from his cheek, he couldn't help but moan.

"Is this what you want?" All he could do, under the power of her seduction, was nod. She struck like a snake, clasping the back of his neck as she kissed him. She tasted like bitter chocolate and chili, sweet infused with something hot and dangerous. Hunger burned within him, and he pushed against her, fumbling at the clasp that held her robe, wanting to fill himself with nothing but her.

When she pushed him to the ground and threw her head back in a haughty laugh, his heart splintered. "Don't be greedy." She tucked a strand of hair behind her ear and winked.

His head cleared as she stepped back from him, and he wiped his mouth with the back of his hand, spitting to rid himself of the taste of her.

"What would your precious Quinn think of you now? I thought you loved her, but your body betrays your heart. Something you and Kaemon have in common." Lilith squatted in front of him, grabbing his cheeks in a vise grip. "Quinn has no idea who you really are, does she? Maybe it's better that way. Should I let her continue to believe you're nothing but a teenage boy, or should I reveal how you betrayed her for your selfish desires?"

"Do what you want with me, just leave her out of this." Aaron jerked away, and she laughed again, deep and grating.

"Oh, I'll do what I want, with you and with her. Mark my words, little boy. I'm only just starting to make you both pay."

"I'll give you anything as long as you leave her alone. What do you want?"

"Oh, so many things, but let's start with your obedience." Lilith stood with arms out, palms up. "I tried to do this the easy way, to pull the answer gently from your mind, but your connection to her is still too strong. Perhaps I can use that to my advantage. In controlling you, maybe I can manipulate her, too."

Aaron spit in her face, and she grinned.

"How human of you." Her full red lips moved as she whispered a chant. The room crackled with power, and Aaron's heart crackled with fear.

Something scuttled behind him, and he jerked to the side, the metal of his chains scraping against the rock as he tried to put as much distance between himself and the creature slithering over the lip of the floor as possible. Four pincers, long as pencils, attached to a lizard head, clattered and snapped beneath multifaceted eyes intent on finding him. A million centipede legs writhed beneath its red, segmented, armored trunk, clacking against the stone as it crawled toward him. Aaron scrambled back and to the left, dragging the heavy chain across the rock, hoping to knock the thing back into the inky pit that surrounded the tiny island that had become his prison, but before the metal could touch it, the beast turned to smoke and re-solidified on the other side. Aaron shook and jangled his tether in a desperate attempt to scare it, but it scurried closer, four great pincers clacking and clicking undeterred by his effort.

Lilith's chanting intensified, and Aaron was hauled upward as an unseen force pulled all of the slack tight, stringing him up between the two posts, his arms outstretched so he couldn't move.

The creature raised the front half of its body as it approached his foot, thousands of silver legs wriggling and writhing in anticipation. He kicked and squirmed as it attached itself to his calf, its spiny legs pricking his skin as it wound its way up his thigh, across his torso, and settled around his neck like a living necklace. Inserting its tail into its mouth, it ate itself up segment by segment until Aaron could feel the edge of the armor plating digging into his Adam's apple. He whimpered as the living collar tightened around his neck and screamed as a million needle barbs penetrated his skin.

"*Kavash*," Lilith spoke the command, and the creature around his neck tensed then released its venom into his body. The venom worked quickly, relaxing every nerve, every muscle, every resistance.

"Sleep now, my angel. Sleep and remember." Aaron sagged against the manacles as Lilith slithered into his mind, sharing every thought and every desire.

"Don't fight it. There will be much pain if you resist. Relax. That's it. Show me what I need to know."

There was no place to hide. The venom pumped into his system by the control collar suppressed his fight. Resistance was impossible. She controlled him body, mind, and spirit.

13

Marcus looked down at Quinn and offered her a hand. The cuffs of his navy suit were caked with mud, and his eyes were glazed, confused. Her dagger lay half-buried in dirt. She quickly kicked some leaves over its glowing blade and prayed no one would notice.

"You okay?" Marcus asked.

Quinn nodded, unsure what to say.

"Well, I'm glad somebody is." Marcus rubbed the back of his neck. "My head feels like it's been hit with a month's worth of hangovers all at once."

"Yeah, every part of my body aches." Reese stared at Quinn.

"Mine, too." Jenna smoothed back a strand of chestnut hair and frowned. "What the hell happened? A freak earthquake or something?"

Shame and contrition churned like tainted food in Quinn's stomach. Secrets and lies were all she knew anymore, and she was tired of keeping them. Quinn opened her mouth, then closed it, then opened it again.

You don't want to bring them into this. Azrael's voice, one part lightning, two parts thunder, filled her head.

I need them. Why couldn't she make Azrael understand? She owed all of them her life, owed them the truth. *They're my friends.*

Go ahead then. Tell them what you can do. See if they believe you. And even if they do, what then? He folded his arms over his chest, black wings spread wide. *They have nothing to offer but fashion advice and snarky comments.*

Don't talk about my friends that way. What do you know of friendship? You aren't even human, she ridiculed.

That hurt. Azrael placed a hand over his heart, an oddly human mannerism, and Quinn guessed he was mocking her.

Did it? she taunted.

No. I'm not human, remember? Nor, from what I've seen, would I want to be.

Quinn didn't care what Azrael said, she was tired of feeling so alone, so isolated. *I'm sick of supernatural beings telling me who I can and can't trust. You can't stop me. I'll talk to whoever I want.*

Of course, you will. You are nothing but trouble and stubbornness. The glow beneath Azrael's skin flared along with his temper.

If I'm so much trouble, then leave me. Concentrating on her intent, she pushed against Azrael's intrusion, but the fight had left her drained. *Get out of my life and get out of my head!*

Do you think I like being bonded to you? That I like hearing your whiny thoughts every second? Azrael gripped the pommels of his swords, his jaw tight, wings flaring behind him. *Learn to control your emotions and your powers, and I won't be able to hear the meaningless drivel that floats through your head.*

The tension was so thick she was almost afraid to breath. Quinn thought about the knife buried at her feet. One nick and the Qeres poison would rid her of him.

You can try, Azrael growled

Leave me. She gathered what was left of her tattered strength and gave Azrael one final push. *And don't come back until I call you. That's a command.*

Azrael bowed low; wings spread wide. She felt rage rolling off him in hot waves. *As you wish. But don't say I didn't warn you.* Then he took to the skies, the beat of his wings kicking up a dust cloud in their wake.

"Quinn, you felt it too, right?" Marcus asked, bringing her attention back to her friends.

Jenna's eyes bored into her, expecting, demanding answers. She trusted Reese and Marcus, but Jenna? They all stayed silent as if sensing Quinn wanted to spill.

Quinn stared at her hands, suddenly unsure again. What if Azrael was right? What if they didn't believe her? Always torn between the seen and the unseen, she wanted her two worlds to merge. She couldn't go on like this anymore. Admitting everything that had happened the last few months would be so freeing. If only she could find the right words.

"What do you remember?" Quinn asked, letting them lead the conversation in hopes that it would open a natural segue.

"You said Aaron was here, and then you fell to the ground convulsing in some sort of fit." Jenna folded her arms across her chest. "You scared us. It wasn't funny, Quinn."

Small chunks. Aaron first, demons later. "It wasn't a joke. I saw him standing right there." She pointed to the spot beside Marcus. "And then he disappeared." It wasn't everything, but at least it was a start. Quinn bit at her bottom lip, waiting for their reaction.

"You really think you saw him?" Jenna asked, a mixture of hope and sarcasm in her voice.

"He's in trouble. I can feel it," Quinn insisted.

Reese shook her head. "Do you know how crazy that sounds?"

"Yes. I do." Quinn's fists balled at her sides. She still didn't understand how she could see him or why, only that she had.

"One third of all drowning victims suffer neurological damage. More like he's a hallucination brought on by your water-logged brain." Jenna tapped a finger on her forehead.

Reese shot daggers at Jenna.

"What?" Jenna shrugged. "You know you were all thinking it. I'm the only one brave enough to say it. I mean, you saw her! She was convulsing and writhing on the ground for God's sake. If that's not brain damage, I don't know what is."

"And how do you explain the missing time?" Reese asked. "I don't remember how I got mud on my dress or leaves in my hair. One minute I was standing next to the headstone, and the next my face was in the dirt. We couldn't all have had a seizure, could we?"

"I'm telling you, it wasn't a seizure." Quinn thought about pulling the dagger from its hidden spot, showing it to them, explaining everything, but something held her tongue. If she couldn't convince them about Aaron, they would never believe demons lurked in shadows and angels flitted through the heavens.

"Shared delusion, like the girls in Salem. I read all about it while doing research on the witch trials." Jenna cocked her head, confident in her assessment.

"Now who sounds crazy?" Quinn wound a short strand of blond hair around her finger. "If you're not going to help me, you can leave."

"I am helping you. Convince me this isn't some seizure episode, or some brief mass hysteria brought on by grief, Quinn. I want to believe, but I don't," Jenna challenged.

Could Jenna be right? If seeing Aaron were part of some injury from drowning, it would explain why Azrael didn't sense him. Could all of this, even Azrael, be the result of brain damage? She hated to admit it, but Jenna might have a point.

"What if Quinn's right?" It was the first thing Marcus had said in minutes. "What if Aaron's communicating with Quinn?" His eyes twinkled, and he looked over Reese's shoulder straight at Quinn. "A ghost or maybe a psychic link?"

Hope surged inside Quinn, and she grasped onto Marcus with all her might. A ghost? Maybe, but according to Azrael, ghosts couldn't exist in this realm. The essence of a human soul resonated on a different note after it disconnected from the body. That soul then traveled to the realm most suited to its true tone. Like music sorted by genre. What people think of as ghosts were really demons disguised to trick and manipulate humans. But if the image of Aaron was a demon, Azrael would have dispatched it with a wave of his sword. What did that leave? A psychic link made sense. If she connected with Azrael, why not Aaron? Maybe angels weren't the only ones she could communicate with after all.

"Seriously? Psychic links? You're grasping at straws." Reese shook her head.

"I know what I saw. Aaron was here." There must be something she could say to convince the rest of them. "Don't you remember seeing that story a few years ago about a boy who had fallen into a well?" She chewed her thumbnail. "His mother kept seeing him in the kitchen, in the yard, covered in mud. They found him alive, and he'd been communicating through some sort of dream state. Like an out-of-body experience or something. What if Aaron's trying to contact me?"

"You've watched one too many episodes of 'Mysteries Unexplained' or whatever," Reese huffed and threw her hands in the air. "I can't even believe we're having this conversation. You are seriously pissing me off. We've come to say goodbye to our friend." Her chest heaved, and Marcus pulled her into a hug, patting her on the back.

"Stranger things have happened," Marcus said. "We should at least have an open mind."

"Not you too." Reese pushed Marcus away. "I don't want to hear anymore. We should all move on. He is dead. D E A D."

Marcus reached for her, but she slapped his hand.

"If you're going to be angry at someone, be angry at me," Quinn said.

"Oh, I am." The hinges of the rusted gate nearly came loose as Reese gave it a shove. Shoulders hunched, she stalked back to the car, slamming the passenger door behind her.

Jenna shoved her hands into the pockets of her navy pea coat and stared at the ground. "I'm sorry, Quinn. I miss him; you have no idea how much. I believe that you believe you saw him today. Your face tells the truth of that. I'm convinced something happened, but I'm not convinced he's alive. I'm sorry. If there was any chance—"

"There is a chance," Quinn insisted.

"If there was any chance at all, I wouldn't hesitate. Look, I know you and I haven't exactly started out on the best terms, but I'd like to try to be friends. I mean it. We should all lean on each other now. Aaron would want it that way. So if you need anything, call me." She gave Quinn one last pat, hugged Marcus, and left.

Quinn turned to Marcus. If anyone wanted Aaron back more than she did, it was him. "I know it sounds crazy, but I know what I saw, I just can't explain it."

Marcus grabbed her shoulders and pulled her to his chest. His overly muscled arms squeezed her close, and she could feel his heart beating strong and steady. No wonder Reese loved him so much.

"You might not have convinced them, but you've convinced me. I believe you." Marcus looked over his shoulder at Reese frowning at him from the car. "I never paid much attention to it before, but what you said got me thinking. Aaron used to know things he shouldn't, and he seemed to sense what I was thinking or feeling, even when I didn't know myself."

"Like what kinds of things?" The hairs on the back of Quinn's neck stood on end. She wanted to grab on to Marcus' theory and cuddle it to her chest like a security blanket.

"Like asking how my grandmother's chemo was going when I hadn't told anyone about her illness. Or the time he congratulated me on beating my personal best in the 100-meter fly. I was alone in the pool for training that afternoon. Nobody knew my new time. I didn't pay much attention to it then; it was just part of who Aaron was. But looking back, there are lots of similar little moments that make me wonder." Marcus rubbed the black stubble on his chin.

Quinn's mind reeled with the possibility. She'd experienced the same thing. That night they spent beneath the stars, the thought that he'd been sent there just for her had been almost too strong to ignore.

"And then there's the unexplained attraction to you." Marcus raised his hands in a please-don't-shoot-the-messenger way. "Not that you aren't a fine female specimen. What's not to like?" His eyes raked up and down her body, a grin playing across his lips. "I'm not talking about your physical assets. I mean the way he fell for you the moment he saw you. He's always had a little bit of a hero complex, but with you it was relentless, like he couldn't let you go, like he knew something bad would happen to you." Marcus shook his head. "Now I'm the one who sounds crazy."

"No, it's not crazy. I've felt it too, the way he just knew

what I was thinking sometimes." Was that why the demons had threatened her? Could he have been hiding something from her like she'd been hiding from him? Maybe it wasn't her power contacting him at all, but his own. The picture started to snap into place, and she became more determined than ever to get answers.

"If only we had proof." Marcus snapped his fingers. "His journal. Why didn't I think of it before? He was always writing in this black leather notebook, song lyrics and stuff. Maybe there's a clue in there, something that might help us. We have to try."

"Marcus, you're a genius."

"I won't give up if you don't." Marcus pulled her into a tight hug. "I'll go over there tomorrow, ask Josh."

"Would you? I would go myself, but I don't think I can face him right now."

"Of course." Marcus stroked her hair, and Quinn cried. Her tears wet the collar of his white shirt, releasing the smell of starch and fabric softener.

"You know I cared about him, right? Everything that happened with Jeff, it was a mistake. I was so scared to let Aaron in. I wish I could go back, change it all."

"I know," Marcus said. "Oh, don't think I didn't want to rip your heart out at first, but your best friend happens to be my girlfriend, and she understands you better than you know."

Quinn wiped her nose on her sleeve. Of course, she did. "God, I'm such a crappy friend, Marcus."

"Yeah, sometimes, but nobody's perfect, and we both love you. Once we get proof, Reese will come around. She's just trying to protect us both from the grief. But she's hurting too." He patted her on the back and kissed her cheek. "Come on now. I think we've all had enough of this place."

"You go. I want to be alone for a few minutes."

"You sure that's a good idea?"

Quinn nodded.

"Okay, I'll call you once I talk to Josh."

Marcus joined Reese in his white Jeep and waved as they drove away, but Reese refused to look at her. Give her time, that's what Marcus said, but the rift between them seemed an endless chasm now, and Reese would have to meet her halfway.

Once the Jeep was nothing but a white dot in the distance, Quinn bent down and retrieved the Qeres dagger from beneath the fallen leaves and returned it to the sheath inside her boot.

Kneeling on the spot she'd last seen Aaron, she pressed her palm into the ground and whispered, "I won't give up on you. I promise. I'll find you. No matter what it takes."

14

"Kavash," Lilith commanded the control demon wound tight around Aaron's neck. It obeyed its mistress, releasing another round of venom through its needle-like legs and into his veins. Each dose made it harder for Aaron to think. The venom stripped away his barrier, layer after layer, like paint from a wall, leaving him completely vulnerable to Lilith's mind search.

"Kaemon, my sweet. I know you're in there," Lilith whispered in his ear.

At the sound of his other name, Aaron's insides twisted. His heart pounded against his ribs.

"Come out, come out, wherever you are. Don't let this human suppress you anymore. If you want to protect Quinn, you'll come out and give me what I desire."

Picturing a solid brick wall blocking Lilith from his thoughts, he tried to rebuild his barrier before she burned a hole in his brain so big there would be nothing left.

"Your psychic gifts are strong, but not as strong as mine. Stop fighting me, Kaemon."

"My. Name. Is. Aaron." He fought for every word, spittle running down his chin.

"*Kavash.*" A million volts of lightning coursed through him, lighting him on fire from the inside out. His brain churned into cream. His thoughts sloshed around, thick, cloudy, and intangible. Screams went on and on, reverberating in his head for so long that he couldn't remember if they belonged to him or someone else.

"Stop, please, you won't find it because I don't know the answer," Aaron begged. "I don't know anything."

"It's not you I want answers from, my pet. The knowledge I seek is in there somewhere, hidden deep within you. And I will find it." More venom swam through him. "Now, close your eyes and remember."

Aaron didn't want to remember, didn't want to see whatever was buried inside, but there was no choice. Toxins ate the last of his resistance, and his eyelids became lead weights he could no longer hold open.

"That's it." She shushed and cooed until his head lolled to the side. His body collapsed to the floor when she loosened his bonds. Lilith pulled him into her lap, and he curled into a ball. Long nails ran through his hair.

"Remember who you are, Kaemon. Show me what you did with it," Lilith encouraged, her lips cold against his ear. "Show me the box." Claws tore through Aaron's memories, ripping away chunks of his experiences to get to Kaemon's, digging deeper and deeper until they seized on what she wanted.

Flashes of a life Aaron didn't recognize rose and fell before him. Dreams and memories all a jumble. A sword, dark swirling shapes, a battle, Quinn's face covered in blood, blood, blood, blood.

"Who am I?" Aaron panted, skin glistening with sweat. "Where am I? What's happening to me?"

"Hush…Don't worry about that now. Relax, don't fight it, and everything will be okay." Cradled in her arms, she rocked him, kissed his head, stroked his hair. Aaron's breath caught in his throat as Lilith seized on the memory.

"There it is."

Pain rippled through his body.

"I knew it would still be in there somewhere, wrapped around his essence." There was a tug in his mind as Lilith drew the full memory to the surface.

15

After hours of meandering down back lanes, through unknown neighborhoods, and across stretches of open fields, Quinn found herself staring up at the red 4 Ever Fit sign. How she ended up in the gym parking lot, she had no idea. Working out usually helped clear her head, but she couldn't muster the energy to get out of the car. All her thoughts were mush, her brain tired of thinking, of rationalizing, of theorizing.

Marcus believed Aaron might be communicating through thought. A telepathic link or something else, she couldn't ignore that something strange was going on. Or was Aaron a product of brain damage like Jenna suggested?

Reese certainly didn't believe it. Reese wanted her to sweep it under the rug and get back to normal. Marcus wanted her to keep searching. Azrael wanted her to save humanity. Everyone had different ideas about what she should and shouldn't do with her life, but what did Quinn want? She didn't know. Not anymore. Not with Aaron gone.

Maybe her powers reached out to him somehow. If she could communicate with angels, maybe she could communicate with other essences. If Aaron tried to contact her, she had to at least try to listen. Intent was the key, focus on what you want, that was what Azrael kept harping on about. Clear the mind and picture the outcome. Quinn took a deep breath in through her nose, and then out through her mouth, centering herself.

Focusing on the steady beat of her heart, she tuned out the world around her and sank deep into a state of meditative Zen. The stillness of the car mimicked the stillness in her mind, smoothing out the waves and ripples of thought until a clear nothingness appeared before her. Within the nothingness, she pictured Aaron, letting her barrier relax, she thought of his eyes, his smile, the way he absentmindedly fingered the guitar pick when he was thinking.

"Aaron," she whispered, calling out to him with her mind, searching the empty void for any sign of him. A voice, a scent, anything that proved he still existed somewhere. Quinn let her essence float there for as long as she could, searching, calling, yearning for his touch, his voice, anything, but the same blank space greeted her.

"Aaron. Please," she begged. "I need to know you're okay." Uncertainty lashed at her hope, ripping holes in her confidence. A million tears poured down her cheeks, soaking her dress. He wasn't there, he never was. A wail started in the pit of her stomach and gushed from her mouth and with it all the pain and anguish. All the power in the world couldn't bring him back. She pounded her fists on the steering wheel and screamed and screamed and screamed until her voice was ragged and there was no emotion left. Day turned to dusk, turned into night, as she stared into nothingness. Hollowness lived where her heart should be.

"Hey, Blondie. You okay?" Caleb banged on the glass, startling her out of her stupor.

"Yeah, I'm fine." Quinn gripped the steering wheel,

avoiding eye contact. Maybe if she ignored him, he would give up and leave her alone.

"You don't look okay. You look like you've been in a fight. Did you know you have mud all over the side of your face?"

Quinn looked in the rear-view mirror and rubbed a sleeve on her cheek to get the dirt off. Caleb knocked on the glass again.

"Go away."

"You've been sitting out here all day. Can I at least call someone for you? A friend? If you need a friend, you can talk to me."

Quinn sucked on her bottom lip. Friends were in short supply these days, and Caleb wasn't so bad. At least she didn't have any history with him, which might be a good thing.

"We're not friends," Quinn said, but she found herself unlocking the door.

Caleb ran a hand through his still damp hair and settled into the passenger seat. He smelled of soap and shaving cream.

"You haven't moved since I started my shift this morning. Did something happen?"

Her chest tightened and heaved. Too personal, too quick. The tears were coming again, and he would see her fall apart. For a second, Quinn regretted letting him in. She should have just started the engine, driven off, left him in the dust. How was she supposed to answer that? What would he think of her? And that's when she realized she could say anything she wanted to him, because she didn't care what he thought. A laugh bubbled to her lips as tears leaked from her eyes.

"Are you hungry?" Quinn asked.

Caleb nodded, slow and unsure. Quinn started the engine and slammed the car into reverse. Caleb pressed his hand against the ceiling to steady himself against the sharp turn.

"You drive like you fight, Blondie. All anger and no finesse."

"Did I ask you?"

Caleb shook his head, knuckles white against the dash, and kept his mouth shut until she pulled into a dimly lit parking lot. On the side of the building, the owner had grafitied "Just Tacos" in giant hot pink, orange, and teal letters. Quinn scanned the lot for any cars she recognized, but it looked safe.

"Are we going in, or are you going to make me eat by myself?"

Quinn nodded, and followed Caleb through the double glass door. They settled into a small booth near the back. Piñatas hung over the tables, and the menu was decoupaged to the table along with brightly colored confetti.

"What's with the cagey twitching and downcast eyes? Afraid to be seen with me or something?"

"Something like that." Quinn glanced behind her. The last thing she wanted was to run into anyone from school, especially Jeff or Kerstin. It was why she stayed home at night, why she never went to Tony's anymore. Demons, she could face. Her ex and his pregnant girlfriend were another matter. Sometimes she dreamed of slamming her fist into Jeff's face for his part in Aaron's accident, and if she saw him, she wasn't sure she wouldn't follow through.

"You know, I missed watching you beat your own hand black and blue this morning. Where you been?"

"I don't want to talk about it."

"What can I get you?" The waitress popped her gum and tapped her pen on a pad. The words "Get Taco Or Get Out" blazed across her white T-shirt in bright green letters.

"Just water," Quinn said.

"Water? Seriously, that's it?" Caleb asked Quinn.

Quinn nodded. "I'm not that hungry."

"Brisket and jalapeño tacos. Thanks."

"Coming right up." The waitress scribbled on the notepad then tucked her pen in the pocket of her jeans. Quinn couldn't help noticing Caleb noticing the curve of her hips beneath the tight jeans.

"You can wipe the drool from your chin now."

"Jealous?"

"Hardly." The hairs on the back of Quinn's neck shot up, as if she'd stepped into an electromagnetic field, and she turned.

"What is it?" Caleb asked, but Quinn shushed him and lowered her shield just enough for the invisible to become visible. There, by the door, a lesser demon slid across the wall of the restaurant, a dim stain against the beige paint. A mere scout capable of mischief and not much more, but the girl it was attached to was a bigger problem.

"Crap." Quinn grabbed Caleb's arm and pulled him forward, just out of her line of sight. So much for not running into anyone she knew.

"If you wanted to hold my hand, all you had to do was ask." Caleb grinned.

"I can't face her. I'm begging you, hide me," Quinn hissed under her breath, but it was too late. Ami's squeal at the sight of Quinn hurt her ears.

"Oh, my God, Q.T. Is that you?" Ami, Westland High's favorite gossip, rushed the booth, pulled her up from her seat, and wrapped her arms around Quinn, strangling the life out of her. "Look who it is, Shae!" Shae, Ami's girlfriend, waved from the counter and continued to place an order, ignoring Ami. "How are you? I can't believe I ran into you, here of all places. I wanted pizza, but She wanted tacos. What luck!"

More like dumb luck, Quinn thought.

"Where have you been? Wait, hold that thought." Ami

pressed her head against Quinn's and snapped a picture with her phone. The demon slinked across the room and settled right behind her, smoky lips pressed to her ear. Hunger for gossip dripped from its essence as it fed off Ami's words. Her fingers flew across the screen—posting it to social media, no doubt.

"Why haven't you returned any of my calls or texts? Reese said you were lying low, but really, Quinn, I thought we were friends. I heard about Aaron's memorial this morning. I'm so sorry. We still can't believe he's really gone. Reese said it was a beautiful tribute. I'm sure everyone will be glad to put it behind them now. Does that mean you'll be coming back to school soon? Everyone misses you."

Quinn balled her fist as the demon bent and whispered in Ami's ear again. Caleb stepped forward, put his hand on her shoulder, and squeezed. Quinn shrugged him off, but Ami had already noticed. She looked from Quinn to Caleb. "Oh my god, I'm such an idiot. I'm going on and on, running my mouth, and I didn't even introduce myself. Shae always says I don't know when to shut up. I'm Ami." She held out her hand and Caleb stood to shake it.

"Caleb."

"Nice to meet you, Caleb." Ami cocked her head and the demon mimicked her. "Wait, you guys are on a date, aren't you?"

"No!" Quinn said as Caleb blurted out "Yes" and put his arm around her. Quinn shoved away his arm and took a step sideways. The demon smiled, showing three rows of razor-sharp teeth, each dripping with green saliva. Quinn wanted to pull the dagger from her boot and shove it into the middle of its essence, and then into Caleb for his stupidity.

"Well, I for one am glad to see you moving on, Quinn. Cute couple for sure! Way better than Jeff. Speaking of Jeff, he and Kerstin have done nothing but fight since Homecoming. I kind of feel sorry for her, you know, being preggers and all."

"You really don't know when to quit, do you?" Quinn asked.

"Excuse me?" Ami pressed her lips together and scowled.

Quinn might not be able to draw her dagger in the middle of the taco shop, but she could banish the demon with a word. Clear on her intent, she placed her hand on Ami's shoulder and expanded her barrier. Her gift pushed against the demon's essence, and its name came to her lips as easily as her own.

"Jezeb, it's time to go," she whispered, and the gossip demon recoiled in a hiss of smoke, compelled by her command.

Ami blinked and smiled. "What?"

"I said, Caleb and I have to go, but I'll call you next week. I promise." Quinn put on her widest fake smile and ushered Ami over to the counter where Shae waited.

"Oh, but you haven't even eaten. I was hoping Shae and I could join you."

"Can we get that to go?" Caleb waved at the waitress and laid a twenty on the counter, his face pale as if he'd seen a ghost or something. No, he couldn't have seen it. Could he? Turning to Ami, he held out his phone. "We would love to, but I just got a text from my boss. Someone didn't show up for the midnight shift, and I have to get going. Rain check?"

"Oh, yes, of course. We understand, don't we, Shae?" Shae nodded and took a brown bag from the waitress. "Well, looks like our order's ready anyway. I hope to see you at school on Monday. Bye, Caleb." Ami gave Quinn a big squeeze. "And we will be taking you up on that rain check."

Quinn pinched Caleb hard on the arm as Ami walked away.

"Ouch. What was that for?"

"Thanks to you, she thinks we're dating. Lesson one: never, ever tell Ami MacAfee anything she can turn into gossip, ever."

"Sorry. I panicked." Caleb ran a hand through his short hair. "You could go out with me, and then it wouldn't be gossip anymore."

"I'd rather eat tacos filled with razor blades."

"Too late, you only ordered water, remember?" Caleb grabbed the bag of tacos and shook them. "Come on, let's get out of here. This place is giving out bad vibes." He glanced over his shoulder to the exact spot where the demon had been.

When they got in the car, Caleb wouldn't stop staring at her.

"What?"

"You saw them too, didn't you?"

"Saw what?"

Caleb narrowed his eyes. "Don't play dumb, Quinn. The shadow attached to that girl, when you touched her, a bright light shot from your hands, and it retreated. What are you?" The hair on the back of Quinn's neck shot up.

Holy crap. Holy crap. Holy crap. Meathead could see them too? Quinn's brain could not process the concept. No, she had to be cautious.

"Ha. Demons, right."

Caleb grabbed her wrist. "I never said it was a demon."

Quinn gulped and yanked her wrist away. "Keep your voice down. Yes, all right. I can see them."

"I knew it." Caleb slammed his hand on the dashboard. "I thought maybe you could, the way you stared into the corners at the gym sometimes, right where the demon would form, but I wasn't sure. But then you did that thing to it in there, and I knew. How long?"

"How long, what?" Quinn asked.

"How long have you been able to see them?" Caleb asked.

"Too long." Quinn drew a lazy circle around the edge of the steering wheel considering how much she should tell him. "And can you banish them?"

"What? The demons? No. I only see them. Can you? Banish them, I mean?"

Quinn shrugged and stared at her hands. "Kind of."

Caleb furrowed his brow and stared out the window where Azrael had settled on the hood. "And what about that angel with black hair, two swords at his hips, and the scowl that looks like it could melt pure steel? Is he with you?"

Quinn turned, opened mouthed, and gawked at Caleb.

"You mean you can see him too?"

Caleb shrugged and stared at his hands. "Sometimes."

"So you knew he could see you?" Quinn didn't even bother to talk to Azrael in her head. Why should she? There was nothing to hide anymore. "And you didn't think to tell me that I wasn't alone in this?"

"There was nothing to tell. The ability resides in all humans, but rarely manifests. As your kind evolved, the knowledge of good and evil that Adam and Eve carried in their blood when they were banished became watered down after hundreds of thousands of years of breeding. The gift was all but lost, deemed unnecessary. But like any recessive gene, it pops up in the odd place."

"Are you talking to it?" Caleb looked truly shocked.

"What? You mean you can't hear him?"

Caleb shook his head. "No. I only get glimpses of them sometimes. They don't talk to me."

"See, he is not like you, Quinn. His ability is limited, useless."

"Well, it's not useless to me. You saw me falling apart, alone, freaking out." Quinn waved her fist in the air. "And you!" She directed her attention to Caleb. "Why didn't you tell me sooner?"

"I wasn't sure," Caleb stammered. "It's not like I go around telling everyone I see angels. You should get that." Caleb lowered his voice. "Nobody would believe me anyway. I learned that the hard way."

Quinn thought about Reese, about her reaction to even the slightest hint that Quinn was different, special. Here was someone who could understand her in a way nobody else could. Maybe she should trust him, let him in. She turned to Azrael because, for once, she actually wanted his advice.

"What do I know? I'm just your Sentinel." Azrael ruffled his feathers, pulled the golden sword from his hip, and examined the blade. "But you tell him for me, if he puts you in peril, I will remove his essence from his body so fast he won't even have time to blink."

Quinn turned the engine on and slammed the car in reverse. Startled, Azrael took to the sky, circling above the car as she drove away.

"Azrael says he will kill you if you betray me."

"At this rate, you'll kill me first." Caleb sank back in his seat, clutching the dash as she cut every sharp corner on the way back to the gym.

Ten minutes later, she brought the car to a stop in front of the 4 Ever Fit sign and turned off the engine.

"So, when was the first time you saw them?" Quinn asked.

"The first time I saw the shadows move, I was fifteen. My older sister brought her boyfriend to the house, a real nasty guy. They got into an argument, and the shadows started to shift and change. The angrier he got, the more demons appeared. I could see them feeding off him. One of the demons mimicked a fist, and the hair on the back of my neck stood on end. I didn't even stop to think. I leapt off the couch and stepped in front of my sister before he struck. The blow landed on the side of my head." Caleb rubbed his left temple. "Knocked me out. The next thing I know, the cops are cuffing him and hauling him out of the house."

"My God, Caleb. Did you tell her about the demons? Did she break up with him?" Caleb rubbed his jaw and stared out the front window. "No. She didn't want to hear it. She accused me of being crazy, said that it was just a side effect of the concussion, that I was making things up because I hated her. Demons tormented her too, but there wasn't anything I could do about it. What do you do when someone doesn't want to hear the truth?"

"I know how you feel." Quinn rubbed her thigh. "Even my best friend doesn't believe me. I can't blame her though. I don't think I would believe me either."

"Nope. You wouldn't." Caleb took a taco from the bag and handed it to Quinn. "Do you have any idea how amazing it is to be able to talk to someone about all this? To not be afraid of their reaction?"

Quinn smiled. "Welcome to Club Crazy. We meet every second Tuesday."

"Oh, man. Tuesdays are hard for me. Can we make it Wednesdays?" Caleb smiled, and Quinn tried to hide her grin. It felt good to trust someone, to share a secret.

"You want to know why I sat here all day? Why I had dirt on my face?"

Caleb nodded and started munching on a taco while Quinn recounted the story of what happened at the cemetery.

"I could feel Aaron, as real as you are right now, Caleb." Quinn wiped the tears away as fast as she could, but for every one that fell, two more leaked out. "Nobody believes that he could be alive, that he needs help. Even with all that I've seen, I can't wrap my head around it."

Caleb turned to her, his brown eyes warm as coffee.

"You're not alone." When a finger stroked her cheek, she shivered. "Aaron's a lucky guy to have someone who cares about him so much."

"It's getting late. I should get home before my mom goes ballistic," Quinn stammered.

"Yeah, I should get going too." Caleb cracked his knuckles and stared up at a streetlamp. "For what it's worth, if Aaron appeared to you at the memorial, I wouldn't ignore it. We live in a strange world, Quinn. Seems like anything is possible." He grabbed her cell phone from the console and began typing. "That's my cell phone number, if you ever need it." He opened the car door and paused, leaning on the frame. "See you tomorrow for some kickboxing?"

Quinn smiled and nodded. "Of course. Goodnight, Meathead. And thanks."

"Night, Blondie." Caleb closed the car door, waved, and disappeared behind the glass double doors of the gym.

16

The faint murmuring of Monday morning lectures droned on from behind the rows of closed classroom doors. Westland High felt smaller somehow, like last year's shoes. Being within its four walls pinched and suffocated Quinn. She'd outgrown its florescent-lit hallways full of idle gossip and meaningless social-ladder climbing. What was once the center of her whole life was now nothing but a pointless exercise in fake smiles and faker friendships. Nothing about it felt normal.

Quinn's mother had been as good as her word, going so far as to sit in on her appointment with Mr. Medina, the school counselor. After an hour of listening to two adults arguing and strategizing the best way to get Quinn back on track and across that stage in June, without even so much asking her how she felt, she was released back into the wild with a kiss on the cheek from her mother and a new, easier schedule from Mr. Medina. Out with the advanced placement classes and in with an extra elective. Quinn didn't care. Her phone buzzed as she left Mr. Medina's office, and she pulled it from her pocket.

CALEB: GOOD LUCK TODAY. YOU CAN DO THIS! I'LL HAVE A PUNCHING BAG READY FOR YOU AFTER SCHOOL THOUGH, JUST IN CASE.

She smiled at the text from Caleb. Over the last few days, they'd grown closer, sharing demon stories while training together at the gym. It was the one thing she looked forward to. Spending time with Caleb had become her safe haven, the only place in the world she could truly be herself. She couldn't help but wonder if that's what it would have been like if she had put her trust in Aaron instead of pushing him away.

QUINN: THANKS, MEATHEAD. CAN YOU PUT A PICTURE OF MY COUNSELOR'S FACE ON IT?

In some ways, Caleb reminded her of Aaron. Caring, loyal, willing to put himself in danger for those he cared about, but there was a cynical sarcasm there too that reminded her of herself. The more she got to know him, the more she liked him. Maybe she should feel guilty for that, but she didn't. Aaron was her first priority. She'd made that clear to Caleb, and he accepted it, or at least pretended to.

CALEB: DONE. SEE YOU AT THREE, BLONDIE. AND DON'T FORGET THE NEW GLOVES.

Replacing the phone in her pocket, she adjusted her backpack, took a deep breath, and started walking. She was supposed to be making her way to third period English, but instead found herself stuck in the middle of the long language arts corridor. The squeak of her boots on linoleum slowed as she approached a row of lockers on the right. There was no way to avoid it.

Hugging her literature book to her chest, she tried to ignore the instinct to run. She didn't want to look, but his locker called to her, a lantern against the gray concrete walls, and her feet ignored a plea to keep walking. Condolence cards still clung to the face of the dark purple metal, a rainbow of printed flowers and serene landscapes. On the wall above it hung a sign dotted with hundreds of signatures. In giant red letters it said:

GONE BUT NOT FORGOTTEN.
WESTLAND HIGH WILL MISS YOU.

Scanning the cards, she read the touching messages full of platitudes. People who hadn't even known Aaron poured out their grief in a barrage of meaningless words for a boy few had taken the time to get to know. Wasn't she as guilty as they were? She wiped a tear with the back of her hand.

A few feet to her left marked the spot where Aaron saved her from fainting. Everyone had called him Superman and sang his praises, all but Quinn. Like a fool, she had called out for Jeff, ignoring the best thing that could have happened to her. There wasn't a moment when she didn't wish she could go back in time and change that very instant when she woke up in his arms. Now Aaron only lived inside her head, a ghost in the machine.

The corners of her textbook dug into her chest as she tried to suppress the memory of Aaron smiling at her, laughing with Marcus.

An exit sign flashed red above the door at the end of the hallway. In less than ten seconds, she could be through it and out into the parking lot before anyone knew she was gone. Why should she stay? Nothing here mattered. High school was nothing but a lie, a farce, and she didn't want to be a part of it anymore. Everyone had written him off, but she wouldn't. She couldn't do this, act like everything was all right, move forward with her life. The whole show of it brought bile to her throat.

Her vision narrowed then stretched as dizziness spiraled around her head. Suddenly, her literature book became a ten-ton brick in her arms. She couldn't hold onto it any longer, and it slipped through her grasp, thudding on the hard linoleum below.

Struggling to catch her breath, she wrenched the confining scarf away from her neck and searched for something to steady herself. Her sweaty palm found the cool metal of Aaron's locker door, and she closed her eyes, taking deep breaths to stave off the drowning feeling.

Touching something of his had a calming effect, and her heart stopped throwing punches at her rib cage. She couldn't help picturing Aaron standing with her, a soothing hand on hers, green eyes dancing as he leaned in for a kiss. Regret ripped at the hole he'd left inside her, and she couldn't hold back the flood.

An icy chill ran up Quinn's spine, and she stiffened as the light touch of a phantom finger brushed the tears from her cheek. Her eyes flew open and scanned the hallway. The human realm appeared empty, but her senses picked up slight vibrations, dark disturbances clinging to the shadows, that made her stomach clench.

Aaron's combination lock clanged against the metal frame, as if someone knocked a hand against it. Quinn startled and backed away, her breath coming in sharp bursts as the temperature dropped. An intense feeling of being watched overcame her. Blinking, she watched the lock vibrate, the dial inching to the right until it landed on the number two. A click indicated it had hit the right spot. The dial spun to the left, faster this time, reaching twenty-seven. Another click, and a spin back to the right. When it stopped on seven, the curved shackle popped out of the case and the padlock fell to the ground with an echoing bang.

"Aaron?" she whispered.

The door inched open, and Quinn held her breath, hoping he would appear to her the way he had at the cemetery. She turned in a slow circle, looking for any signs of his manifestation, but if it was him, he remained hidden. It must be him. Quinn whipped around as the door squeaked open another centimeter.

"Aaron is that you?" she whispered again, an invocation.

In response, the door swung wide as if caught in a gust of wind, banging against the adjoining locker, causing her to flinch.

She stared at the open compartment and twisted a short strand of hair around her finger. Nobody had taken the time to empty its contents, and the inside lay untouched, exposing a piece of Aaron she hadn't taken a chance to know. Such a personal space, the inside of a locker, and she was anxious about invading it without him there. There were the usual textbooks, and a collage of pictures and poetry scrawled in his messy hand were stuck to the sides with a collection of small black and white magnets.

Aaron smiled at her, one arm around Jenna, the other around Cade. They stood in front of a drum set in what looked like a garage. His guitar hung from his shoulder, and he looked as happy as she'd ever seen him.

Jealousy bit at Quinn's heart as she thought of dark-haired, beautiful, and no-nonsense Jenna singing with Aaron, wrapping her arms around him in a hug, kissing in the bleachers. There was nothing between them but friendship, but maybe if they were together before that day he rescued Quinn in the hallway, he never would have fallen for her, never would have been at the river that night, would still be alive.

The other picture showed Marcus and Aaron standing back to back, arms folded across their chests, baseball caps on backwards, sporting a pair of fake mustaches with you-know-you-want-some-of-this smirks. An overwhelming need to possess that picture gripped her. Was this what

Aaron wanted her to find? She looked left, then right, to make sure her crime wasn't observed.

When she moved the magnet that held it in place, her sleeve caught on the tip of a spiral notebook. Jerking her arm up and back, the small black binder tumbled to the floor and landed at her feet with a thump. Her hands trembled as she bent to pick up the journal. The handwriting was distinctly Aaron's, a slanted mix of block and cursive. *So that's why Marcus and Josh couldn't find it.* They'd both been through his room half a dozen times looking for it. Quinn had checked the ruins of St. Angeles in case it had been hidden there, and Marcus had even begged Jenna to have a look around her garage. They'd all given up, but here it was. Nobody even thought to look in his locker.

"Aaron, is this what you wanted me to find?"

Nausea tugged at her gut. Even with her guard up, she sensed the change in the atmosphere as something hungry and corrupt approached. The temperature dropped ten degrees in less than a second. Quinn's breath came out in a white mist, as if she were standing in a winter storm instead of in the middle of a warm building. This wasn't Aaron.

A powerful demon entered the hallway, cutting a long knife-like shadow across the floor. It had been manipulating her, playing with her mind.

Behind it walked a girl, red hair like fire blazing in long disheveled curls. Kerstin stared at Quinn, eyes completely jet black, her face full of malice. Her lips curled into a snarl, making the hair on the back of Quinn's neck prickle and burn.

"Welcome back, Quinn Perfect," Kerstin purred with a not quite human voice. "We've been waiting for you."

17

Piercing screams tore through a swirling mist, and the smell of smoke and sulfur choked Aaron's lungs. No, not Aaron's lungs—Kaemon's. Golden wings spread wide; he circled above a large waterfall. The roar of the cascade poured into the river below, drowning out the angry howls of the demons swarming the lush landscape below. The war had begun. Lilith had returned to Eden from the Underworld to take revenge on Adam and his new wife, Eve.

Before Eve, Lilith was Adam's wife, but when she sought the forbidden tree of knowledge for herself, Adam betrayed her to The Light. As punishment, The Light stripped her of her title as Keeper and cast her into the Underworld. Now, she wanted them all to pay.

Kaemon watched as a half-eaten apple fell from Adam's hand, red skin bright as fresh blood against the spring-green carpet of pristine grass. As it hit the ground, the fruit shriveled, the shape caving in on itself. In seconds, it had decomposed, turning brown and then black, like someone had charred the edges of the skin. From the center of the mush that was once a living fruit, a funnel of smoke blossomed. It rose three feet above the ground and cascaded back down in a mushroom cloud before spreading across the landscape.

Hideous creatures erupted from the fog, like worms pushing their way to the surface after a rain. Some slithered, some crawled, and others stood on two legs like men with leathery wings protruding from skeleton-like forms. The garden was breached. Everything the demons touched died and rotted, their presence a plague upon the land, and he could feel their evil intent rolling off them like waves. Hungry, so hungry, they wanted to eat until satiated; life, beauty, meaning, they sought to take it at any cost, for her, Lilith, their mother, their queen, for revenge.

As the smoke cleared, animal carcasses littered the countryside. All the trees in the great forest lay twisted and dead. The taint from the demon horde killed every living thing it touched and turned beauty into desolation.

Dozens of Elite angels followed Kaemon, weapons at the ready. Righteous anger burned in their hearts, fueling their power. Thunder rolled across the sky, dark clouds gathering over the horizon, moving fast. The war had begun.

Remiel, Zephon, find Lilith. I want her essence flung back into the Underworld now. Do you understand? The rest of you, spread out. Take down as many as you can. Kaemon relayed the message through his telepathic link with the rest of the host. *Be careful, the enemy has taken the Qeres fields.*

Eden was the only realm where Qeres flowers bloomed, from which came the poison that killed immortals, angels, and demons alike. Lilith knew exactly where the flowers were cultivated; she tended the garden herself before her banishment and commanded her army to rip out the purple flowers by the roots and coat their own weapons in the deadly juice of the plant. The raw poison wouldn't do as much damage as a proper Qeres blade forged in the fire of the Arcadian sun, but they would be dangerous enough.

Tucking his wings to his side, Kaemon started his descent, circling toward the epicenter of the destruction. What had been grass was now nothing but dust. The evil taint released from Lilith's poisoned apple spread, a black plague across the land.

There, in the middle of the chaos, kneeled a girl in the center of a blackened ring that spread outward for miles. Eve. Adam's new wife. Kaemon felt regret dripping from her like rain. So, this was her doing. Disguised as a serpent, Lilith had led Eve astray. Her emotions pulsed with shame; her heart crushed under the weight of her betrayal. Long, brown hair cascaded against her bare back and past her waist in sweeping curls. In her hands, she clutched the other half of the apple.

Smoke writhed through Eve's fingers, evil trying to escape, but she wouldn't let go of the tainted fruit, wouldn't let the rest of the demon horde touch her beautiful home, not like Adam had. Adam's disgrace drove him back inside the cave to hide from what he'd done, a coward. Kaemon sensed her determination and courage, but he feared her desire to correct her mistake was a little too late.

Refusing to give up, she pursed her lips and grabbed the closest container she could find, a small, carved, wooden chest, and dropped the remaining apple into it. It would take more than that to hold the rest of the demon horde, but maybe it would buy the angelic host a little more time. He had to admire her courage.

On her knees, Eve clutched the container that kept the rest of Lilith's children from being loosed on Eden to her chest. It quaked as the trapped demons pushed the lid, trying to escape. She wept in fear and remorse, tears rushing down her cheeks to fall upon the polished wood. Kaemon watched in awe as a rainbow of phosphorescent runes etched themselves upon the box, a new prophecy writing itself to bring balance back to the realms.

When the tears of Eve have turned to blood and her sins have turned to flesh, the key will fall. For love is bound by the power of the Trinity. Their destiny is written by chaos and betrayal, and on the first eclipse of the eighteenth year, the voice of the sacrifice will break the lock, restoring darkness unto the light. By this promise, be compelled.

Somehow, her regret and desire to right the wrong acted as a catalyst, calling forth an inner power. This was something beyond the control of The Light. An intricate system of checks and balances was in constant play to ensure no one realm dominated over another. Kaemon had witnessed many a miracle that kept the scales from tipping one way or the other for too long. There were loopholes within loopholes, and it was the job of the Dominions to keep track of all the threads and find ways to gain the upper hand.

In the celestial hierarchy, Kaemon belonged to the first order of angels called The Powers, and as a Power, a warrior Elite, part of Kaemon's job was to restore order to chaos. Keep the box away from Lilith, keep her from finding a way to open it and gaining the key to unleashing the rest of her army.

After the last rune blazed across wood, a bright light flashed, sealing the box with magic, and the prediction faded like invisible ink, but Kaemon's memory would never let him forget what he'd read as he hovered transfixed above her shoulder.

Thunder cracked, and a rift opened in the ground before them, startling them both from their stupor. A demon rose from the crack, eight feet in height with hollow eyes, horns like a ram, and a long, skeletal snout curving down into one sharp bone tooth. Spikes protruded from his furry back and shoulders like lances, and his armor appeared to be made of cobwebs and smoke. Another crack opened behind them. Six serpents with bodies as thick as tree trunks slithered through the rift. One reared back to strike the girl, but Kaemon was faster, chopping its head from its body. Black blood spurted from the wound, the tail still wriggling.

He had one simple task. Protect the Keepers until this was over. He should never have let his guard down, even for a second. Wind whipped at his tunic as he took to the air, drawing them away from Eve as best he could. Grabbing her chance at escape, Eve darted to the right, making for the cave, but she stumbled, and the chest fell from her hands. It tumbled end over end until it landed at the edge of the rift.

Leave it, save yourself. Kaemon used his telepathic ability to guide her, but she disregarded him and scrambled to retrieve her charge, putting her directly in the path of the large bone demon. Such a stubborn child. Now he would have to rescue her. Before Kaemon could reach her, the bone demon snatched the box with one hand and wrapped the other around Eve's throat. Holding them both up in triumph, it let out a howl that shook the ground.

Eve choked out a strangled scream, clawing at the exposed bone and sinew on the creature's arm, trying to get loose. But the monster laughed and shook her so hard Kaemon thought her neck might snap.

All the fire of the Arcadian sun raced through Kaemon, and he shot straight into the air. An arc of blue, like a bolt of lightning, cut the demon's head from his body. Smoke poured from its severed neck as immortal poison ate away at his essence and turned him to dust before he hit the ground. The box fell from the ashes of one hand, while the girl tumbled from the grip of the other. Lilith's entire army howled in rage and turned all their attention to him.

18

Quinn pressed her back against the lockers until the metal bit into her shoulder. Kerstin's demon had grown since she'd last seen it. Six feet tall, it towered over her petite frame. Dozens of tentacles whipped and writhed from its shifting body of fog, pushing through Kerstin's chest, wrapping around her arms, curling in her hair like a deadly vine. Smaller threads of the creature connected directly to her skin, reminding Quinn of the strings of a marionette. Quinn hugged herself as her grief intensified, her head pulsing in pain as the beast tried to break through her defenses.

"Kerstin? You have to let me help you," Quinn stammered. She strained to catch her breath as the demon's essence pushed against hers, looking for a crack in her barrier. Sweat beaded on her lip, and she resisted, using all her energy to focus on keeping it out.

The demon laughed from Kerstin's throat. "It's too late for that now. The girl has been the perfect host, such anger and insecurity to feed on. And look how we've grown?"

"Leave her alone." Quinn pushed forward the bubble of

light surrounding her, trying to engulf Kerstin in the protective shield, but the demon was too strong.

"You don't have the power to banish the likes of us, Eol Ananael. I am stronger than you." Smoke slithered around Kerstin, obscuring her from sight. "This one is mine until she dies."

Heat pulsed against Quinn's calf, and she reached for her dagger, but before she could pull it from the sheath, a misty tendril pushed through her defenses. The light barrier cracked around her as the tendril threaded into her chest. Frozen in place, she tried to call to Azrael for help, but the creature's power had wrapped around her gift, suppressing her ability to communicate with her Sentinel.

"Regret," the creature said. "So full of it, there's room for little else inside that soul of yours. We can feel it running through you, calling to us, the grief and guilt. You are guilty, aren't you, Quinn?"

Quinn convulsed as a cold hand squeezed her heart between invisible fingers. Pain exploded through her chest, the beat slowing under the crushing weight of the demon's influence.

"It would have been easier for everyone if you had died in that river like we planned. I could do it now, squeeze until you have a heart attack. So easy." A crooked smile twisted Kerstin's lips. "As easy as watching a stupid boy die for love of you."

Anger filled every inch of Quinn. She could feel her face flush as heat rose in her cheeks. This creature and all his brethren had pushed her and Aaron apart, threatened her, driven her to the brink of insanity. Her biggest remorse was listening to them in the first place.

Your regret is like a black beacon, Azrael had warned. *You must let go of your guilt, let go of the boy.* Azrael was wrong, it wasn't giving up on Aaron that would help her, it was holding him close. Quinn gritted her teeth and reached for the spark of light deep within. A kiss under the stars. The melody to Aaron's song thrummed through her, and she felt the demon's grip weaken.

Power, hot and white, burned within Quinn. Blue lightning crackled around her, aching to be released. A deep breath focused all her energy into her intent, and she released the blow into the demon. The demon jerked backward, pulling Kerstin with it. Together, they flew six feet down the hall, slammed into a row of lockers and crumpled to the floor, energy sparking around Kerstin's skin like tiny fireworks.

"Your name, demon," Quinn demanded, her confidence growing with her anger.

"I'll never tell you." Black eyes wide, the demon hissed.

"Eudmhox?" Like a flash, the demon's name was on her lips. "Jealousy, is it?"

"No, you can't make me leave. This one called to me, wanted me." The creature hugged Kerstin close. "You have no right."

"Do you know what this is, Eudmhox?" Quinn pulled the glowing blue dagger from its sheath and pressed the tip to the hollow of Kerstin's throat. Kerstin's body convulsed with its touch and Quinn grinned.

"That old thing doesn't have enough poison in it to kill one such as me."

"We'll see." Quinn dragged the dagger across Kerstin's skin and the demon screamed and shrank back. Kerstin's eyes flashed from black back to blue as his dark influence wavered. Seizing the chance, Quinn wrapped her power around Eudmhox's essence, ripped his shadow from Kerstin, and threw him across the hall. In a blink of an eye, Eudmhox shrank into a tiny black fly and then zoomed through the roof and out of the building before Quinn could invoke the banishment.

Well done. Azrael stepped through the row of lockers behind her, swords drawn, a grin on his face.

He got away. Quinn returned the dagger to her boot.

Azrael nodded. *You will have another chance. His hold on the girl is strong.*

Coming back to herself, Kerstin blinked and looked at Quinn, confused. "What are you doing here?" She glanced around, forehead knitting in worry.

"Heading to class. You?" Quinn offered a hand, but Kerstin pushed her away and pulled herself up on the edge of Aaron's open locker.

Be careful. Even now I feel a small piece of him squatting inside her like a virus, Azrael warned.

"None of your business." She stumbled, and Quinn grabbed her elbow to steady her.

"Are you feeling okay?" Quinn asked.

"Why?" Kerstin jerked away and glared as if Quinn were the devil himself.

"Well, I wanted to make sure you're all right, that's all. You look a little green around the gills."

"Look, you can drop the goody-goody attitude. Keep your friends close and your enemies closer, is that your game? We're not friends." Kerstin smoothed a stray curl with the palm of her hand.

"Paranoid much? There is no game; that's what I'm trying to tell you." Quinn tried to re-assure her.

"As if. You say you don't want him because you know he loves me, not you. I know you'd like nothing better than for me to disappear, me and the baby. Don't worry, Quinn, I won't give you the satisfaction." She thrust a hand into Quinn's face. A diamond the size of a pea sparkled under the florescent lights.

Quinn rolled her eyes. A few months ago, the sight of Jeff's engagement ring on Kerstin's hand would have sent her over the edge, but not now. Truth was, it all seemed so stupid and juvenile—the fact that Kerstin slept with Jeff, his lies, the pregnancy—like something that happened to another Quinn in another life. She still cared about Jeff, but because of what they had, not because she wanted something more. And Kerstin, well, she realized that she and Kerstin were a lot more alike than she wanted to admit.

Quinn shrugged. "Congratulations. I hope things work out between the two of you. You both deserve to be happy."

"Oh, we're very happy. And don't think that just because you're back anything's going to change." She rubbed a hand over her belly.

"We've both been through hell, Kerstin. Don't you think it's time to put it all behind us and start over? I don't want to fight with you. Honestly, all I want is to get through the rest of the year and get out of this hell hole and forget everything that's happened here."

A remnant of the demon surged through Kerstin, turning her pupils into black saucers. Azrael drew his sword, but she stayed his hand.

She's not going to hurt me. The spirit's hold has weakened. I'm fine.

Azrael ruffled his feathers. *For now, but no doubt it will return. She is a gaping wound, an empty vessel waiting to be filled.*

She's a human.

She's a pawn of the Underworld.

A pawn, which is all the more reason to try to help her. She didn't envy the confusion and pain that came with that darkness, no matter how she felt about Kerstin.

"What would you know about my life? You don't have any idea what I've been through, and don't pretend to give a shit. I don't care about your little sob story. I have it pretty good compared to you," Kerstin continued on her rant. "I'm not the one who leapt off a rock in a desperate attempt for attention. I'm not the one who killed Aaron."

Kerstin reeled as Quinn's palm slammed into her cheek. "Don't you ever mention his name to me again. Do you hear me?" Quinn's warning escaped in a growl.

And you wanted to help her?

Quinn gave Azrael a dirty look. He shrugged, sheathed his blade, and disappeared through a wall and back out onto the Westland campus.

"What the hell?" Jeff sprinted to Kerstin and cupped her jaw in his hand.

Great. Quinn should have known he wouldn't be far. They were like conjoined twins, the two of them. Quinn crossed her arms over her chest and braced herself. There would be no way to defend her position. All Jeff had seen was Quinn slapping his pregnant fiancé. Never mind that Kerstin had been harboring a demon and had started the fight, or that all Quinn had wanted was to lay low. Kerstin wouldn't let her. Quinn would get the blame and Kerstin would get the sympathy. *Welcome back to Westland High, Quinn.*

"God, Quinn. Look at this!" Jeff turned Kerstin's cheek so she could see. A red mark stung the skin but would quickly fade. She hadn't hit her that hard, but Kerstin was out to win an Emmy for best performance with her tears, and the gloating smirk on her face when Jeff wasn't looking made Quinn want to smack her again.

"I want to go home, Jeff. Please, take me home." Kerstin sobbed and pulled at his sleeve, a child begging a parent. "Tell the nurse I'm too sick to drive myself. I need to get out of here, I need you."

"Fine. Go wait for me in the car," Jeff said.

"Aren't you coming?"

"I have a few things I need to say to Quinn first."

"I'm not leaving you alone with her." Kerstin's eyes flashed from blue to inky black.

Jeff gave Kerstin a hard look that Quinn had never seen before, his patience running thin. The fog rolled around Kerstin, thick and black, but she didn't argue. Instead, she turned and stomped down the hall. Jeff waited until she had disappeared around the corner then turned to Quinn.

"Nobody's seen you for weeks. Reese said you locked yourself away like Miss Havisham from that Dickens novel. The whole school's been worried. I've been worried. Now you show up, and within five minutes Kerstin's been assaulted. What were you thinking? She's pregnant, Quinn."

"Yeah, no need to remind me." Quinn rubbed the toe of her shoe on the back of her jeans and stared at the ground.

"I don't even know who you are anymore," Jeff said.

"Of course, you don't. I'm not the same Quinn you dated for four years and then cheated on, or the Quinn who foolishly fell right back into your arms because she was too afraid to trust herself. You can't go back, Jeff, and frankly, I don't want to anymore."

"I'm sorry, for what it's worth, about Aaron, about everything." Jeff rubbed at his temples. "I know those words are a little too late, and not nearly good enough to erase the damage that's been done. I was running too, from the mess I made. I didn't know how to handle it."

"Yeah, well, we've all made mistakes." As much as she should hate him, hate Kerstin, none of it mattered anymore. Jeff was the past, and her future didn't have room for him. "Let's forget about it."

Jeff nodded. "I still care about you, I'll always care, but I think it would be easier for everyone if you stayed away from Kerstin and me from now on."

Quinn nodded. "I think that's for the best."

A knot twisted in her gut as Jeff disappeared down the

hall. Maybe she shouldn't have let him go without warning him. No, nothing good could have come out of him knowing. He had made his choice, and no matter what Quinn said, he wouldn't believe her. Besides, she had other things to focus on, and none of it had to do with school.

Aaron's journal lay beneath his still open locker. She bent to pick it up, along with the photo of him and Marcus. Quinn fanned through the book. The pages were filled with a few other entries along with poetry, guitar chords, and sketches of gardens, angels, and her own face.

The handwriting on one particular section drew her attention. It looked so different than the other pieces of scrawled notes and poetry. The lyrics to "Starlight Memory," the song he'd written for her, were neatly printed in blue ink, filling the blank space as he had poured his heart onto the page for her, for them. Each lyric had been carefully put on the page, with purpose. She traced the lines of the lyrics with a finger, the haunting melody playing along with the words.

Another page turn revealed a letter in the same hand. At the top of the left corner was her name, printed in blue ink. It looked as if he had written it over and over in the same place, the letters overlapping each other, her name bold against the stark white. Jagged white teeth edged the sheet where it had been ripped from the binder and hastily replaced with a small strip of tape. It looked as if it had been crumpled and then smoothed out again, the author torn on whether or not to keep it. When she looked at the date, she understood why.

September 15th, the night of their first date, the night she stole Marcus's Jeep and Aaron walked in on her and Jeff kissing. It had been the beginning of the end.

Quinn,

That night under the stars, you said something that got me thinking. You wondered if I had come back from the brink of death for you. What if it's true? What if you're the reason I'm supposed to be here?

Quinn remembered curling her body against his, the way he had given her his trust, shown his true heart without hesitation, and how she let herself fall in love so completely in that moment that she had been willing to ignore the demons bent on keeping them apart. Looking back, it was the one and only time she let herself believe their connection was more than a crush, that it was magic, dangerous, and exciting. What if he had been sent back for her? Fate or destiny, all the things the cynicism of adult reality had ripped from her the minute her father had left, the second Jeff had cheated, restored with Aaron's kiss, his arms around her.

But the spell cast that night faded as the shadows of fear and doubt settled on her, whispering in her ear. She had been so distracted, she never stopped to consider why the demons would fight so hard to keep her away from Aaron if he were nothing more than an ordinary boy. Had they known something she had been too blind to see, or had she been too much of a coward to see the truth?

Such a beautiful little fool, Quinn thought to herself. Daisy's statement to Nick and Jordan in her favorite novel took on a frightening new relevance. Rubbing the ache above her chest, she went back to the entry.

I hope today is the day for a new beginning for us. It's hard for me to put into words how I feel about you, so I decided to do what I do best and say it with a song. I hope you were surprised by Starlight Memory and all that it expressed. Music and you are the only two things that make me feel centered in this world. I don't know why I'm drawn to you, but I am. Your smile, your happiness, means everything to me. You inspire me.

Yours always,
Aaron

She couldn't change the past, but it didn't mean she

couldn't make it right. She could make this right, listen, believe, stop being afraid. The future wasn't written yet. She flipped to the next page. The entry was short and not so sweet, the handwriting chaotic, angry.

September 16th

When I reach out with my ability, there's nothing there. Not a thought, not an emotion, nothing but an endless black void. I can't feel her in my mind at all anymore.

Marcus had been right. Proof that she and Aaron had some sort of psychic connection. Heat rose in her cheeks, and she gripped the edge of the journal.

I keep asking myself why I even care, why I feel such a weight of responsibility for her, but there is no reason, only this nagging sense of dread in my gut that won't go away. I can't help her. She won't open up to me, and I can't read her mind, even with the help of my gift, I can't see anything clearly. So full of secrets that it's hard not to want to rip them from her. I keep reminding myself that she doesn't even want my help. She's thrown the truth of it in my face enough.

Having read enough, Quinn closed the journal and hugged it to her chest as if it might bring them closer together. Proof that Marcus was right about Aaron's gift couldn't be denied. Reese would have to believe her now, they would have to help her look for him. Her heart turned upside down, draining all the sorrow and pain she'd been trying to hold back ever since she'd emerged from the river. Tucking both journal and picture in her purse, she sent Marcus a text.

QUINN: MEET ME IN THE SCHOOL PARKING LOT IN FIVE.

Not wanting anyone else to have access to Aaron's private space, she closed the metal door and replaced the lock. The shackle clicked into place and Quinn started for the nearest side exit before anyone else noticed her.

19

Kaemon held firm as they advanced, pushing the girl behind him for safety, but she refused to move, standing her ground in defiance of the darkness destroying her home. Picking up rocks, she started throwing them at the approaching enemy. Kaemon was torn between laughing at her foolish attempt and admiration for her warrior spirit.

Kaemon picked up the girl and placed her under his arm. Nothing but skin and bone, she kicked and screamed, scratching him with sharp nails, but Kaemon held tight. He glanced around for an escape route. The trees above trapped him to the ground, the cave wall was at his back, and the demons had him surrounded on three sides. The only way out was straight through. Suicide, especially with over a hundred gleaming poisoned blades heading right for him. He tensed his muscles and took a deep breath. Spreading his golden wings, he dug in his heels and sprinted forward, the Elite battle cry pouring from his lungs.

Rallied by Kaemon's battle cry, the Elite warriors of the heavenly host descended on the darkness in a bright mass of wings and weapons. Distracted by the incoming attack, the demons turned, and Kaemon seized the opportunity. Flourishing his blade in a figure eight with one hand, the girl still held firm with the other, he pushed his wings outward, knocking a path through the enemy line. Any left standing found the sharp end of the Qeres sword, their essence shriveling to dust and scattering to the wind.

A war raged behind him as the forces of light and dark collided, but Kaemon sheathed his weapon and took to the skies while the host engaged the enemy. More than a hundred angels dressed for battle descended into the smoke, swords swinging wildly, cutting down the enemy where they stood. Balls of fire rained from above, like comets, destroying everything in their path and setting what was left of the trees on fire.

Linked with his fellow warriors, he understood their rage, knew each movement, and felt every death. And there were many, Qeres eating away at their immortal souls like acid. Need coursed through him, the call of war hard to resist, but Kaemon couldn't turn back.

Keeping the girl and the box safe was more important. She had stopped fighting the minute they lifted off the ground. Holding her around the waist, they circled high above the battlefield, keeping clear of danger. He thought she would be afraid, but instead excitement and exhilaration pulsed through her as strong and steady as her heartbeat. A smile lit her face, and the wind caught at her long, dark hair. For a moment, Kaemon thought she was the most beautiful thing he'd ever seen and regretted that soon he would have to let her go and send her to a new realm with the boy, Adam.

Can we go higher? Her wish was easy enough to fulfill, and he beat his wings, taking them high into the clouds and across the gardens.

Surveying the damage, he felt the pain bloom inside her, regret and guilt eating away at her happiness.

All because of me. He heard Eve's thoughts through their psychic link.

Kaemon couldn't argue. It was her fault, all of it, but Lilith could be convincing, he knew.

As they flew over a ridge, Kaemon spotted Lilith surveying the devastation of her forces, a black dot on a silver steed. Shadows writhed around its hooves as it pawed the ground. His brethren reduced her army to nothing but ash. Catching his eye, Lilith pushed back the hood of her inky cloak to reveal raven hair and silver eyes so stunningly cold they would freeze the heart of any who dared gaze into them too long.

The dozen or so angels left gave chase at Kaemon's command. In defiance, Lilith reared her horse. Racing over the ridge, wings outstretched, the angels descended, but she was quicker, urging her steed into a portal and disappearing back into the Underworld.

The boy, Adam, emerged from the cave as Kaemon and Eve landed, and Kaemon wondered how such a coward had been named First Keeper of Eden. No wonder Lilith refused to be bound to him for all eternity, choosing banishment to the Underworld instead.

"What do we do now?" Adam asked, surveying the desert of ash that was once a thriving paradise.

"We can't stay here." Eve ran her thumbs over the polished wooden box as if making sure it was still locked tight. "Can't you feel it? The taint has soaked every inch of soil. Nothing will grow here again, and we are no longer Keepers. We are something else entirely."

"This is our home." Adam stomped his foot like a spoiled child. "I told you we shouldn't eat the fruit from that tree. The Light forbade it."

Eve glared at him and tapped out an impatient rhythm on the side of the box with her fingers. "And yet you ate it anyway. I didn't force you to eat it. It was your choice as much as mine. Don't lay all the blame at my feet."

"It was your idea!"

"And you were stupid enough to listen to me!"

Adam raised his hand as if to slap her, and she flinched. Kaemon stepped between them.

"That is enough. Look at yourselves, pointing the finger, placing blame on one another. The garden is not the only thing that is tainted. Eating the fruit changed you both and Eden will no longer accept the frequency at which your essences now resonate."

Eve bowed before him. "I'm sorry. The serpent said the fruit would give me secret wisdom, wisdom I would need to be a good Keeper of the garden. She said Adam and I both needed to eat it. That it would please The Light. Please don't make us leave."

"And did it? Give you secret wisdom?" Kaemon asked, already knowing the answer.

Eve nodded, her hair covering her face. "Eating it showed me many things, both strange and terrible, things I dare not repeat. All these thoughts are clouding my mind. There is a strange fight going on inside of me, both beauty and despair. I've never been ... afraid before." The word was foreign on her tongue and in her thoughts. "I no longer feel safe."

"What is twisted cannot be straightened; what is lacking cannot be counted. This world is not a safe place anymore. You saw to that. Such is the burden of wisdom. Lilith knows how to manipulate even the strongest of creatures." It was a half-truth, but it seemed to comfort the girl.

"What do we do now?" Eve asked.

"What you do with the knowledge you have is your choice alone. I am sorry, Eve. You are the master of your new fate, as is Adam. Harmony is broken, but you will have to hold yourselves together as best you can."

"What about the garden? Who will look after it?"

Kaemon turned back to the garden. The devastation was immense. Everything withered and died; even the two suns were drained of their light, leaving the garden draped in shadow. Bones crunched beneath his feet, dead animals that once freely roamed the place of paradise. "The garden is dead. You will be banished to a new realm. The gates will close. No one will be allowed in. It is poisoned beyond repair."

As an Elite warrior within the order, it was now up to him to restore the balance and find them a new home, a realm where their taint would be contained.

Eve wiped a tear from her eye and straightened her spine. "There is nothing I can do?"

"You've done enough. Your retribution is just beginning. Your new realm will not be quite the paradise you're used to. From this day, you will forever stumble in dark while seeking The Light. Some days it will elude you, some days you will find it, but have faith always. Now, Adam, give me your hand." Kaemon drew his sword, and Adam shrunk back, but Eve stood tall, looked him in the eye, and gave him hers instead.

"No, little one, it is his turn to feel the weight of his actions." Kaemon motioned Adam to come forward. Adam took a tentative step toward him, glaring at Eve. Using his sword, Kaemon sliced open Adam's finger, letting his blood soak the dying ground. His blood would create a new realm for them to live in, one suited to the resonance of their new essences.

With the last drip from Adam's finger, a portal opened before them, revealing a young garden with grass pushing through the arid land in small tuffs. A waterfall trickled down a cliff, and beyond, a beach looked out into a vast ocean. Their new home was a rough copy of the realm they had desecrated. A mix of the old and the new, just like their souls. It would do.

"You cannot stay here another moment." Kaemon stepped through and offered his hand.

Adam clung to Eve and shook his head, but Eve lifted her chin and stepped over the threshold into the new world, dragging Adam behind her. With a snap, the portal closed behind them, and Adam ran, fear driving him into the familiarity of a nearby cave. Eve didn't even look back. Instead, she watched Kaemon with eyes the color of night, the box clutched to her chest.

"What about Lilith. Will she return?"

"I am afraid that your taint makes you vulnerable. The very knowledge you carry can both repel the darkness and draw it to you. Finding your own way is crucial. Because of your betrayal, the veil is thin between this realm and the Underworld. But it also falls under the jurisdiction of The Light, as Eden did. Now, give me the box."

Eve looked at the polished wood. "It was a gift from The Light on my naming day, the only thing I have left from my home."

"You know what it holds inside. Lilith would not hesitate to release the rest of her horde into your new world. I cannot allow you to keep it."

Eve nodded and handed him the box, the runes glowing bright as their hands touched. "What does it mean?" Eve asked.

"It is nothing to concern you. It will be safe. That is all you need to know." The box lay cold and unassuming in his hands. He turned it over, examining all sides. The runes faded, and there was no latch, no way to open the box. Who would ever guess it housed Lilith's evil spawn within its walls? "I must go. I have a duty that requires my full attention."

"Can't I stay with you?" She swiped a tear from her eye. "I don't want to be left alone with Adam. There is a strange look in his eye. One I have not seen before, and I am afraid."

"That is called anger. You will feel it, too. It is part of the taint, part of this humanity you have both become. Do not worry. It will pass, and he will love you again. Forgiveness will be learned by both of you."

"I don't want him to love me." Eve wound a strand of hair around one finger. "I would rather stay with you."

Kaemon cupped her cheek with his hand and sent calming vibes through his link. What was this girl doing to him? He shook his head, concentrating on the task at hand.

"Your duty is to your husband." Kaemon swallowed a lump in his throat. "Do not fear him. You will need to work together to survive. He will give you many children, and you will forget you ever knew me."

Eve shook her head. "I'll never forget."

"You must." Kaemon rubbed at a pain in his chest and took to the skies of this new Earth. She would be fine; a warrior's spirit thrived inside the frail, skinny body of a girl. Eve could take care of herself, but he wasn't sure about Adam. No concern of his—he must put his mind from Eve and back to the task. Taking the box to the Dominions to study in Arcadia was the logical thing to do, but Kaemon didn't run on reason, he ran on instinct, and instinct said no one should possess such an abomination, not even The Light. There was only one thing to do.

"What did you do with the box, Kaemon?" The pressure in Aaron's head increased as Lilith's voice wrapped around his memory. "If you didn't take it to the Dominions, where did you take it?" Lilith's presence in his mind burned like acid. "You must know."

20

"Hey, hey, look who's here!" Marcus grabbed Quinn around the waist, lifting her off the ground in a giant bear hug. "School hasn't been the same without your fine frame to look at."

"Hey, Marcus." His hug was the first thing that had made her feel normal all day. When he finally put her down, a real smile graced her face.

"Glad you're finally out of the house. I know not everybody has delicious brown skin like mine, but you're seriously starting to make vampires look tan. You're not going to burst into flames with all this fresh air and sunshine, are you?"

Quinn rolled her eyes, but couldn't suppress a giggle, glad for the lightened mood. She could always count on Marcus for a good laugh. "So, does Reese know I'm here?" Quinn sucked at her bottom lip.

"Yeah, I told her the minute I got your text. I need to warn you, she's still kind of pissed. Especially since you didn't tell her you would be here today," Marcus said.

"That's because she's been giving me the silent treatment

since the memorial." Quinn sighed. "I'm stuck. I can't move forward, and I can't go back. She doesn't understand."

"She might if you'd let her in," Marcus said. "How are you really feeling?"

Quinn rolled her eyes and sighed. "Fine. Great. Perfect. Okay, maybe not perfect, but great."

"Your nose twitches when you lie."

"I don't belong here anymore. I can't pretend that everything is okay and go back to cheerleading and gossiping with Ami. That night changed me, and I can't undo it. I'm an outsider now, and I don't want to go back in there." Quinn waved a finger at the double doors leading back inside.

"You don't have to, not today anyway." Marcus pulled her into the crook of his arm, the way Aaron used to do, shielding her from the world. "What say we go grab some pizza instead? I'm sure Mr. Navarro can make it through physics without me."

"Best idea ever. Plus, I have something to show you. You're not going to believe what I found."

"So what's the big emergency?" Reese let the metal door slam behind her as she stepped out into the parking lot.

"Hey." Quinn took a step forward.

"What are you doing here? Aren't you supposed to be at the gym or still in your pajamas or something?" Reese replied, her eyes straying to the ground.

"I thought I would surprise you." Quinn shrugged and held out her arms. "Surprise?" she squeaked.

"I don't like surprises."

An awkward silence stretched between them. Quinn chewed on her lip while Reese tapped her foot on the floor.

Marcus elbowed Reese. "Aren't you going to welcome her back?"

"Why? I wasn't expecting her today. Actually, I wasn't

expecting her ever," Reese said, arms crossed over her chest. "She sent *you* a text, not me. What kind of friend does that?"

"Of course, I sent him a text. You haven't replied to any of my messages since the memorial." It was hard not to sound defensive, but Quinn couldn't help it. They both had played a part in the unraveling of their friendship. "The phone works both ways, you know."

"Yeah, Quinn, it does. How about finding out from Ami that you're dating some guy that works at the gym? She seems to think you make a cute couple and keeps asking me about it. How would I know? You don't tell me anything anymore. Is that why you've been ditching school? Ditching me? For some guy?"

"I'm not dating anybody. He's just a friend."

"Come on, girls. Can you two hug it out now? All this fighting is making me hungry." Marcus grinned. "Or maybe kiss it out? Go ahead, I'll watch."

Reese tried to hide her smile, but Quinn saw the gleam in her eye. "God, Marcus, you really know how to ruin a good BFF fight, don't you?" She sighed. "I'm tired of being angry at you. And I'm sorry I haven't returned your calls. I have missed you, but the whole thing with Aaron at the cemetery freaked me the hell out. You freaked me out." Reese embraced Quinn in a tight hug.

"I'm sorry I freaked you out." Hugging Reese was like coming home. "You have no idea how much I missed you. And I'm sorry I didn't tell you about Caleb, but there was nothing to tell, really."

"Now that we're all friends again, want to grab some pizza with us?" Marcus asked. "We've decided to take a half day."

"I really shouldn't. I've got an economics quiz." Reese glanced back at the side door of Westland High.

"Please, Reese, I can't go back in there." Quinn bit her

bottom lip. "My hand kind of ran into Kerstin's face."

"What?" Marcus and Reese said in unison.

"She said Aaron was dead because of me. I snapped." Quinn left out the part about Kerstin being possessed by a demon. "If people thought I was psycho before, today will be the nail in my coffin. Besides, you're already late." Quinn bumped her hip on Reese's. "Please?"

Reese put her arm around Quinn and squeezed. "Fine. One slice, but I want to be back before physics. We're making special glasses for Thursday's solar eclipse."

"Oh, I forgot about that. Be sure to make one for me too, okay?" Marcus winked. "And can you add X-ray vision to mine? You know, to help me with human anatomy?" He waggled his eyebrows.

"If you mean girl anatomy, I think you know enough." Reese punched him on the arm and grinned. "And no, I won't do your homework for you."

"So, you're just going to let me go blind staring straight into the sun without that paper box thing?"

"You won't go blind. You'll just damage your retina beyond repair. It doesn't hurt or anything, you'll just get afterimages that look like flocks of crows in your vision. You would know that if you had been paying attention in class last Friday instead of passing me drawings of Mr. Navarro in awkward situations."

"Hey, those drawings might be worth something someday. I think I've got some real talent." Marcus opened the car door for Reese.

"I think you better come back for physics with me if you know what's good for you." Reese patted his cheek.

"Hey, do you guys mind if I invite Caleb to join us?" Quinn pulled her phone from her purse and replied to his latest text. "He gets off work in ten minutes. I think you both will really like him."

"We would love to meet your new friend." Marcus mimed quotation marks with his fingers when he said the word friend. "Right, Reese?"

"Yeah, I guess. At least maybe Ami will stop asking me about him if we do." Reese hopped into the passenger seat. "Well, come on, let's go."

TONY'S WAS PRACTICALLY EMPTY. Quinn guessed that not many people ate pizza before noon. Quinn slid into the booth beside Reese and across from Marcus. Putting her arm around her friend, Quinn sensed how happy Reese was that they were finally doing something normal, but if she could see Azrael standing just outside the window, she would know that life for Quinn was anything but.

"Before Caleb gets here, I have something I want to show you." Quinn placed Aaron's journal on the table.

Marcus picked up the notebook and held it reverently in his hands. "It's his song book, all right. Josh and I looked all over his room for it. Where did you find it?"

"In his locker."

Marcus sat up straight in his seat. "No way. I walked past it on my way to class this morning. I always pat it with my hand. My way of saying I haven't forgotten him. It was totally closed. The padlock was locked."

Quinn traced an invisible pattern on the cover with a finger, avoiding eye contact. "Someone must have unlocked it."

"Weird. I should have known that's where it would be." Marcus skimmed through the pages. "Did you read through it yet?"

Quinn nodded. "Here, September sixteenth." She flipped to the final entry.

Marcus read through the entry and grinned. "I knew it."

"Let me see that." Reese grabbed Aaron's notebook and started reading herself, flipping pages and shaking her head. "This is getting too weird." Reese sat back in her seat, crossing her arms over her chest. "Lockers that open by themselves, messages from beyond the grave, it's like some low-budget movie on the SyFy channel. Next you're going to tell me you have some special powers." Reese snorted at her own joke, and Quinn winced.

The perfect opportunity to come clean had presented itself. Quinn opened her mouth, ready to spill.

"What can I get you?" The waitress approached the table and slammed three glasses in front of them, water spilling over the sides and pooling in a ring around them. Quinn slumped; the moment shattered. Too much too soon. Maybe it was a sign that it wasn't time just yet.

"Want to hear the specials?" The waitress cocked her head and grinned at Marcus.

"No need. I'll take one extra-large meat feast with extra meat, two diet sodas, and a chocolate milkshake. What do you girls want?" Marcus grinned back at the waitress, his eyes wandering over her tight white T-shirt and short red shorts.

"Ignore him," Reese said to the waitress. "That's what everyone else does."

"A couple of extra plates will be fine," Quinn added and thanked her.

"Coming right up." The waitress scribbled on the notepad then tucked her pen in the pocket of her shorts.

Reese waited for her to leave the table and then leaned over to pop Marcus on the ear.

"Ouch!"

"You can wipe the drool from your chin now."

"I was staring because I can't believe how ugly she is. Did

you see the gap between her front teeth?" Marcus lowered his voice and looked at the waitress with a sidelong glance.

"She doesn't smile with her chest, Marcus. Don't think I didn't see exactly what gap you were looking at, and it wasn't anywhere near her teeth."

"Busted, but her legs and butt aren't nearly as nice as yours." Marcus took Reese's hand in his. "Picturing you in that cheerleading skirt makes me want to skip lunch and go right for dessert."

Reese thumped his ear again, and Marcus raised his hands in defense. "All right, woman, I get the hint. You can lay off now." Marcus placed an elbow on the counter and cupped his chin in his hand. "I miss Aaron. There's too much estrogen in my life without him here."

"I know I'm no Aaron, but maybe I can help even out the hormones for today, at least."

"Hey, Meathead." Quinn stood and gave Caleb a hug. "Glad you could make it."

"Hey, Blondie. Thanks for the invite." Caleb held out a hand. "You must be Marcus."

"Nice to meet you." Marcus shook his hand, then moved over and offered him a seat. "Want a Coke or something?"

"Iced tea would be great." Caleb took a seat next to Marcus, leaving a few inches between them.

"One iced tea for my new friend, Caleb." Marcus motioned to the waitress and clapped Caleb awkwardly on the back. Caleb tried to hide a flinch, and Quinn wondered if this had been a bad idea. Too late now. She couldn't very well uninvite him. Besides, she wanted him here. Quinn looked from Reese to Caleb and back to Reese again.

"Oh, right. I'm Teresa, but everyone calls me Reese for short."

"I know. Quinn never stops talking about you." Caleb smiled, and Reese cocked her head at Quinn.

"Funny," Reese said. "She never mentions you."

Quinn poked her in the ribs with her elbow. "Be nice."

"I'm always nice." Reese put on her best smile. "Glad you're here, Caleb."

Marcus tapped his fingers on the Formica, Reese stared out the window, and Quinn could feel Caleb's leg bouncing beneath the table. New friendships take time. Once they got to know each other, they would all be best buds, right?

"So, we were just talking about Aaron," Quinn explained. "Remember what I told you about the journal?"

"Wait, you told him about that?" Reese asked. "Exactly how much time have you been spending with him?"

"Well, I had to talk to someone, since my best friend didn't believe me. Not to mention the fact you wouldn't answer my texts." Quinn tore her paper napkin into long strips.

"Now you see why I need another guy in the group," Marcus whispered to Caleb. "Can we get back to Aaron, now?"

"So, what do you think?" Quinn asked.

"I think he's definitely trying to contact you, and we should stop waiting around for him and contact him ourselves." Marcus looked at Reese,

"And how are we going to do that?" Reese swirled her Diet Coke around with a straw.

"A spirit board," Marcus said.

"A what?" Reese asked.

"One of those boards that mediums use to contact spirits," Caleb explained.

"Marcus, you're a genius." Maybe she could use the board to enhance their connection somehow. It was worth a try.

"Nobody's ever called me that before."

"There's a reason for that," Reese quipped. "So, where do we get one?"

Quinn bounced her leg. They were really going to help her contact Aaron. This could work.

"My little sister has one of those Ouija games, she and her friends mess around with it when they have slumber parties," Marcus said. Sometimes I flash the lights and stuff to scare them. You should hear them squeal."

"See, even Marcus admits it's just a silly party trick. Everyone knows whoever is touching the planchette is controlling the board." Reese's voice oozed with skepticism. "Remember when we had the spirits tell Ami she was going to marry Horace Wheeler?" Reese chuckled. "Talk about looking horrified."

"I think it's the only time I've ever seen her speechless." Quinn grinned. "But this will be different, Reese. We're not nine anymore, and I doubt any of us would fake communication with Aaron. What harm can it do?"

"Spirit boards are dangerous. You might contact a *demon*, or something worse." Caleb stressed the word demon and kicked Quinn's leg under the table, but Quinn ignored him.

"You're supposed to be on my side." Quinn kicked Caleb back, and he scowled.

"I'm with Caleb on this. I think it's a bad idea." Reese shook her head.

"Thank you, Reese. At least someone's making sense around here." Caleb sat back and crossed his arms over his chest.

"Come on, Reese. Don't you want to help your best friend and ridiculously hot boyfriend find closure?" Marcus cocked his head and raised an eyebrow. "It's not like we're going to ask inane schoolgirl questions. We know who we want to contact. If nothing happens, we've spent an hour hanging out with each other, but if something *does* happen, maybe we can get some real answers."

Reese impatiently stirred her drink with her straw. "If I

do this and it doesn't work, which it won't, will you finally let go?"

Quinn placed her hand over her heart. "If it doesn't work, I won't mention it again." That didn't mean she would give up, but she would let Reese go on with her life and get answers on her own. "Are you in, Caleb?"

"Yeah, I'm in, Blondie, but I still think it's a bad idea."

"Thanks, Meathead."

The words "Breaking News" caught Quinn's attention as they flashed across the television screen mounted to the wall above the counter. Quinn sat up straight to see over Marcus' head. A dark-haired reporter stood in front of a familiar row of houses surrounded by cop cars and an ambulance. A body bag lay on the concrete.

"Hey, can you turn that up, please?" Quinn asked. The waitress stood on her tiptoes and adjusted the volume.

"... the street on Valley Road when the altercation turned physical."

Marcus and Caleb turned in their booth.

"Isn't that Jeff's neighborhood?" Marcus asked Quinn.

Quinn nodded, her guts twisting into tight knots as Reese squeezed her hand.

"Neighbors called the emergency services when the shouting started. One witness said the girl became violent after her boyfriend threatened to leave her and their unborn child, launching herself at him and digging into his skin with her nails. Another witness claimed the girl acted like a rabid animal, wrestling him to the ground. Witnesses from a nearby house caught the entire altercation on video."

The story cut to a grainy video of a couple standing in the street, obviously filmed on a cell phone from a neighbor's window. The witnesses recorded the spectacle from the safety of their own house, unwilling to put themselves in the middle of a domestic dispute but not too proud to film it.

Kerstin's red hair clung to her pale face as she paced, agitated. Jeff stood by the open door of his truck. The sound was almost non-existent, but Quinn didn't need sound to see the truth.

Gaaperi, a demon known to intensify both love and hatred, slid between the couple and faced Jeff. Bigger than Kerstin's own demon, the beast's name and purpose came to Quinn as it materialized on screen and solidified into a black mass so dense it looked like a CGI image. Smoke writhed around its legs as it stood a head higher than Jeff. Dreadlocks of mist shrouded its face, and its shoulders and neck were as thick as a bull's. Jeff couldn't see its long fingers reaching for him, drawing him closer, but Quinn could.

She sucked in a breath as the demon's fingers transformed into five razor-sharp needles. Her stomach twisted as the demon dug its hand through Jeff's shirt and into his belly, injecting its essence into his body. She wanted to scream at him to run, but it was too late. The demon grew smaller and smaller as it pushed itself into the chosen vessel until not one speck of the eerie fog remained visible. Nausea rocked Quinn as Jeff grabbed Kerstin by the arm and twisted it until she doubled over.

"Oh, my God!" Reese screamed and covered her mouth. "Please, Jeff, let her go. Just let her go."

Marcus grabbed Reese's hand. Quinn's friends were oblivious to what was really happening. Caleb turned his brown eyes on her, grabbed her hand, and gave her a knowing look.

"Did you see that?" Quinn asked, and Caleb nodded. Quinn gulped. She wasn't the only one who could see what crossed the veil. They both saw the real horror as it unfolded.

Kerstin's own demon, Eudmhox, had returned in full force. Dark tears stained her face like streams of ink, her eyes flickering from blue to jet black as the demon bent her will to its own. Then her face changed, twisting, morphing into that of a beast. She snarled and launched at Jeff. He flew backward, hitting his head on the frame of the open door and falling half in, half out of the truck. As he lay dazed and vulnerable, she pinned him to the passenger seat and wrapped her hands around his throat.

"Make them turn it off," Reese whimpered and buried her head in Marcus's chest, but Quinn couldn't tear her eyes away. She could see the dark beings absorbing Jeff's fear.

Jeff's eyes bulged, and his face turned red and then blue from lack of air. His legs thumped and flailed against the concrete, but Kerstin held him firm and fed on his pain, sucking the life from his body and pulling it into her own. One hand clawed at Kerstin's face while the other fumbled for the glove box. Something silver flashed in the sunlight.

"Dear God." The witness holding the camera dropped it as a gunshot echoed through the neighborhood.

Quinn's hand flew to her mouth, and she heard Marcus and Reese gasp.

"Did he just..." Marcus stammered.

"After shooting his pregnant girlfriend, the unidentified boy ran into his home and began boarding up the windows." The reporter droned on, unfeeling, uncaring. "As police arrived on the scene, witnesses reported hearing several more gunshots coming from the house. Upon entering, they found the young man dead, having committed suicide. Some are calling it self-defense while others are crying murder. We will be here with live coverage..." The television flicked to black as the waitress turned it off.

"I need to go home. Marcus, please. I need to go home now." Tears streamed down Reese's face. Marcus nodded.

Caleb turned to Marcus. "You get Reese out of here. I'll make sure Quinn gets home."

Marcus nodded, wrapped his arm around Reese, and

ushered her out of the restaurant.

"Quinn. Come on. It's time to go." Caleb tugged on her sleeve.

Numb, Quinn let Caleb guide her outside and into the passenger seat of his white pick-up.

"I'm so sorry, Quinn." His sincerity broke the dam, and she cradled her head in her hands, letting the tears pool in her palms. Caleb pulled her head to his chest and ran his fingers through her hair as she cried.

"Better?" he asked, kissing the top of her head.

Quinn nodded, wiped her tears, and pulled away.

"You saw them too, didn't you? The demons. They killed them, Caleb. And we're the only ones who know the truth." Quinn balled her fists, digging her nails into the palms of her hands. If only she had been there, if she hadn't antagonized Kerstin this morning, maybe she could have stopped it. No matter how she felt about Kerstin, she never wished her dead.

"It's not your fault. There wasn't anything you could do to stop it." Caleb turned on the engine and the radio blared to life. Another reporter interviewing a witness. He pressed the power button, silencing the news.

What good was being Eol Ananael if she couldn't protect the people she cared for? And where were all the warriors Azrael kept going on about? They were supposed to be protecting humankind. How could The Light let this happen?

"The world has never been a safe place, but this? I've never seen so many demons in one place before. God, Quinn, what the hell is happening?"

Azrael's words floated in her mind through their psychic link. *Things are accelerating much faster than anticipated. Elite forces are engaged on all fronts, your entire realm is under attack. This incident doesn't even compare to the devastation and darkness* going on in the rest of your world. Do you see why your role is so important now? The power in the Underworld is growing.*

Azrael reached through the window and switched the radio back on.

"Hey. Just because you're an angel doesn't give you the right…"

Azrael opened his wings to their full span, casting a shadow over the truck, and Caleb's mouth fell open. "Okay. The radio is yours."

The stations began to flip from news report to news report. A child murdered in Chicago, girls kidnapped in Nigeria, genocide in Sudan, nuclear threat, each account worse than the last.

Quinn covered her ears. "Please, Azrael. I don't want to hear anymore."

This is what we fight against, Quinn. What happened to your friends today is happing all over the world. This is what I've been trying to impart to you. Humanity depends on you defeating the darkness and re-sealing the veil. Azrael pressed the urgency into her mind, and the magnitude of the situation started to sink in.

I am being called to help push back the hordes. In the meantime, stay home. As soon as I'm back, you must go to Arcadia. We must begin preparations.

"Fine, when you get back, I'll go." She might not be able to ignore her calling much longer, but she wasn't going to Arcadia without at least trying to get through to Aaron. She would have to put her plan into action now, before Azrael got back.

I will be back soon. If you need me, I am just a call away. You will always be my first priority. Azrael bowed to her then shot upward and into the sky.

"Go where?" Caleb asked.

"To my destiny."

21

Quinn looked at her watch. Half-past six. They had agreed to meet here half an hour ago. Where were they? It would be dark soon, and she wasn't sure how long Azrael would be gone on his mission for The Light. No doubt, he would put a stop to her plan if he found out. This might be her only chance to contact Aaron before Azrael whisked her away to fulfill her destiny, whatever that meant.

The sound of tires on gravel made her turn around. Marcus's Jeep appeared around the corner and pulled up next to her, the tinted windows obscuring the sight of any passengers. Quinn's heart sank when he got out. Reese hadn't come.

"I can't believe you picked this place for our experiment. It has some seriously bad juju." Marcus kissed the gold cross hanging around his neck and mumbled a prayer of protection.

"Where's Reese?"

"The whole thing with Kerstin and Jeff really freaked her out. I still can't believe it. She says sorry, but she can't face anything else tonight." Marcus looked away and shoved his hands in his pockets. "To be honest, I'm not sure I can either. Maybe we should have ordered pizza and watched funny movies. Try to forget all this pain."

Quinn couldn't blame either of them for wanting to hide. She'd been doing plenty of that herself over the last month, but this couldn't wait. Tomorrow Azrael would drag her kicking and screaming to her destiny, and any chance of finding Aaron would be gone.

"What about Caleb?" Marcus asked.

"He's not coming either. His mom's out of town, and he didn't want to leave his younger sister alone, not with everything that's going on."

"Yeah, I can't blame him." Marcus scratched the side of his jaw.

"Marcus." Quinn took his hands in hers and squeezed, looking him dead in the eyes. "I know it's going to be painful, but I need to do this. Aaron needs me, but you don't have to be here. Give me the spirit board and go back to Reese. She needs you, and there's no reason I can't do this myself."

"No. Aaron wouldn't want me to leave you." Marcus shook his head. "Reese wants everything to be the same, to ignore the possibility that he could be out there, hurt, or worse. She doesn't get it. I can't stop replaying every second of that night over and over."

"Me, too. The guilt is like a swarm of ants crawling over my skin. Every time I think I've shaken them off, another one bites me." Quinn stared at her hands. They'd fit perfectly in Aaron's. She should never have let go.

"Right? I know it's not my fault. It's definitely not yours either, although I know you think it is. If I'm thinking it, I can't imagine how you must feel. Do you play 'What If'?" Marcus leaned against the doorframe of the Jeep and ran a hand across his scalp.

"All the time," Quinn admitted.

"The thoughts always start with him telling me we should separate to look for you. I should never have left him, I should have run faster, swam harder, tried to carry both of you." Marcus balled his fists. "I should have insisted, seen how weak he really was. Sometimes I can't sleep because I'm analyzing every moment. My brain knows I did everything I could, but my heart—my heart's broken."

"Mine too."

"That's what Reese doesn't understand. You're the only one who gets it. Did you know I haven't been back in the pool since? I can't face it. The thing I've trained for, worked for my whole life, it's meaningless. If I couldn't use it to save my best friend, what's the point in it?"

"You saved me." She smiled and Marcus looked away, wiping his cheek with the back of his hand.

"Aaron saved you," Marcus corrected.

"You both saved me. I'm the reason he's gone, Marcus. Not you. None of us should have been in that river that night. If I had followed my heart and gone to Homecoming with Aaron, this never would have happened. It's my fault. He should never have come after me. I wish he had let me die in that water. I would give my life for his if I could." Confessing to Marcus freed something within her, gave her hope. Knowing she wasn't alone in her grief, in her contrition.

"Don't say that. You don't mean it."

"I do mean it. I can't go back and change the past, but I need to make peace with him, somehow."

"Me, too. That's why I'm not letting you do this alone," Marcus continued. "I'm scared that it won't work. Or that it will work, and he'll give us some terrible message from beyond the grave. But no matter what happens, we do this together. He needs us both now. I can't explain it, but I have this feeling I can't ignore. This can't wait; we have to try to get to him."

"Thank you." Quinn rushed forward, tackling him in a hug. "I'm scared, and I didn't really want to do it alone."

"If there's a chance to save him now, we have to try." Marcus stroked her hair and then let go. "Let's do this before we both change our minds." Marcus grabbed a backpack from his passenger seat and locked the Jeep.

Shadows darted through the trees, demons, following at a distance as they headed down to the riverbank. The dagger tucked into her boot pulsed against her shin, and her hand itched to pull it from the sheath. A steady breath fortified her shield, and the glowing bubble surrounding her solidified. She reveled in the power of her gift. Controlling when and where she spoke to the demons made her happy. Well, maybe not happy, but their distraction kept her from curling up in a ball and sobbing into her pillow every minute of every day.

"I think this is it." Marcus rubbed the back of his neck and swatted at a fly. "I haven't been back here since that night. Everything looks so different now."

With the river back to its soft, trickling pace instead of bursting its banks, it was hard to tell. In her best guess, this was roughly the spot where Aaron disappeared.

"Close enough." Quinn settled on a rock outcropping, folding her legs in front. Cold seeped through her jeans, sending a shiver through her bones, and she zipped her black hoodie all the way to her neck.

"And why does the man always have to carry the bag? This doesn't even go with my shoes." Marcus tossed a pink and purple backpack to Quinn and settled across from her, taking the same cross-legged position.

"You're always going on about your muscles. Wouldn't want them to go to waste, right?" Quinn unzipped the backpack and took out a rectangular wooden board, roughly the size of a laptop, and placed it on the flattest surface of rock she could find.

All the letters of the alphabet were engraved in two arching lines across the middle, with a line of numbers at the bottom. In the top corners, the words *Yes* and *No* were printed beside illustrations of a sun and a moon. *Hello* and *Goodbye* completed the spirit board's bottom two edges, along with a weeping angel and dancing imp.

"What about the planchette?" Quinn asked

"I thought it might be better if we used something personal." Marcus fished in his pocket, bringing out a rectangular bit of white plastic with the artwork from John Lennon's *Imagine* album printed on the side. "His favorite, from his guitar case."

"Now what?" Quinn asked.

"Well, in the movies, they always put their fingers lightly on the planchette and then ask the spirits if they want to communicate."

Quinn placed her index finger on one of the three sides of the guitar pick and frowned. "It's too small for both of us to touch at the same time." She studied the board, unsure where to put her hands. "Maybe we touch the edges of the board instead? That way, we know the planchette is moving on its own and not because one of us nudged it with a finger."

"Worth a try." Marcus picked up the board and scooted forward until his knees touched Quinn's. Setting it back down across both their laps, he positioned his thumbs at the halfway point, long fingers slightly curling around the edge. Quinn positioned the pick in the dead center of the board and placed her thumbs opposite his. They both stared at the board.

"Should we close our eyes or something?" Marcus asked.

"How should I know? I've never done this before." Quinn suddenly felt awkward and silly. She wanted to believe that, somehow, this piece of wood and plastic could boost her own gift and reinforce a connection with Aaron, but doubt ate away at the edges of her faith.

"Well, since you seem to be the one he's trying to contact, I think you should call out to him or something. Urge him to manipulate the board and let us know where he is."

"Okay, tell me if it starts moving." Quinn shut out the world around her and tried to relax like Azrael taught her. Tension in the body led to tension in the mind, which led to less control over her abilities. Breath by breath, she moved through the defensive layers of the barrier that separated her from the unseen shadow world and restricted her sight. It had taken weeks to master holding her defenses in place. What had once been like a thin, delicate bubble, ready to pop at any minute, became an intricately woven, invisible shield, which she manipulated to reveal as much or as little of the other world as she wanted.

The air around her took on a slight hum. The essences became clearer as she stripped away armor, leaving herself naked and vulnerable. A strong scent of sulfur made Quinn jerk her head and cough. Sweat beaded on her temples and dripped down her cheek while the hot, moist air stilled around her. She felt a strange shift in the surrounding energy, something she couldn't quite put her finger on. Electric sparks exploded beneath her closed lids, a firework display of orange and yellow against the black. Marcus's hands froze beneath hers with the sound of plastic scraping across wood.

22

Kaemon did know, and now so did Aaron, but together they managed to bury the image of the box being thrown into a vast ocean seconds before Lilith seized it. An ocean whose water receded over millennia, leaving fertile land in its wake, land the founders of Westland had called home, and so did Quinn.

When the tears of Eve have turned to blood and her sins have turned to flesh, the key will fall. Quinn's flesh contained the very essence of Eve, her tears, her blood. The words of the prophecy took on a terrible new meaning. Fate, destiny, none of it was coincidence. Loopholes upon loopholes, the universe aligned as prophecy predicted, and it was only a matter of time before the box made its way back to her, if it hadn't already. No denying the dramatic irony of it all—Aaron was trapped in the middle of it, tortured, helpless.

No, not helpless, Kaemon whispered. *We can do this. We must do this. Quinn has no idea what's coming.*

And then what?

We find Quinn. Warn her.

How?

"I taste your fear, sweet and full of flavor. You know something. I sense the answer flitting in that tiny brain of yours. I will find it, Aaron."

Hurry! I can't keep her out much longer. You have to help me shield the location of the box and Quinn's connection to it.

Aaron's breath came in quick spurts as he focused all his energy on hiding the information she sought. Using his gift to turn the psychic link back on her felt like banging his head against the side of a mountain, but even the slightest vibrations had an effect. A speck of dust, a pebble, a boulder, a landslide, enough to pull her attention elsewhere while he transformed the vision of the box into a hummingbird, sending it on a whirling, frenzied path through his mind.

"Clever, very clever. Your ability to manipulate the psychic plane is impressive, but you won't keep it from me for long." She charged the memory, and it dashed away. Charge, zig, chase, zag, always staying half a step ahead. Mind against mind, will against will.

"You saw for yourself. That's all there was." Aaron had to convince Lilith, throw her off the path no matter what.

"You think you can fool me? Your deceit, your manipulation, will get you nowhere." She grabbed his chin in her hand and squeezed.

Aaron braced himself. Her lightning bolts seared his veins, turning them into a thousand crackling wires beneath his skin. Convulsions rocked his body with each new shot.

"Bring it back, and I'll make the pain stop."

Aaron gritted his teeth. "I will never give you what you want!" He had to keep her from finding this box of Agathe. Quinn's life depended on its secret staying buried. Not just her life, he feared, but all of humanity.

"You will give me what I want in the end. *Kavash!*"

Mauling his mind, she clawed and ripped at every thought that bubbled to the surface until long strands of thick red blood dripped from his nose, his ears, his eyes. Such agony, torture, screams bringing him to the brink of madness.

"I tried to be gentle, but you had to fight me. Tell me!"

The hummingbird zoomed in chaotic patterns just out of her reach, but she would catch it soon. There wasn't much left of his mind to search, nowhere left for it to hide. Even Kaemon's power waned. She was too strong.

Lilith's laugh rolled and thundered as her power wrapped around the hummingbird and ripped it from his mind. A thousand volts of energy exploded through Aaron, and he lolled to the side, foaming at the corner of his mouth. Nothing but pain and screams and more screams, and a memory of her face. He failed. Quinn would die, the box would be opened, and Lilith's demon horde would be unleashed. The human realm would become another Eden, tainted, ruined, and it was his fault.

Quinn. I'm so sorry. If I had known. Quinn. Her name, an apology, a mantra, a ward, but nothing could protect either of them now.

Lilith retreated from his mind, and he sagged against his bonds, sucking in shallow breaths to clear his thoughts. Her pale face swam before him, the venom making it hard to focus. Blood dripped from Aaron's nose, the tang of copper filling his mouth, making him gag.

"So, that little bitch is even more than she seems. Eve's blood runs through her veins, does it? No wonder The Light sent his best Elite to protect her. I should be angry that you hid that from me for so long, but never mind. Your good intentions have paved her way to hell." Lilith's touch prickled his skin as she patted her new pet. "Now that I know where to find the box, I can move fate along as it suits me."

Lilith pulled her cloak from her shoulders and laid it on the ground in front of her. Faceless skulls writhed within the smoky fabric, moaning, pressing against it.

"Hello, my pretties," she cooed at the shadowy, featureless souls trapped within her cape, willing slaves that would do anything for their master's attention. "Find her for me. Go. Find me Quinn." The cloak rippled, and at her command, the spirits trapped inside whispered louder and louder to one another, swirling in a frenzied circle. Then, one by one, they disappeared back into the depths of the inky black fabric until it was still as obsidian glass. Lilith cocked her head, silver eyes intent on whatever her minions were showing her.

"Ah." With a wave of her hand, Lilith beckoned one of the faceless demons from the depths of her cloak. It thrashed and gurgled. "There she is. Seems she thinks you're still alive somewhere. Nothing but Aaron, Aaron, Aaron on the brain. Her whole essence quivers with your name. She's looking for you right now, in fact." A smile twisted across Lilith's face, striking fear into his heart. "Using a spirit board, no less, and on the very shore where Kaemon thinks the box is buried. Looks like fate is on my side after all."

The demon disappeared within the cloak. With one fluid motion, Lilith swirled it from the floor and back on her shoulders, fixing it with the silver serpent broach. "I can't cross the veil into the human realm, not yet, so she will need to bring the box to me, and I know just the trick. She would do anything for you. Follow you to the ends of the Earth, to me, to her death. Is it her blood or her tears that will unleash my dark children back into the world and help me cross the veil into the human realm? Either way, I can arrange to make her cry and bleed. And you, my pet, will help me with both. Revenge on two for the price of one."

"I'll never help you," Aaron growled.

Lilith smelled of a coming storm as she approached. Forcing his head up, he straightened his shoulders and met her cold gaze.

"You will." Grinning, she cupped his cheek. "All she needs is one more small push in your direction. Her mind is open and vulnerable. Do you think Quinn inherited Eve's proclivity for being manipulated?"

He jerked away and spit in her face.

She laughed as his saliva dripped down her cheek, and she wiped it away with the back of her hand. Another twisted smile crept across her lips. She turned up her palm and began another chant.

Electric shocks rocked his body as silver threads of power leapt from her fingers and pierced his skin and into his heart. Every nerve was on fire as she wrapped her dark sorcery around his essence.

"All I need is a little bit of your essence. Just enough to make her think it's you." He felt a tug deep in his chest. Lilith's chants grew louder, and Aaron balled his fists, determined not to give her what she wanted. He lunged for her, twisting his wrists to free himself, but his chains held him tight.

"Stop struggling. You won't win." Silver eyes found his, two pools cold as ice, freezing him in place. "*Kavash,*" she whispered to the control demon around Aaron's neck. Another shot of fire entered his veins, the creature's venom dulling his resistance.

"You won't miss that little part of you."

Aaron screamed and arched his back as she clawed a tiny piece of his essence from him and drew it from his heart. He slumped forward, head lolling to the side, his manacles the only thing keeping him from falling face first to the ground. A thin thread of gold, a part of his gift, his spirit, hung in the air between them, pulsing with brilliant light. Lilith covered her eyes, shying away from the brightness.

"Just enough of your essence to disguise my own." Puckering in disgust, she opened her mouth and swallowed the bright piece of him. "You taste awful." She gagged as her darkness absorbed the light, her skin pulsing with a golden glow. Within seconds, her black curls shortened around her ears. Eyes blinked silver to green, and her striking cold face morphed into that of a boy. Not any boy—Aaron stared into his own face. He smiled at himself, malice dripping from his lips.

"Do you think she will trust that I'm you?" Lilith turned, arms outstretched, showing off the completeness of the transformation, even down to a T-shirt and jeans.

"I will not be your bait." Aaron rattled his chains, and she laughed.

"You have no choice. I already have what I need from you." Lilith held up the likeness of his own finger, making a dramatic show of pricking it with the tip of the silver broach that had previously held the shadow cape around her body. Blood dripped from the tip, and she dragged it on the ground, enclosing them both in a circle of dark red.

"Don't worry. You'll be reunited with your precious Quinn soon enough. When she hears from your own lips that you're in my clutches, she'll find a way to come to the Underworld. And when she does, I might even kill her first and let you watch. I'm sure you'd like to watch, wouldn't you? Consider it a gift, a thank you for all you've done." Another command to the control collar, and fire ate through his blood.

"I will die before I let you touch her." Instead of sounding strong and angry, his words came out slurred.

"I'm just giving her what she wants. Where's the harm in that? I'll be sure to say hello to your precious Quinn for you."

The mirror of his own Adam's apple bobbed in her throat. Aaron wanted nothing more than to wrap his hands around it and squeeze and squeeze and squeeze. It was his last thought before another shock of electricity splintered what was left of his mind into a million tiny pieces.

23

Quinn watched, jaw wide, as the guitar pick levitated six inches off the board, twisting and spinning as if caught in a whirlwind.

"Please tell me you see this, too." Marcus didn't answer. He sat frozen, eyes closed, full lips parted in a half-grin, and hands clasping the board. His usually rich brown skin looked pale and ashen against the cloud-laden sky.

Quinn jerked her hands away, but her body didn't move with her. Instead, it mirrored Marcus's, still as a statue, fingers still gripping the board, forehead creased in concentration.

Whoa! So that's what an out of body experience was. Was she in some sort of trance? Her translucent spirit shimmered ghostlike, somehow connected to, yet separate from, her physical form. Quinn swallowed the panic rising from her stomach. Had she done this, or was it something else entirely? She took three deep calming breaths and surveyed her surroundings.

It was as if she'd stepped into a sepia-toned photograph.

Everything was frozen in time, all but the spirit board. The once ordinary letters adorning the surface radiated a strange, iridescent, glow-stick green, the only color among the reddish-brown landscape.

"Is anyone there who wants to communicate?" She tried to sound confident, in control as she asked, but her voice squeaked.

Letters floated off the board and joined the plectrum in a swirling light show.

"Aaron?"

In answer, the letters mixed and spun until they arranged themselves into a single word.

Quinn.

Her heart became a thunder of hooves within her chest. "Aaron? Is that you?"

Quinn.

Characters flew in and out, pulsing and dimming.

"Where are you? Are you hurt?"

Instead of a direct answer, the letters morphed into strange runes like those on Azrael's sword. She focused all her attention on them, trying to make sense of what they could mean. What kind of language was it anyway? Sanskrit? Sumerian? She was a teenager, not some expert in linguistics.

"Seriously, how am I supposed to read that? It could say anything for all I know," Quinn huffed in frustration.

As if by magic, the symbols started to unravel, pulling apart and morphing back into letters she recognized, rearranging themselves into words, faster, a frantic cyclone of glowing green.

When the tears of Eve have turned to blood and her sins have turned to flesh, the key will fall. For love is bound by the power of the Trinity. Their destiny is written by chaos and betrayal and on the first eclipse on the eighteenth year, the voice of the sacrifice will

break the lock, restoring darkness unto the light. By this promise, be compelled.
Be compelled.
Be compelled.
Be compelled.
"What does that mean?" Quinn asked.
Seize your destiny.

The letters arched above her head like a comet and dove into a small pool near the river's edge. She hadn't remembered seeing that pool before leaving her body. It only seemed to exist in this strange alternate universe. Quinn glanced at her corporeal form still sitting cross-legged with Marcus. What would happen if she strayed too far from her body? Surely walking a few yards away wouldn't hurt anything. Both her body and Marcus would still be within sight. Giving up now wasn't an option; she had to see this through.

Her heart hammered as she inched down the bank of the river and approached the place where the comet fell. She stood looking down into a hole about three feet in diameter and half as deep.

Myriads of gold, blue, and green shimmered beneath the murky puddle, reminding her of fireflies dancing in a darkened field. She rubbed her chest at the ache the memory evoked. At the bottom, the source of the mysterious light beckoned to her. A box, half-buried in silt, flared bright as the letters, once on the spirit board, now etched into runes along the sides and top. A sense of déjà vu brought a sick feeling in her stomach. A forgotten dream, and something more, something older. Visions of her handing the box to an angel with golden wings flashed before her then vanished just as quickly. This was *her* box.

Quinn shook her head to clear her mind. Impossible. Yet

it wasn't. She gritted her teeth and dipped a finger into the water. The colors of the runes shifted faster and faster, from green to gold and back to blue. Swallowing her fear, she lowered her hand into the cool water and wrapped her fingers around her destiny.

24

   Tingles of electricity coursed up her arm as she pulled the box free. The same runes that had flown through the air now adorned the wood. They blazed bright against her pale skin as she traced them with a finger. A bright flash made her blink, and then the symbols faded, leaving nothing but scorched marks along the sides and the top.

  Six inches long and four inches deep, the box looked wooden but had the weight of stone. The sides and top were worn smooth except for the now darkened symbols engraved on the domed top and across the sides. Petrified black with bits of dark mossy green and light gray running with the grain, it looked old, an artifact that should have been displayed behind museum glass instead of at the bottom of the river.

  A memory of a forgotten dream fluttered to the surface of her mind. Aaron handing her a box just like this one, an angel with wings the color of molten lava standing against a dark wasteland, a horde of demons at his back. Finding this box on the bank near where Aaron drowned had to be a sign.

"Aaron?" Rubbing her arms against the sudden electrical charge in the atmosphere, she straightened.

The air before her shimmered and thickened as every molecule around her prickled in anticipation. Before falling asleep each night, she imagined what she would say when she came face to face with him again, but as Aaron's essence manifested into being, her heart held her words captive.

"Quinn. Thank God you're here." Two strides, and he closed the gap between them, standing so close she could see the rise and fall of his chest beneath his shirt. Ripped and soiled clothes clung to his pale, thin frame, and his hair hung in long black cords around his ears. Like Quinn, he was a soul outside a solid body, but his spirit took on his earthly form.

"Aaron? Is it really you? Are you okay? What happened to you?" All the questions Quinn had been holding in spilled out at once. "Are you hurt?" What she really wanted to know was, was he dead? The word choked her, and she didn't dare ask for fear of the answer. A thousand apologies ran through her head, none of them right, none of them good enough. She wanted to pull him into a kiss, to wrap her fingers through his hair, to hold him and never let go, but all she could do was stare into his bright green eyes. "I thought I would never see you again," she sobbed.

"Me neither." The essence of Aaron's hand brushed a tear from her cheek, and she flinched. Something about his touch felt off, wrong.

"Quinn. It's me." Aaron frowned. "What's wrong?"

"Nothing." Quinn tried to smile, but she couldn't suppress the dread rising in the back of her throat. "This place, it's just unnerving." She forced herself to stay still as he came closer, his eyes wandering from her face to the box in her hand.

"Where did you get that?" Aaron cocked his head, and a

deep hunger pushed against Quinn's essence. She clutched the box to her chest and took a step back.

"Here, between the realms. It was buried over there in the riverbed. The storms must have washed it in from the Gulf."

"Can I see it?" Aaron grabbed for the box, and she pivoted just out of reach. Something about the way he smiled, the left side of his mouth slightly twisted, forced, frightened her. Afraid of Aaron? Ridiculous. Aaron would never hurt her.

"Don't you trust me?" Aaron asked. The pained look on his face broke her heart. Of course, he could sense her distrust, as she sensed his hurt at her betrayal, through this strange link they had.

"Of course, I trust you." Taking a deep breath, she forced herself to relax and held the box out to him. Before he could touch it, a spark of lightning leapt from it to his essence, and he drew away his hand.

"Damn thing bites," Aaron hissed and rubbed the place where he'd been shocked.

"Never mind the box." Quinn tucked it into the pocket of her hoodie and out of sight. "Where are you? What happened?"

Aaron looked into the woods behind them and ran a hand across the back of his neck. "The Underworld. I don't know how I got here, Quinn. I'm scared. She's holding me prisoner." He hunched his shoulders and lowered his voice. "I think she's going to kill me. I can't take any more of her torture."

"Who?"

"Lilith," he whispered. "The demons call her The Dark Mother." His voice, ragged and full of fear, pierced her to the very core.

"Demons?" Cold dread prickled at the base of her spine.

He nodded, and she sensed his fear and pain.

"You don't know what it's cost me to get to you. She's powerful, more powerful than me. Every time I try to make contact with you, she..." he swallowed, "... stops me." The way he said "stops me" froze the Quinn's blood. "Something distracted her, and I managed to sneak away. I wasn't sure you would hear me. I tried so many times before." He shivered.

"How do I get you out? There must be away."

"I think there is. That's what I've been trying to tell you. We're connected. I felt it that day I fell into your nightmare. I didn't understand it then, but I know now." Aaron's eyes flicked to either side. The ground rumbled beneath them. "Oh, God. She's found me. It's not safe. You have to go. She knows."

"No. I'm not leaving you." Heat spread through Quinn as lightning crackled through her, filling her with dread. Another quake opened up small cracks around them, and the tether binding them together started to unravel.

"Those demons you saw, they're nothing compared to what's down here. Please, Quinn. You have to help me. I'm scared. I want to come home. To you." Aaron's green eyes filled with tears, and Quinn swiped at her own cheek. "You don't know what she's capable of. You have to get me out of here, please. You're the only one who can."

Panic clamped Quinn's stomach at the thought of losing him again, but she was powerless against the forces bent on ripping them apart. Not now, not yet. There were so many missing pieces she needed him to fill in, but the thread that bound them grew thinner and thinner with each passing second.

"Please, Quinn. Promise you'll come for me," he begged. His fear, cold and hard, sliced against her essence, and she wrapped her arms around him, as if that could anchor him to her forever. The tremors were getting stronger, making it hard to stay on their feet. "I don't know how much longer I can last."

"You have to hang on until I find a way." She touched her forehead to his. "I'll come for you. I swear."

Another quake ripped a gash beneath his feet, and he screamed.

"Aaron!" Quinn grasped for him, but she wasn't fast enough. Her fingers found nothing but dust as his face, twisted in fear, disappeared into the gaping darkness below, and the hole snapped shut.

"No!" Quinn beat her fists on the ground. "What do you want? I'll give you whatever you want if you bring him back."

The world around her growled and shook, violent and angry. Dark gashes, like thick fissures of ink, scarred the entire sepia landscape. Shadows swarmed from the cracks and crawled out from the abyss. Their essences pushed against hers, agitated, excited. She was a fly, the encroaching darkness like two hands converging to trap her inside. No time to think, she had to get back to her body, but ever-widening fissures ate away the land between her essence and her flesh.

Muscles tense, she ran. A tendril of fog exploded next to her. Dodge to the left, roll to the right. Instinct took over fear. Her body sat less than six feet away now. A crack opened in front of her and her essence leapt, landing an inch from the edge. Three feet. Almost there.

She glanced over her shoulder. A dozen or more demons, different from the ones she'd seen before, were closing in. She'd never seen anything so frightening. All the demons she'd met up until now looked like sweet kittens compared to these. With their approach, the box shivered and knocked against her, making it impossible to hold, and it tumbled from her pocket and across the ground. Quinn scrambled after it, catching it with the tips of her fingers, and she shoved it back into the pocket of her hoodie.

Another burst of speed, and she slid into home, but

coming out of her body was much easier than going back in. Knee to knee, finger to finger, nose to nose, no matter what she did, her essence would not merge back into her flesh.

Please let me back in. Please.

The demons were closer now, mere feet from her and Marcus. Elongated bodies, roughly the size and shape of a Doberman Pinscher, were held up by ten long, spider-like legs. Red-needled spikes poked through bruise-colored, armored skin. Their tails curled above them like a scorpion's, menacing and dangerous. Quinn didn't want to think what kind of poison they might carry. She could sense their intent: they would attack, and she was too vulnerable with her guard down. Torn between fear and desire, she wrestled with the urge to flee, but where would she go?

Hundreds of faceted, red eyes gleamed around her. Giant pincers protruded below them, clicking and clacking as they scurried closer and closer. Tears poured down her cheeks. She tried to quiet her mind, to focus, but her failure spurred them on. Inches separated them, their rotting smell choking her. She had no choice. He wouldn't be happy that she'd been trying to contact Aaron, but she didn't know what else to do.

She formed his name on her lips and screamed her psychic call for help.

"Azrael!"

His named boomed like a shockwave, silencing the clattering of the demons as they stopped to look at the sky. Quinn looked, too. Half a dozen golden lights ripped through the smoky blackness.

Azrael, followed by five other angels dressed in armor, hurled downward into the waiting throng. Azrael landed in front of Quinn, his swords flashing blue and gold against the sepia sky, and shouted commands in a language that sounded like something the elves spoke in *The Lord of the Rings*. The small angel army advanced, swooping down and raking their weapons across the backs of the scorpion-like demons. The demons spit cannonballs of glowing red poison from their pincers, but the angels were nimble and quick, evading the balls of fire by banking left and right, coming in from new angles, wearing them out.

"Stay behind me. And for all that is holy and good, get back inside your body and get your shields up!" Azrael's face was all sharp edges, and his voice hard as flint.

"I can't," Quinn pleaded. "I don't know how I came out of it in the first place.

The look on Azrael's face said it all. She was in big trouble now. Before she could say anything in her defense, his hand connected with her essence and shoved it backward. Being forced back into her body felt like being squeezed into a too-tight dress, restrictive and oppressive. Her essence squirmed and writhed under her flesh, trying to readjust to being tied up inside skin, muscle, and bone again.

"Sometimes I think you are more trouble than you're worth." Azrael bowed before her and shot into the sky to join the others in battle. As the two sides collided, the insects' screams were like the twisted metal of two cars crashing. Swords gleamed with blue and gold.

A rainbow of colors whirled with her, the human realm coming back to life around her. She heard Marcus suck in a breath, his hands warm beneath hers as her eyes flew open.

"What the hell?" Marcus stared at her. "You look like you've seen a ghost? Did it work? I didn't see anything. What's that?" Marcus pointed to the box lying in her lap. "It looks like something my grandmother would buy at a flea market."

Suddenly aware of the cold, Quinn's whole body quaked, and her teeth chattered. Marcus grabbed a bag of chips from the backpack and began munching as if they were on a picnic.

"Man, all this medium, hocus-pocus stuff has made me hungry. Should we take silence as a failure or a success?" Marcus shoved another fistful of chips into his mouth, unaware of the battle raging around them.

Behind him, one of the demons reared up on two of its hind legs. An angel with silver-green wings dive-bombed it, hacking off three of its legs. The demon howled in rage as it fell on its face, body twisting in pain while its unattached appendages flapped and flailed around it. Purple goo spurted from the demon's wounds, covering the angel, teeth bared, as he delivered the killing blow, turning the demon into ash. Then he was off in a flash of green and gold and on to his next target. He looked totally in his element, ready to take on all the evil in the world with a smile and a laugh.

"What's next?" Marcus asked. "We could try a real medium." The angels were too busy to notice that a shadow had detached itself from one of the lifeless legs, but Quinn watched in horror as it and slithered over Marcus's shoulder.

"Mm-Marcus," she stuttered. "I need you to give me your hands."

"What? You want to hold my hand again? Did you like it that much?"

"Please, trust me. Give me your hands, now."

He grinned, offering her an upturned palm just as the shadow darted into his ear. His eyes went wide, the whites filling with oil as the demon took hold, and he dropped the bag of chips, crumbs spilling down his sweatshirt and across the rock.

Quinn pushed her barrier up, extending it out in a wide arc. Marcus shuddered as light inched along his arm like a golden glove. Her body trembled with exertion as she tried to expel the demon's essence, but it was wrapped tightly around Marcus's, so much so that Quinn couldn't tell where the demon ended, and Marcus began. Not to mention the fact that she had no idea what its name was. Without its name, she couldn't expel it from Marcus's body.

"You do not have the power to banish me, Eol Ananael." The demon's voice crackled like fire. "Not yet." Hearing it speak through Marcus made her blood turn to ice.

"My name is Quinn."

"A little name for a little being. Perhaps you are not who we thought you were."

"Get out of my friend's body now, and I'll let you live." Quinn tried to sound brave, but her voice squeaked out.

"I will leave when I am good and ready, be that in a minute or a decade. This body is strong and fierce. I might just keep it."

"You wouldn't dare."

"Wouldn't I?" The demon laughed, rising to stand above her. "You are playing with powers you know nothing about. Were you not the one who crossed into the realm between your world and ours to stand within the veil?"

Quinn grabbed the box and scrambled back as the demon advanced. "You, a beacon in the darkness, dared to delve into the shadow world and scream his name." The demon used Marcus's foot to crush the spirit board beneath his heal. "Did that smug protector you call a Sentinel not warn you? You are the one who seeks the boy—the one you let die so that you could live."

The reminder was like a slap, and Quinn winced at his words. Even worse coming from a friend's face, a face she had shared grief with, who had told her she shouldn't feel guilty. "What have you done to Aaron?" Quinn got to her feet, refusing to let him intimidate her.

"I have done nothing to him. My mistress gets to have all the fun. He is too important to her to let one as lowly as I play with her favorite pet." The demon pouted with Marcus's face and Quinn shivered. "No, he is all hers."

"Please. I will do anything."

"Anything?" The demon arched an eyebrow. "Yes, she thought you would say that."

"And? What does she want? Spit it out."

The demon stared at the box clutched in her hand, and she felt a need, a bitter craving, rise in his spirit.

"You mean this?" She looked at the strange container in her hands. Could this be the distraction Aaron had been talking about? Had her finding the box been coincidence?

The demon eyed the box. "We've been waiting for this moment for a long time." It licked its lips, slow and steady, its hunger for this precious object growing by the second. "She of many names, Lilutu, Zahriel, Kakasha, Ardad Lili, The Dark Mother, demands you return that which is hers." The demon voice emanating from Marcus sounded like the buzz of a million bees, angry and annoyed. "You have until the solar eclipse to comply."

"And if I don't?" Quinn hugged the box to her chest and stuck out her chin.

"Then the boy's soul is hers forever. Do you know what she does with her playthings?" The demon cocked Marcus's head and studied her. "No? I do not imagine your small human mind could fathom the terrible things she has planned for him. Thousands upon thousands of years of rather creative experimentation have perfected her art for misery." The demon ran a tongue over Marcus's lips. "Revenge, torture, agony. These words are but poor definitions of the eternity of hell he will experience, all because of you. There are worse things than death. Won't it be lovely to feed off the guilt you'll have, knowing you've damned the boy you love to an eternity of torment?"

"But the eclipse is only a few days away. I don't know how to get to the Underworld. I need more time."

"There is no more time. I'm sure you will find a way, Eol

Ananael." The demon turned Marcus's mouth upward into a wicked grin.

"Get out of his body!"

"You dare command me? You don't even know my name."

"She doesn't, but I do, Nysrogh." Azrael swooped down, chest heaving, wings settling at his sides. He looked fierce and frightening. The tip of his golden sword found the hollow of Marcus's throat. Saliva dripped in long strands from the sides of his mouth, his body shook.

"Stay out of this, angel, lest you suffer Lilith's wrath," the demon sputtered, but his voice was reduced to nothing but a ragged whisper, his power waning under the point of Azrael's sword.

"Where did you get that?" Azrael's attention was drawn to the box still in her hand. She thought she saw a flash of fear in his eyes, and then it was gone.

"Over there." Quinn tried to steady her voice.

"That box belongs to my mistress," Nysrogh hissed.

"Hush, Nysrogh, or I will pry your essence loose from the boy piece by piece if I have to. You will be so broken that it will take you a millennia to knit yourself back together." Azrael pressed the tip farther into her friend's flesh. Quinn wasn't sure if it was the creature or Marcus himself that gasped as blood blossomed at the base of his Adam's apple.

"No! Don't! You're hurting him." Quinn grabbed Azrael's wrist, but he flicked her away as if she were a mosquito and stepped back, chanting under his breath.

"I will deal with you when I'm done," Azrael growled at her between chants.

A trickle of red tainted with a trace of shadow fell onto Marcus's shirt. Drawn forth by Azrael's power, gray threads floated upward from the blood, the demon's essence separating from the human's.

Marcus's face twisted and morphed into the true shape of

the monster within. His eyes bulged, and he snarled, revealing three rows of sharp teeth. Azrael flourished the golden sword, moving the tip in a tiny circular motion, winding the shadow strands around the blade. The cords, attached to Marcus at one end and wound tight around Azrael's sword at the other, writhed and squirmed.

While the golden sword extracted the evil squatting inside her friend, Azrael held the blue one above his head as if ready to strike. Once the threads were fully in his grasp, he struck down with the blue Qeres blade, cutting the demon off from its host. Poison worked its way through the demon's essence, hissing and popping with electricity until every inch of the demon dissipated.

Marcus's eyes fluttered, returning to their natural brown state. "What the hell was that?" Quinn launched herself forward, wrapping her arms around him, tears soaking his shirt.

"Well, hello to you, too." He patted her on the back and rocked her, his arms awkward around her. "Did I miss something? What's going on?"

The last demon standing screamed as a violet-winged angel drove a sword through its eye. With its death, the five Powers of the heavenly host turned and bowed to her before taking to the air. Only Azrael remained. He shook his head and glared at her.

"Marcus, there's something I need to tell you."

25

Left to drift through the ruins of his own psyche, untethered and trapped between consciousness and unconsciousness, Aaron succumbed to the bleakness of his situation. Another attack would wipe the slate of his mind clean. There wasn't much left as it was, just a jumble of random images and thoughts he couldn't hang onto for more than a few seconds at a time, but that wouldn't stop her. Once Lilith finished with Quinn, she would be back. Not that it mattered; he no longer had the strength to fight her. He was a rag doll she could play with and throw away—no feelings, no life. He wasn't real anymore.

All he could do was wait, suspended in his torturous purgatory with no way out. Better not to worry and embrace the feeling of numb apathy instead. No need to think about that, no need to feel, it wouldn't do any good. Just float. Float and forget. Let it go, all of it.

Billions of stars winked in and out around him, dust, fragments of his shattered mind left in the wake of Lilith's attack. We are all made of stardust after all, even our musings.

Muse.

The word, familiar one second, foreign as ancient Sumerian the next, echoed through his empty shell of a mind and knocked something loose. Words from a long-dead language bubbled to the surface.

Sumerian. As familiar as Quinn's face.

He shouldn't know Sumerian from Greek, but somehow, he did. This life. Another life. This time. Another time. To not know who you were, where you were, what you were. What could be worse? He was lost, a soul without a body, a body without a mind, never to be whole again.

Quinn.

Something prodded him to try to piece his mind back together while he had time, but he ignored it.

Quinn.

Retrieving all the pieces would take too much effort, he reasoned. What was the point anyway? Each thought was as intangible as a whisper of wind on his face. Once there, and then gone.

Quinn.

His thoughts looped back around to that one word. A song stuck in his head, driving him crazy.

Quinn.

Cinders of his lost mind swirled and danced, taking the shape of her face, her hair. Something awakened deep within, a part that burned as bright as the sun at noon. If he could harness it, maybe he could regain consciousness.

Focusing on that growing spark of faith, he reached for the closest particle and pulled it back into himself. Then another. Piece by piece, he rebuilt himself, exploiting the potential power growing inside him until every memory, every grain, was back in place. Evil may have taken his mind, taken his flesh, but he wouldn't go down without a fight. If he could get free, he might break Lilith's connection with

Quinn. Giving up was not an option. Rage burned through Aaron, overriding the effects of the drug. Mind clear and renewed with energy, his eyes snapped open.

Lilith, still disguised in his essence, grinned up at him and gracefully rose to meet his dagger glare. A bomb ticked at Aaron's core, ready to explode as more flashes of a past life mixed with his present. Lilith had wanted him to remember and remember he did. She had trapped a weak human in bonds but awakened a powerful Elite angel and all that came with it.

"Well now, that's a pleasant surprise. I didn't expect you to ever wake up. Seems your mind is stronger than I gave you credit for, if not your body. You look positively exhausted." With a wave of a finger, she loosened the slack of the chains that bound him. His arms dropped to his sides as the metal links pooled at his feet. Not complete freedom, but enough that he might be able to gain an advantage. "See, I can be forgiving when it suits me."

She thought him weak, subdued. She had no idea what she'd awakened within him. Good. Playing the part, he sank to the floor and curled into the fetal position, resisting the urge to snap her neck.

"Masquerading as you was too easy." Lilith's features rippled and morphed back into her own, T-shirt and jeans replaced with tight bodice and shadowed cloak. "She didn't expect a thing." She circled him, watching his reaction, but Aaron refused to give her what she wanted and kept his body still and his mouth shut. He could sense her frustration growing, a tide of anger ready to devour him.

Patience, Aaron, patience.

"Did you hear me?" Lilith raised her voice, but still he gave her nothing but mute indifference. Squatting in front of him, she squeezed his cheeks and forced his jaw up to look at her.

Lilith gasped; her eyes wide silver pools as he grabbed her wrist and twisted hard. He locked his glare on hers and rose to his feet, dragging her with him.

"*Kavash,*" the command seethed from her lips, and the demon around Aaron's neck tightened its grip, ready to release more drugs to subdue her enemy.

Before it could act, Aaron let go of Lilith and wrapped his hand around the demon control collar. He suppressed a scream as a thousand needles ripped from his throat as he pulled the creature from his flesh, breaking Lilith's hold over him and restoring him to his full senses. Venom spurted from a thousand wriggling legs, coating his hand in blood and amber slime.

Ragged breaths caught in his lungs, but he was free from her clutches. The creature writhed in Aaron's hand, legs digging into his skin to make him let go, but Aaron tightened his grip. He couldn't let the thing escape. It had one task: obey its master and bind Aaron to her power once again.

Narrowing his eyes, he held Lilith's gaze and squeezed the life out of the monstrous control demon, black blood oozing between his fingers and down his arm. When the beast fell silent, he dropped it at her feet.

"I am tired of this game." Flicking her shadow cloak, she raised her hands and began chanting. Smoke poured from the bottomless pit that surrounded his island prison. It curled and spun, the wisps taking shape into a circle of demons, each heavily muscled, blue-black veins pulsing with hate, heads of eagles, sharp spears at the ready. "Take care of him," Lilith commanded, and the demons advanced.

Aaron twisted in his manacles, backing away as the demons approached. The only way to help Quinn was to get free and contact her himself. He couldn't wait any longer.

Come on, Kaemon, he begged, *don't let me down now.*

If he could keep Quinn from coming to the Underworld

and keep her away from Lilith, he had to accept that he was part angel.

I know you loved her, too. Do it for Eve, for Quinn.

Aaron panted. It was working—he could feel the strength growing inside him, more than even the strongest man on Earth possessed.

The skin beneath his shoulder blades itched and burned as if a thousand spiders crawled below his flesh, biting, stinging, and pushing their way free. He scratched at his back, rolling on the ground and tearing his nails across skin. He clawed at the soft tissue until blood oozed from his wounds, but the itch intensified, driving him mad.

Aaron rolled onto all fours and dug his fingers into the hard, stone floor as the sharp edge of his shoulder blade sliced through his scapula. Foam gathered in the corners of his mouth, and he howled, back arching as layers of tissue and muscle separated, birthing two long wings covered in golden feathers. Spanning twelve feet, Aaron stretched his golden wings to each side. Metal popped and groaned as he tugged on the chains. A few more seconds, and he would be free.

Two demons ran at him from either side, and like flicking flies, he brushed them over the edge with a swipe of his wings, and they tumbled into the abyss. Lilith shrieked commands at her army. Spears came at Aaron from all sides, but the light boiling inside him made him quick as well as strong. Twisting and turning like he'd seen a million times in the martial arts flicks he and Josh used to watch, he trapped each spear point in a section of chain, pulling them from the demons' grasp. Aaron delighted in his new powers, grinning as he kicked an oncoming attacker in the chest. Was this what it felt like to be invincible?

Pain ripped at his left shoulder. Three demons had come up behind him. One grabbed him around the waist and pinned his wings to his sides while the other two grabbed his arms. He fought against them, their strength no match for his own, but before he could break free, three more beasts tackled him, six demons pinning him to the ground.

Aaron's chest heaved as he pushed against them, but they held him tight. Lilith stood above him, a control demon scurrying up one of her arms, across her shoulders, and down the other. Directly above Lilith's head, a tiny light in the domed ceiling winked at him. The control demon reared up on a thousand tiny back legs, its pincers clicking as it approached. Taking a deep breath, he focused on the light and dug deep. Power flooded through him, and the explosion of a million suns burst through his pores. Demons screamed and scattered back, and he was free. Without thinking, Aaron ran for the precipice and let his wings unfurl. Air caught beneath him, and within seconds, he soared up toward freedom and Quinn, leaving Lilith in his wake.

Aaron circled the top of the domed ceiling. A sliver of cold, blue moonlight spilled from a small crack in the stone barely big enough for a rat to fit through. If this was the only way out, he would have to exploit the natural fissure and bash his way through to the other side. Tucking his wings to his sides, he dropped, letting gravity carry him as close to the ground as he dared, the wind rushing in his ears as he fell. There were at least twelve stories between the island prison and the top of the dome, and he would need every inch of it for his plan to work. Before he hit the ground, he spread his feathers and soared over Lilith's head, her raven hair blowing in the wake of his flight. Flying came as easy as breathing; it was as if he'd been doing it all his life.

Lilith howled in anger, stomping her foot as he darted to the right, just out of reach of her minions' spears, and beat his powerful wings. Faster and faster, he climbed, gaining speed and altitude. Tucking his chin to his chest, Aaron angled his shoulder, aiming for a point just to the right of the crack. A loud BOOM echoed off the ceiling as he hit his mark. The crack widened as stone and rubble hailed on the demons below. Pain rippled down his shoulder, his bones rattling from the force, but two beats of his wings, and the hurt receded to nothing. Aaron tucked his wings again, ready to make another run. A few more hits like that should bring down the whole dome.

At Lilith's command, millions of small bat-like demons erupted from the depth of the pit surrounding the platform, the whirlwind of leathery wings heading right for him. Aaron set his jaw and dove right into the middle of the storm. Talons ripped at his naked flesh above his abdomen, and he swiped the first creature away with a hand. The demon tumbled away as two more latched on to his leg, their long, razor teeth sinking into his calf. Aaron twisted onto his back trying to shake them off, but a dozen more swarmed him, ripping at his feathers, locking jaws on his naked skin as he plummeted. When one bit his forearm, he grabbed its tail and tore it loose—a lot more painful than ripping off a Band-Aid—and hurled it like a baseball into the stone wall. Stunned, the demon dropped. He plucked another off, and another, flinging them into the wall, the ground rushing closer and closer.

Inches from the stone floor, he flipped back onto his stomach. His wings spread out behind him, and he rocketed upward, tucking his chin and focusing on the widening fissure above. What was left of his attackers scattered in his wake. Nine stories, ten stories, eleven stories, he climbed.

Right before impact, a bolt of silver lightning flashed just above his head, and he had to roll right at the last minute to miss it. Unable to stop his momentum or correct his trajectory, Aaron hit the side of the dome instead of the crack he was aiming for. The stone walls shuddered at the force of his collision, and the opening widened, but it still wasn't wide enough for him to fit through.

Another silver lightning bolt crackled across his left shoulder. The smell of burning feathers and skin made him gag. Aaron flew in a circle, trying to extinguish the flames that caught at his golden plumage, beating his wing against the stone until they finally went out.

The horde of demon bats rallied for another attack, angling upward to meet him. He would give anything for a Qeres blade. He couldn't think of anything more satisfying than separating their heads from their bodies and watching the poison turn them to dust, but he would have to rely on Kaemon's strength, his own wits, and their determination to get them through this together.

Lilith let off another silver explosion, this one barely missing his head. He ducked and banked left, trying to make himself a smaller target, but he couldn't pull in his twelve-foot wingspan unless he wanted to fall to his death. Twist left, pitch right, zoom up, dive down—he dodged energy bolt after energy bolt. And then the demon bats were upon him again, a black cloud of screeching and flapping. Talons scratched at his flesh, tearing his skin until blood trickled from his wounds. He couldn't keep this up much longer, Kaemon was strong, but even an Elite Warrior could tire.

Aaron dug deep, ignoring the beasts biting, stinging, and screaming in his ear. He tuned out the explosions of light ripping through the dark. Escaping and warning Quinn, even if it was just for a moment, was the only thing that mattered. If they killed him after that, he didn't care. Once he broke through the ceiling, he would be free; he could contact her through their connection. Kaemon understood how it worked; he could get to her if Aaron let him. Together, they pictured her face, her body pressed against his, her soft voice calling his name. This time, when his shoulder hit the target, it yielded. A sound like a bomb exploding rebounded from the impact down to the foundations of the dungeon as the entire dome caved in.

Aaron didn't hesitate as he shot through the hole and out into the ceaseless night of the Underworld. His prison hadn't been in a tower, but in an underground dungeon deep within the mountain. Rubble continued to rain down on his enemy, angry screeches growing fainter as he darted up and away. The domed ceiling now stood as a gaping hole at the edge of the ridge where Lilith's palace ended, and the desolate terrain of the Underworld began.

Maybe Lilith would be crushed in the avalanche with them. Kaemon knew better; she would have blinked away before any harm came to her. Besides, she was immortal. Nothing could kill her here in her own kingdom.

Three spired towers of varying heights loomed against the stark and barren landscape, casting shadows over her entire domain. Thousands of obsidian glass windows spiraled up and around the towers, shining dark eyes in the gaunt light of twin blue-hued moons. From any vantage point, it would be easy to spot a lone angel flying in the distance, golden wings a torch in the darkness. Everything was quiet, too quiet, as if he were trapped in a bubble, no wind, no sound, only the thump of his heart and the beat of his wings.

At least there were no guards walking the ramparts, no armies gathered in the streets. Lilith had no need for defenses. Nothing could touch her here, but that didn't mean he wasn't watched. Demons were like roaches. Where you saw one, hundreds more were hiding and scurrying in the walls, infesting every dusky corner. As soon as Lilith regained control, she wouldn't hesitate to send a new horde to find him. He had to find shelter, and fast.

Swerving right, he soared over Lilith's castle, which jutted upward from a rocky cliff, and scanned the area for a safe place to land—a copse of trees, a cave, someplace he could conceal himself long enough to complete his mission—but miles of lifeless earth stretched to the horizon, reminding him of pictures he'd seen of the surface of the moon or dead lava fields of Iceland. Nothing but dust and rock under a bleak sky, nowhere to shelter, nowhere to hide. And then he spotted it, a deep crater in the distance. It wasn't ideal, but it would do.

Landing wasn't as easy as flying, and as his feet hit the ground, he stumbled forward, stretching out his arms to take the impact, and ended up face first against the pitted, black rocks. Gulping, he tried to catch his breath. His palms stung from scraping the rough surface of the crater, but he didn't care. He pushed up and ran under a small overhang, hoping it would provide enough cover to buy him time. With Kaemon now fully awake, he could close his eyes and see her essence, hear the whisper of her thoughts. It wouldn't take much. Pulling his wings in against his chest, he pushed his essence up and out through his psychic link, called her name, and prayed she would answer.

26

*A*zrael circled above Quinn and Marcus. Onyx wings a sharp silhouette gliding along the shore of Bluebonnet Creek. She didn't care what Azrael thought. He may be her protector, but this was her life, not his. He had no idea what it was like to be human, to feel so alone in grief and confusion. She needed someone to know what she'd been going through, all of it, and despite Azrael's arguments that it was his job to be there for her, he wasn't enough. Disapproval emanated from his essence as she confessed everything down to the last little detail to Marcus.

Marcus surprised her. He didn't crack a joke, not even once, as she paced along the shore, telling a truly unbelievable story. When she got to the part about the demons warning her away from Aaron, she choked.

"He should never have come after me." Quinn couldn't stop the flood of emotions dripping down her cheeks. "It would have been better if he had let me die. He would be here now instead of trapped in the Underworld with that monster."

"Don't say that. Of course, it wouldn't be better." Marcus

brushed a stray strand of hair from her eye and smiled. "It all makes sense now. Don't you see? It was his destiny to save you. This goes beyond everything, Quinn. When that thing was inside me, I could feel it digging for my deepest fear. It kept playing Aaron's death over and over in my mind, trying to make me weak, to suppress my, what did you call it?"

"Your spirit essence."

"Right. My essence. It got into my head and twisted my thoughts around to the point where I didn't want to fight back anymore." Marcus shivered.

Foolish. Stupid. Careless. Rash. Azrael's lecture went on and on. *You do not know the first thing about the evil you are dealing with. Bad enough that you risk you own life in a futile pursuit of a boy you have no hope of saving, but you refuse to go to Arcadia where you'll be safe, You put your friend at risk, too. Stubborn. Yes, add stubborn to the list. And did I mention stupid? If only I had leave to drag you to Arcadia kicking and screaming, I would.*

I'm not leaving Aaron there. I told you.

I will not allow you to risk everything to go to the Underworld.

"What if they're not just here to cross the veil and create chaos, as Azrael says. What if they're here to destroy us?" Marcus scratched his forehead. "Look what they had Jeff and Kerstin do to each other. Look at the wars we're having, the sick things happening all over the world. You have to stop them, Quinn, before it's too late. I can't watch my family and friends suffer like that. Maybe Azrael's right."

The boy understands far better than you do. You should listen to him.

Quinn ignored Azrael's interjection but didn't ignore the fear in Marcus's voice.

"Marcus, how can you say that? She has Aaron." A million iron bands squeezed at Quinn's chest, and her breath came in quick spurts. "You didn't see him, didn't talk to him. He's being tortured." She paced.

"And what's in that box? This Lilith chick wants it pretty bad, which says to me you shouldn't give it to her." Marcus ran a hand through his hair.

Something dark. Something dangerous. Something you should not be in possession of. Agitation laced Azrael's voice.

"If I don't give Lilith what she wants, he'll be trapped for eternity." Quinn stopped in front of Marcus and squared her shoulders. "Giving her the box means we can have Aaron back. You can have him back, Marcus. Isn't that what we both want more than anything?"

Do not be foolish, Quinn. Lilith is older and more powerful than you can imagine. If you set foot in the Underworld, you will not return. Your world will fall. Everything you love will die. And for what? The soul of one boy?

"How can you ask me to leave him there?" Quinn shouted at the sky as Azrael zigzagged in agitated patterns above them.

You can't even be sure it was Aaron. Lilith is a master of deception and manipulation. Even Eve was not immune to her lies. The box, Quinn. It must be taken to Arcadia. Azrael spoke through his bond. *It must not fall into her hands. Do you understand? I beg you to deliver it into my care.*

"Marcus, he's your best friend. You couldn't leave him there, could you?"

Marcus dug the toe of his shoe in the dirt and shoved his hands deep into his pockets. "I don't know, Quinn. I don't think Aaron would want you to risk everything just for him."

Yes. See? You should listen to your friend.

"What does that angel of yours say?" Marcus asked.

"He agrees with you. He thinks I should let him take the box to Arcadia for safe keeping and that I should go with him." Quinn flung her hands in the air. "I can't!"

"That demon said you have until the eclipse, right? That's

three days away. We have time to figure it out. Come up with a plan."

No. You are both fools. I won't let you throw all this away. There is no time. If you do this, you are on your own. Azrael flew in erratic circles around her head. *Do you hear me? I will abandon you.*

No. You won't. And we both know it. That seemed to shut him up, for now at least.

Quinn turned the box over in her hands. "Three days."

"Well, whatever you decide, I'll stand with you. And you have to tell Reese."

"I can't bring her into this. I shouldn't have even told you."

"You can't do this alone. Let us help you. It's our world, too."

"Okay, I'll tell Reese, but there's someone else I want to bring into this."

"This is your show, just think of me as your backup dancer." Marcus did a spin and slide, and Quinn couldn't help but laugh.

"With those kinds of moves, we're sure to win this fight." He unzipped the backpack and eyed the splintered spirit board. "I guess I'll be buying my little sister a new one of those."

He handed the backpack to Quinn, and she placed the box deep inside, zipped it all the way up to make sure it was secure, and slung it over her shoulder.

"Come on. I'll call Reese, and we can meet at my house. My parents are out tonight, so we'll have complete privacy. Now, let's get out of here. This place is nothing but trouble." Marcus put an arm around her and guided her back up the hill. "You're not alone anymore. We'll figure this out, together."

Hot, white fury rolled off Azrael, but he followed, his bond to her too strong to do anything but.

Quinn bit her lip as she pulled into the circle drive of Marcus's house. Beneath the porch light, Reese leaned against the archway, waiting. Quinn turned off the engine and looked in the rearview mirror. Where was Marcus? In the time since they had left Bluebonnet Creek, she had gone home, showered, and changed. Plenty of time for him to pick up the pizza and make it home. He'd promised she wouldn't have to face Reese alone. No time. She couldn't just sit in the car and wait. That would make an awkward situation even worse.

Come on, Quinn, this is your best friend. Not like she's going to bite. Get out of the car. That's it. See? Was that so hard?

"Hey," Reese walked down the stairs, rubbing her arms, "I'm so glad you guys called. I was going crazy at home alone." She dabbed her eyes with the cuff of her cream cardigan. "My dad's off doing damage control with the sheriff's department, and Ami won't stop texting me. She seems to think I'm her new best friend. I even had to turn the television off. They keep showing repeats of Kerstin attacking Jeff and him shooting her. If I hear one more 'expert' analyzing why this tragedy happened, I'm going to go postal."

"About that..."

"Looks like you started the party without me." Marcus slammed his Jeep door, two boxes of pizza balanced on one hand. "I brought snacks. We can play a little Zombie Island while we figure out how to rescue Aaron." Marcus handed Quinn the pizzas and fumbled with his keys to unlock the front door. "There's this one level where you stumble onto a crashed airliner. You have to open the door to get to a quest item, but when you do, all the dead passengers swarm you and try to eat your brain. It's awesome."

"What do you mean, rescue Aaron?" Reese asked. "Wait. That spirit board thing didn't actually work, did it?"

"You mean you haven't told her yet?" The key clicked into place, and Marcus motioned the girls to enter. Azrael slipped in behind them and slinked into a dark corner of the living room. Arms over his chest, he rested his sullen gaze on Quinn. At least he was keeping his thoughts to himself.

"I was just getting to that." Ignoring him, Quinn grabbed Reese's hand and pulled her over to the couch. "You might want to sit down for this."

Reese looked at Quinn and then at Marcus. "You're joking, right?" She settled into the sofa and sighed. "Okay, I'm sitting. Go ahead."

"Do you want to, or should I?" Marcus bounced on the balls of his feet.

"I think she'll take it better from you."

"Oh, for God's sake, somebody tell me what's going on."

"My idea worked, Reese. Quinn contacted Aaron, and then these demons showed up." Marcus waved his hands, acting out the whole scene for Reese's benefit. Reese, ever the skeptic, stared at him and rolled her eyes, totally not buying it. "They possessed me."

"Demons. Right. We just had two more friends die, and you want to make jokes. I'd rather be home alone than listen to this bull for one more second."

Marcus squatted in front of Reese and took both her hands in his. "It's true. I saw one of those demon things with my own eyes. It was nasty! All fangs and hair, and the smell! It was worse than that time the boys swim team had a farting contest in the back of the bus on the way to regionals. Nasty!"

"Stop it, Marcus. You're scaring me." Reese jerked away from him.

"You should be scared." Marcus's sober expression

stopped Reese from heading for the door. "They're the reason Jeff and Kerstin are dead, why Aaron is missing. I wouldn't joke about that, I swear."

"You're both crazy," Reese said, but she didn't leave. Instead, she looked from Marcus to Quinn and back to Marcus, tapping her foot on the concrete. "Next, you'll be telling me Quinn is some alien from the planet Zulu."

"Or a teenager who can see angels and demons and was born to save humanity from ultimate darkness?" Marcus pounced at the opportunity.

Reese burst out laughing. "Good one. One Slayer born to kick a little vampire butt back through the Hellmouth."

"Not vampires, demons. And it's called the Underworld, not the Hellmouth." Quinn waited for her friend to calm down. "I'm serious."

"No." Reese looked at Marcus. "Is she?"

Frustration welled up in Quinn. How could she make Reese believe her? It sounded so far-fetched. Maybe Caleb could explain, but why would Reese believe a boy she barely knew. No, there had to be another way.

Azrael. If Reese saw her Sentinel with her own eyes, she would have to believe. Why hadn't she thought of it before? A minute ago, he'd been sulking in the corner, now he was nowhere to be seen.

"Azrael?" Although she could speak to him telepathically, Quinn chose to speak out loud so her friends could understand what she was doing. "Where are you? Show yourself. I command it."

No need to shout. Azrael floated through the ceiling, landed softly beside them, and tucked his wings to his side. *They cannot see me. Their sight does not resonate at the correct frequency. No matter how much you command, I cannot reveal myself.*

"Where were you?" Quinn asked.

Patrolling the perimeter, as is my duty. You seemed too busy with this wearisome teenage chatter to be worried about demon attack.

"Who are you talking to?" Reese looked around and shrugged.

"Azrael, he's my Sentinel, my guardian angel. I commanded him to show himself to you, but he says he can't."

"Of course, he can't. Guardian angels can't show themselves to just any old humans, only those destined to save the world. Everyone knows that." Skepticism laced Reese's voice, but Quinn wouldn't give up on her plan.

"Give her a minute." Marcus put his arm around Reese, and she snuggled into him.

"I'll give you five, and then I'm out of here." Reese pulled her cell phone from her pocket and began surfing.

"There must be a way. You have to tell me if there is a way." Quinn pushed her will onto Azrael. She was his boss, not the other way around.

Don't let your power go to your head. Pride comes before a fall. Light pulsed around Azrael, and he grimaced. She could feel his desire to resist, but her wish overruled his. *Perhaps there is a way, but I don't know if it will work.*

"Tell me already." Quinn wondered if she looked like some of those mentally ill patients she saw in New York, talking to imaginary people. Maybe they weren't crazy after all. Maybe they were like her.

Encompass them within your barrier and use your energy to include them in what you see. If they are within your bubble, you might be able to influence their essences and let them see what you see. Use your energy to manipulate their perception, so to speak.

"And how am I to do that?"

Azrael shrugged. *You are Eol Ananael, not me. I am doing what you asked: telling you what I think might work. Since I do not* know for sure, I am putting forth a theory. In theory, it should work, but there is no guarantee. And for the record, I still don't think this is a good idea. It is against the edicts of the Dominions. They will not be best pleased.

"I don't care if the Dominions are best pleased. Am I Eol Ananael or not? Besides, you never think any of my ideas are a good idea." She looked over to Reese and Marcus, explaining, "Azrael says there's something that might work. Give me your hands."

Marcus stood and took her right hand while Reese gave him a sidelong glance.

"Oh, come on." Marcus grabbed Reese's wrist, took her phone, and pulled her forward.

"Okay! I can give her my hand myself, thanks." Reese jerked away from Marcus, and then held her arms out and nodded. Quinn stepped forward and took one hand while Marcus took the other.

"Will this hurt?" Reese asked.

"I don't think so." The circle complete, Quinn closed her eyes. As her essence brushed against theirs, she could feel the tension and skepticism in Reese like a block of ice against her energy. Marcus on the other hand, was so open that it was easy to push her bubble of protection out and around him.

"Dude. That's awesome!" Marcus exclaimed a few seconds later.

"What? What's awesome?" Reese asked.

"You should see him, Reese. He's so ... bright."

Impatient frustration coursed down Reese's arm and into Quinn's. "Why can Marcus see him and not me?"

"Relax, Reese, or at least try to have an open mind. Like meditation. Focus on your breathing."

"Do I have to chant or something? This feels so silly."

"No, just..." Just what? Quinn didn't even know what she was doing. How was it so easy for her to influence Marcus and not her best friend? "Let me in. Think about something fun we shared, like when we went on that road trip to Magic Island." It was working. She could feel Reese's essence unwinding, and she heard Reese giggle at the memory. "That's it."

Reese gasped and let go of Quinn's hand, and the bubble burst. "What the ... Where did he go?"

"If you want to see him, keep holding my hand. It's not easy for me to do this." Reese joined the circle again, and Quinn concentrated on expanding her barrier to include them. Then she worked to tune their essences into Azrael's frequency. It wasn't as hard as she'd imagined. Instincts led her where she needed to go as she experimented with how to manipulate their desire to see Azrael into reality.

Within seconds, she sensed Azrael shimmering into focus. She let go of their hands and opened her eyes. They would only be able to see him when Quinn was near. The change she made to their essences depended on her being close. It was similar to the way she pushed out her barrier to defend her mother from the demons. If they stepped out of the bubble, he would disappear.

"I can see him now! Oh, my God, Quinn, you weren't lying. He is so beautiful." Quinn remembered the first time she saw Azrael and wondered if her face had looked like Reese's right then.

"I'm sorry, Quinn. We're supposed to be best friends, but all this talk of ghosts and psychic powers, it spooked me, you know? I wanted to believe you but couldn't let myself. It was all too scary." Reese and Quinn fell into a tangle of hugs and tears.

"No, I'm sorry. You were right when you said our relationship was nothing but lies and secrets and that I didn't trust you. I was afraid you wouldn't understand."

"I wouldn't listen. No wonder you kept secrets from me.

God, Quinn, I've been so stupid. But I'm here now." A flash of fear mixed with wonder rumbled through Reese's essence. "Is he dangerous?"

"Only to demons."

Azrael stood before them in all his glory, hands gripping the pommels of his swords, a hard look on his face. He did not like being her dancing monkey. He didn't even try to hide his distain from her.

"Azrael, this is Reese and Marcus. Guys, this is my Sentinel, Azrael."

"I know who they are." Azrael pulled his sword from his scabbard and began picking dirt from beneath his nails with the tip. Reese and Marcus both backed away.

"Play nice, Az."

"Don't call me that, and maybe I will."

"Ignore him. His bark is worse than his bite."

Azrael snarled, and then grinned. Quinn rolled her eyes.

Reese circled Azrael, studying him as if examining a work of art. Quinn couldn't blame her; he was an Adonis to look at, though his personality was completely lacking. Azrael ignored Reese like a cat ignored its owner, preening himself and looking smug.

"And you started seeing him after you drowned?" Reese asked. "Why didn't you tell me?"

"I didn't know how. Would you have known how to tell me something like this?"

Reese shook her head. "I guess not. What does this have to do with Aaron?"

"Long story short? He's trapped in the Underworld by Adam's first wife, Lilith. She wants this box I found in exchange for Aaron."

"A box that, when opened, will unleash the rest of Lilith's horde into the human realm and rip the veil to pieces." Azrael flexed his jaw, wings fluttering in agitation. "Lilith will no longer be trapped in the Underworld. You are being foolish and selfish. You would risk the lives of your friends, your family, their families, for the life of one boy?"

"I have until the eclipse to bring it to her or damn him for eternity." Quinn didn't know what the Underworld looked like, but she imagined it was a terrible place. She pictured Aaron alone and in pain, and her heart shattered all over again.

At the thought of his face, pain crackled through her body like a million volts of electricity running under her skin. "He's here," Quinn whispered. Although she couldn't see him, the magnetic draw of his essence pulled her to him. She sensed his urgency pushing across from the Underworld.

"Don't. You do not know what is contacting you." Azrael took two giant steps toward her, intent on keeping her from Aaron. Quinn raised a hand, palm out, and directed all her focus at Azrael. "You will let me do this. Azrael, Sentinel of Arcadia, I bind you to my command and order you to hold your position."

"You do not know what you are doing." Azrael growled.

"I know exactly what I'm doing." She didn't need to think about it anymore. Accessing her power was as easy as breathing. Wish, and it will be.

Before Azrael could say another word, Quinn commanded him to be silent then slammed a barrier between them so he couldn't follow her. He paced like a caged animal, repelled by the wall she put between them. Satisfied he wouldn't be able to interfere, she dropped to her knees and projected her essence out of her body and into the astral plane, the seam where the fabric of the Underworld and her realm joined.

27

Time slowed, and then stopped. Reese and Marcus stood like carved statues, concern and fear etched on their faces as the world bleached of color. Hues of gray and black replaced the white walls of Marcus's living room, and then Quinn stood between her realm and another, darker world.

Shadows bathed the astral plane, and the air smelled of a strange mix of sulfur and grass. A thousand fingers pinched at her heart. Gray smoke writhed in the corners, creeping closer, but Quinn held firm.

"Aaron," she called to him. His essence was close; its familiar scent wrapped around her like a warm blanket. Breathing in, she savored the sweet, earthy smell, like a warm summer night.

Light rippled before her, and the shadows parted like a curtain. Aaron stumbled through, his bare chest heaving with exertion, and Quinn's breath caught in her throat. Although their physical bodies remained anchored in other realms, here in the seam, on the astral plane, their essences appeared just as they would in the real world, as flesh and bone on a blank canvass. But this Aaron was more than just flesh and bone. Golden wings unfurled from his shoulders, each feather flickering like a flame from a candle. Quinn's jaw dropped, and she gasped. An angel! He was an angel! How the hell did that happen?

"Quinn? Thank God." Aaron spread his wings wide, fluttering them the way Azrael did when he was agitated. "Are you okay?" Only Aaron would be more concerned about her than he was for himself.

Quinn nodded. The awe of seeing him in his new form tied her tongue in a knot. Even Azrael paled in comparison, and she wondered what his feathers would feel like against her fingers. Would they be warm to the touch? She took a tentative step forward. Aaron moved to meet her, stopping just shy of touching. Heat radiated from his skin. Being close to him was like standing in the sun on a warm spring day, and she wanted to soak it all up before winter came to steal it away.

Aaron brushed back a matted strand of black hair, not meeting her gaze. Blood seeped from a gash above his eye, streaked his torso, dripped from an open wound on his side and down his left thigh. It was then she realized he was completely naked. Blood rushed to her cheeks, and she snapped her eyes back to his face. How long had she been staring?

"Sorry," he stammered, his face turning a deep shade of cranberry as he realized. A tip of a golden wing rushed to cover his exposed skin. "Give me a second to, um, dress." With nothing but a wish, jeans wrapped around his legs and fastened around his waist. "There's so much I need to tell you, but I don't know where to start." Rubbing the back of his neck with a hand, Aaron glanced over his shoulder, brow furrowing. "I didn't think I would ever see you again." He blinked, but not before she recognized the tears threatening to fall.

"That wasn't you at the river." There was no need to explain—Aaron's thoughts flowed into her own, their bond stronger than ever. "It was a trick?"

Aaron nodded.

"How could I have been so blind?" Now that the true Aaron stood in front of her, she could sense it. The difference in his essence and the one she'd met in the seam just hours before was like the difference between ice cream and frozen yogurt.

"Don't blame yourself. She's a master at manipulation."

She cupped his cheek, examining the long scratch running from his ear to his chin. Sweat dripped from his thin body, and scratches covered his arms, highlighting the long scars that twined from his wrist to his elbow. A dark red ring circled his throat as if he'd been strangled, and his hair hung in matted strands around his dirt-streaked face, making him look older.

"And torture?"

Aaron shivered and looked away again, brow wrinkling into two faint worry lines. Hiding wasn't an option anymore. On the astral plane, their connection exposed his emotions to her. Tears slid down her cheeks. His thoughts were open to her and hers to him, as if they were one being, and she caught glimpses of chains and demons and a dark-haired woman with silver eyes.

"Lilith." Aaron shook his head and rubbed a thumb to his temple, banishing the vision from both their minds. His uncertainty beat against her essence like a thousand wings. She wanted to press him further but sensed he wanted to forget for a moment and feel safe in her arms, and she needed to respect his wishes as he would respect hers.

"Aaron, I'm so sorry, for everything." The words

tumbled from her like heavy boulders rolling off the side of a cliff, a load she'd been carrying for a long time. But even voicing her apology didn't change the guilt that etched itself on her heart. She ran the back of her hand down his cheek and across his lips, drinking in the truth of what she'd done to him. A fate worse than death. Guilt and shame stabbed her heart. Aaron should have been the chosen one, not her. Courageous, loyal, selfless—everything she wasn't. "If it hadn't been for me, you..." Quinn began, but Aaron shook his head and pressed a finger against her lips.

"Let's forget all of that. We're here now, together." Though his words whispered of forgiveness, she sensed the sting of her betrayal buried not so deep within his essence. Trust was a fragile thing, and she had wounded him deeply.

"I'm not completely blameless for what happened, Quinn." Aaron looked away.

"What do you mean?" Her heart contracted as the truth started to bleed from his essence into hers.

"I know now why I came back, why I didn't die in the car accident, why my suicide was futile. Meeting you wasn't chance."

Quinn felt Aaron push a memory into her mind, and she saw the reality, all of it, as if she had witnessed it herself. Her hands flew to her mouth, and she backed away. No, it couldn't be true. Aaron wasn't just a boy. He had been a Sentinel. Not any Sentinel—hers.

"Everything that's happened to you, the demon attacks, the nightmares, it's all my fault. Or at least half mine, Kaemon's half." Aaron reached for her, but she swatted him away.

"You knew? All this time, you knew what I was, and you didn't say anything?"

"No. It's more complicated than that."

"How can it get any more complicated than you masquerading as a human and lying to me for months?"

"I didn't know what I was, Quinn, just as you didn't know what you were. You have to believe me."

"Believe you? You abandoned me. Left me unprotected. You left me at the mercy of those things."

"Look, I know you're angry and confused. I was too, at first, but in Kaemon's defense, Azrael tricked him. He used Kaemon's love for you, his wish to become human, to lure him into a trap, to get close to you. Kaemon's essence was supposed to die along with mine, but something went wrong. Together, we survived."

"No, that can't be … " Quinn turned away, but Aaron put a hand on her shoulder.

"Azrael's been manipulating us both, Quinn. In your heart, you know it. That sword he carries? The blue one? It belonged to Kaemon. That night in the river, he drew it across my throat. He's the reason I'm trapped in the Underworld."

All of Azrael's actions replayed over and over in her mind. His reluctance to believe Aaron was alive, his aversion to direct questions about her purpose, it all made sense, but he also trained her, protected her. How could that all be a lie?

"You can't trust him." Aaron's expression darkened as he revealed each manipulative deed Azrael had committed, including Aaron's death.

Breaking away, Quinn shook her head, unable to process everything. Kaemon's betrayal, Azrael's lies—it seemed to her the angels weren't any better than the demons. At least with demons, she knew what to expect. Evil was their nature. What was the excuse for the servants of The Light?

"I don't know what Azrael's excuse is, but I can explain Kaemon's. His essence was drawn to yours the way he was drawn to Eve that night in the garden. You saw for yourself the spark between them. When he was assigned to you, and you wrapped your tiny hand around his finger, he recognized her essence in you, and he thought maybe this was the plan all along, that The Light gave him a chance he could never have with Eve. His desire to be with you condemned him, but it saved me, twice. I can't believe that was coincidence either. Kaemon did it because he fell in love with Eve, with you. Now I understand why I did too, and Azrael used that love to trick Kaemon. We are meant to be. We're stronger together. I know you feel it. You have to trust me."

Quinn covered her ears and shook her head. She did feel it, the undeniable pull to him. *When the tears of Eve have turned to blood and her sins have turned to flesh, the key will fall. For love is bound by the power of the Trinity.* She was the Trinity, the Eol Ananael, the essence of Eve, the perfect balance of human, angel, and demon, just as Eve was, the moment she'd eaten the apple.

Memories of herself as Eve standing at the portal as Kaemon closed it to seal her away from Eden flashed before her. Eve loved the fierce warrior angel even then, and if he had asked her to run away with him and leave Adam forever, she would have, but duty came before love. They made their choices and moved on, but neither of them forgot the other.

Aaron nodded. "I know, it's confusing, but the one thing I'm certain about is how I feel about you."

Quinn stared at her feet.

"Look at me." He cupped her cheek, and she felt him open up to her as she stared into his eyes. "Quinn, I'm not Kaemon. I'm still Aaron. What I feel for you goes beyond time and space. It is eternal. This is not Kaemon's choice; it is mine, Aaron's. Everything I've done, I've chosen. And I would do it again, even knowing the outcome."

. . .

Maybe he was right. The past didn't matter. Eve, Kaemon, they didn't exist anymore, not fully. They could make their own decisions as Quinn and Aaron. Destiny was nothing more than a choice. If she wanted, she could turn her back and walk away from it all, or she could decide to follow her heart. The choice was hers and hers alone. But after everything she'd put him through, could he really forgive her?

"Forgiveness isn't the same as forgetting, Quinn. It's not possible to erase the past, but that doesn't mean we have to live in it. We've all made mistakes." Aaron smiled and brushed a strand of hair behind her ear. She reached up, and her hand found his. Pressing his palm to her cheek, she let the tears flow freely.

She'd pushed everyone away for so long that she didn't know how to trust anyone else. For the first time, she realized she didn't just want Aaron, she needed him, not to rescue her or love her, but as someone she could share her life with. They were stronger together. All the reassurance she needed was her own heart, beating in time with his. This was Aaron, the boy who saved her more times than she could count. He would not abandon her, and she could never desert him either. The past was unchangeable, but the future was yet unwritten, and this time she would do whatever it took to keep him safe.

"When did you get to be so wise?" she asked.

"Finding out you are part angel ages a person." Aaron moved closer until his soul pressed against hers.

Essence to essence, the electric energy between them hummed in perfect tune. His hand cupped her neck, and he tilted her face upward. Eyes tinged with sadness gazed into her own. Calm hummed through him, and she felt his heart slow to match hers. She was afraid to move, afraid the bubble that held them would burst, and he would disappear. Neither of them knew how much time they had together in this realm. Seconds, minutes, it didn't matter. This moment belonged to them alone, and she wouldn't waste it wondering.

"Quinn," he murmured. She thought her name never sounded so beautiful. "I love you. I've always loved you. Don't you know that?" Hands stroked her hair, his touch so gentle it sent shivers down her spine.

Quinn pressed closer, brushing her lips against his. His mouth opened to hers as she kissed him, soft and slow. He tasted of sunlight and summer, heat pulsing from his skin and into hers, melting all the fear and regret she'd carried for so many months.

Arms pulled his hips to hers, and he let out a soft moan. Aaron deepened the kiss, his nails digging into her waist, and she pulled him down with her until they were both on their knees. She let him guide her to the ground, her back pressed against the golden grass as he used his power to paint the perfect scene. With nothing but a thought, their field sprang to life around them, complete with starry sky. Aaron hovered above her, arms holding him inches away.

"Are you sure?" he asked.

In answer, she cupped the back of his neck to bring his lips to hers once more. Love and relief washed over them both in waves, and she felt his desire as strong as her own. When she was with him there was no room for darkness, nowhere to hide in the light of his love. For the first time, she didn't want to hold back anything from him. Emotions transcended words; there were no secrets between them. He saw all of her, the dark and the light, and he loved her anyway, and she him.

When Aaron pulled away, desolation crept between them as stark reality bound them like a heavy iron chain. None of this was permanent. They were both nothing more than energy connecting on an alternate plane.

"What is it?" Quinn asked.

Aaron put a finger to his lips and cocked his head. Then she heard it too—the sound of hooves pounding on stone approaching.

"She's found me. I'm out of time." He rushed to his feet, pulling her with him. They both stared at the wall of fog that devoured the horizon. Through the thin veil separating the seam from the Underworld, Quinn could make out an army of demons, weapons drawn, and at the front, a silver stallion, legs made of twisting shadows. On the horse sat a woman with raven-black hair. Lilith.

"You have to leave, Quinn. Now. No telling what she'll do if she finds you here." Aaron pushed at her essence, begging her to return to her own realm, but she shook her head.

"You must get back to your body. Flee to Arcadia," he argued. "Tell The Light what you know about Lilith's plan. Let Azrael think he's still your Sentinel, and whatever you do, don't come to the Underworld. She can't open it without you, and she can't cross the veil to get it. You are the key, Quinn. Without you, she has nothing."

"No, I won't let you go. Not now." Quinn had made up her mind. She wanted him with her as her partner. "We're stronger together. You need me. Let me help you."

"No, don't even think about it." Panic fluttered through Aaron's heart and into hers.

"But she'll kill you if I don't give her what she wants."

"It's too late for me. I'm already dead."

And there it was. The thing they both tried to ignore made real in words. Quinn shook her head and dragged her fingers through her hair.

"Deep down, you knew this was only a moment, one that couldn't last." Aaron's sad smile broke her heart into a million pieces. "I can never come back. My human body is gone, my essence has become something more. I'm trapped here in the Underworld, bound to her realm. There is no way out for me, I can't cross the veil."

"There must be a way, and I will find it. I won't leave you here. I won't let you risk everything for me."

"Don't you know by now that I would jump to save you a million times over? It is my destiny to protect you, and I do it gladly," Aaron whispered, his voice ragged with emotion. "Please, don't cry." He wiped a tear from her cheek. "Everything happens for a reason. Besides, Kaemon and I have a few tricks up our sleeves. She won't get us that easy."

Quinn wished she believed that, but Lilith's reach was far, her power great. Where could one angel hide in the Underworld? There would be no sanctuary, no allies. They both looked past the swirling fog and into the Underworld. Webs of lightning crackled across the darkened sky. Even in the seam, the ground shook as the demon horde approached.

"Remember what the garden looked like after the taint? What they will do to the realm of men will be far worse. Reese, Marcus, everyone will be their slaves, food for her children to feed off. Do you want that?"

"I don't care. I'm not leaving you. Aaron, please, there must be a way. I can't do this without … "

Lightning struck when his lips pressed against hers, hard and urgent, silencing her mouth and her thoughts. He wound his arms around her waist, drawing her close. Wings caressed her back, brushed against her cheeks. Her fingers twisted through his hair as the heat rose between them. She clung to him, willing him not to leave. Grief mixed with desire seeped from his every pore, filling her with anger. His kiss said the goodbye that his voice couldn't. She wouldn't accept it, wouldn't let him go. But before she could protest, he pulled away and shoved her backward so hard she fell on her backside. With two beats of his wings, he launched upward.

Stunned and hurt, she watched him circle overhead, just out of reach.

Don't do this! Please, Aaron.

One more circle overhead, and his essence shimmered and blinked out as it returned to his body back in the Underworld, leaving her alone in the seam. She sensed him retreating from her mind too, the intensity of his emotions becoming nothing more than a dull ache. In seconds, Aaron would be nothing more than an impression. He tried to sever their connection, but Quinn refused to let him go.

Don't leave me! she begged, fighting to stay joined, to haul him back, to anchor him to her, but his gift was stronger than hers.

We can figure this out. I'll fight her, Quinn cried to him through their rapidly disintegrating link, but silence met her pleas.

Quinn pressed her essence against the thin veil separating the seam from the Underworld. Through the gray mist, Quinn could just make out Aaron's sun-kissed wings as he zoomed toward the approaching horde, drawing Lilith's attention away from the astral plane, away from Quinn.

You can't do this!

In response, Aaron sent a burst of power through their link, like a psychic shove, so hard it jarred her essence to the core, and then a wall, thick and dark, slammed between them before she had the chance to retaliate.

Silence.

Aaron was gone.

28

*B*eyond the veil, Quinn watched as an eclipse of demons took to the sky, black leathery wings tracking Aaron's golden ones as he led them deeper and deeper into the Underworld and away from her until they were nothing but tiny dots over the horizon.

Her fists beat against the ethereal barrier, kicking up particles of fog, which danced and swirled around her as she screamed his name.

Anger and revenge welled up within her, and her power swelled, ready to erupt. No, not helpless, not anymore. Quinn paced in front of the thin wall between the seam and the Underworld. If she could see Lilith through the veil, maybe she could kill her. She was Eol Ananael; she had to try. Hands pressed against the barrier, she centered herself, calling on the light within. Buzzing filled her head, and the wall of fog vibrated beneath her touch.

Lilith! she called.

The sound of hoof beats on stone echoed in the distance, turning Quinn's way. A silver steed, legs enveloped by smoke, raced across the bleak landscape of the Underworld. On it, a woman, cloaked in shadow dragged a body behind her.

Quinn's heart hammered against her ribs, and she tried to calm herself with three deep breaths. Aaron, encased in a cocoon of spider webs, thrashed and kicked, the burnished feathers of his wings pushing against his bonds as his body was trailed across sharp rocks.

I swear, if you hurt him, I will kill you. Do you hear me, Lilith? I will fucking kill you if you so much as scratch him.

Laughter echoed across the veil. *You dare threaten me? Bring the box to me before the eclipse, and I might let you live. As for the boy? His fate is in your hands, Eol Ananael, as his blood is on the hands of your Sentinel. Remind me to thank Azrael for his little gift.*

Quinn swallowed, fighting not to take the bait. Lilith first, then she would deal with Azrael. Putting questions about her Sentinel out of her mind, Quinn focused on the task at hand: to release a killing wish and end Lilith's life once and for all.

A few more feet, and Lilith would be at the border, close enough for Quinn's power to reach. Lilith skidded to a stop before the wall of fog, her horse rearing under her command. Silver eyes, so cold they made her gasp, locked on Quinn's and wouldn't let go. It was now or never.

Power surged from the pit of Quinn's stomach, hot and angry, but before Quinn could release it, a shockwave of energy rocked her mind, casting her out of the seam and thrusting her back into reality. Colors swirled to life as time resumed, and she was back in her body, arm outstretched, Aaron's name on her lips.

"No!" Quinn screamed as the world came rushing back to life. Unfrozen, Reese and Marcus ran over to her, but she pushed them away, intent on one thing and one thing only.

The power that built up inside needed release, and if she couldn't have Lilith, she would have the next best thing.

Sensing her intent, Azrael's eyes widened, and he spread his wings to take flight.

Quinn stretched out her hand and released her command as a bolt of white light from her fingers. Azrael hung in midair, a snarl on his face. "Stupid girl," he hissed.

"What are you doing?" Reese asked. "Quinn? I thought you said he was your guardian."

"Are you, Azrael?" Quinn asked.

Azrael didn't even squirm in her grasp. His defiance pricked her essence like thorns, but her strength had grown, and anger fueled her now. She wouldn't let go until she got answers.

"You betrayed me. You knew where Aaron was all along." Quinn gritted her teeth and used her energy to squeeze an invisible hand around his throat. His eyes bulged, and he pawed his neck.

Marcus patted Quinn on the shoulder and whispered in her ear, "You're killing him."

"Immortals can't choke to death, but I'm sure it's uncomfortable to have your essence crushed. There's only one way to kill an immortal. Give me your blade, Azrael. You know the one I mean, the one you stole from Kaemon when you tricked him into Aaron's body, the one you used to slit Aaron's throat after he jumped in to save me."

Shock cut Reese and Marcus' faces.

"Aaron would have lived if it wasn't for him," Quinn said to Marcus.

"He would have died anyway. I have told you before, it was his destiny." Spittle flew from Azrael's mouth.

"A destiny you chose for him. You could have saved him. Now, give me Kaemon's blade." Azrael's arm shook as he tried to resist her, but in the end, he reached into his scabbard, pulled the Qeres blade from its sheath, and handed it to Quinn.

Drunk on revenge, Quinn positioned the tip of the blade to the hollow of his throat. "Aaron showed me everything. I can still feel the pain of the poison running through his body. Our bond let me feel the depth of your betrayal, Azrael. Do you know what Qeres really does to an immortal essence?" Quinn pressed the cold star-blade into his skin. "Time to experience it firsthand."

Azrael didn't flinch. He stared at her with his golden eyes. "Go ahead and finish it then. Have your revenge, but I know what you really want. I feel your desire radiating from you like sunlight. It burns hot inside you; this need to bring him back. I might know a way."

"Tell me." Quinn tightened her grip on his essence, and the light beneath his skin flickered in pain.

"Release me," Azrael panted. "Let me take you to Arcadia until the solar eclipse has passed, and I will help you rescue the boy."

"No, you will take me to the Underworld. Now."

"I can't let you." Pain etched lines into Azrael's usually smooth face.

"Let me? You have no hold over me, Azrael." She pushed the tip of the blade a little farther into Azrael's skin, and he flinched.

"Don't be foolish. Lilith will kill you. You've read the prophecy. You are Eve's tears and her sin turned to flesh. The Trinity refers to your essence, the perfect balance of human, demon, and angel. If you fall, descend into the Underworld, Lilith will have what she needs to break the lock. You are the sacrifice. We must leave for Arcadia, tonight. There is no other choice."

"Lilith can't do anything without the box, Azrael, and I have the box. It's my bargaining chip. It's my life. I hold all the cards here." Quinn cocked her head. "There's something you're hiding. I can sense it." Quinn forced her will upon

Azrael, using their link to dig for an answer she wanted, but his thoughts were evasive. Like a breeze, they were constantly changing, moving, flickering, to the point she could never quite get a hold of one.

"If you are going to meet the Queen of the Underworld, you will need to do the same. Keep your thoughts flowing, do not let her pinpoint any specifics."

"I am not in the mood for lessons." Quinn forced her will upon his essence, and his eyes widened. "You will keep your mind still and reveal what you're hiding." Seizing on a fleeting thought in Azrael's mind, she flexed her fingers around the hilt of the sword and pressed the tip once again into the hollow of his throat.

"When did you take it?" Azrael shuddered as she ran the tip of the blade across his bare chest. "You will show me." Quinn growled. Even though he didn't resist, she tore through his mind anyway, without a care for his feelings. He didn't care about hers. There. She seized the moment and replayed the image of Azrael reaching a hand through her car and into the bag while she and Marcus tried to convince Reese that demons were real. So that's where he had disappeared to.

"Where is it now?"

"I gave it to one of her minions," Azrael said with labored breath.

"The part in the prophecy about chaos and betrayal, it refers to you, doesn't it, Azrael?" It took everything she had to keep from cutting his heart out with Kaemon's blade. "Did you know about the box all along?"

"No, I believed the box of Agathe to be nothing more than a myth, until today. Even though the Dominions knew of the prophecy, they weren't sure the rumors coming back from Eden were authentic. But all myths are grounded in truth, and I recognized it the moment I saw it in your hands. *It* found *you*. Don't you understand? Destiny drew it to your essence, to Eve's essence incarnate. Once the box revealed itself, I saw an opportunity."

"An opportunity for what? Betrayal?"

"To keep you from going to the Underworld and killing us all." Fear spilled from Azrael's essence, not just for her, but of her. She could taste it, bitter and metallic on her tongue. Good. Let him understand how much he underestimated her. "And you thought you could give Lilith the box, and I would just run off to Arcadia and leave Aaron there to rot?"

"I didn't think it would be easy, but I planned to drag you to Arcadia kicking and screaming if I had to, until the eclipse was over, ensuring the prophecy would not come to pass. That box means nothing without you; so as long as you stay away from it, Lilith's plan will fail. Everything I did was for the greater good." Azrael actually believed what he'd done was right. Quinn could sense his conviction "Everything I did was with The Light's approval."

"And did The Light tell you to kill an innocent boy?" Quinn asked, digging deep into his mind to root out the answer. "How did killing Aaron that night in the river serve the greater good? And Kaemon, my real Sentinel, what about him?"

He tried to hide the truth from her, but she was stronger now, her power surging. Azrael had interpreted his orders as he saw fit. As long as it got the job done, The Light turned a blind eye. After all, he was chosen because of his penchant for bending the rules.

"You killed them both out of petty jealousy?" Tears streamed down Quinn's cheek and she swiped them away with the back of her hand.

"It's not like that," Azrael begged. "The Dominions watched Kaemon's bond to you grow. They feared he would be distracted, that his feelings for you would cloud his judgment. His unwavering love made him reckless, made him weak. I should have been your Sentinel to begin with, but the Dominions chose Kaemon because they thought he might lead them to the box. For me, they cast a darker, more sinister role."

"You were playing both sides?"

"As I was commanded." Azrael's agitation showed in the ruffling of his feathers. "When the Dominions began to lose trust in Kaemon, they saw an opportunity to kill two birds with one stone, so to speak. I would take care of their Kaemon problem in the guise of leaving you unprotected for Lilith's attacks, and they would restore my rightful place as your Sentinel in exchange. But prophecy has a strange way of fulfilling itself. Aaron, Kaemon, they were factors unaccounted for. With Kaemon's essence still in the human realm, our plans failed. A human can only have one Sentinel after all, and Kaemon was still bound to you, even in a mortal body. Nobody foresaw this outcome."

"So, Aaron, Kaemon, they were collateral damage in all this? I'm so sick of lies, Azrael." Quinn flourished the Qeres blade in his face, the tip just shy of cutting into his eye.

"Aaron would never have survived without Kaemon's essence. Kaemon should have perished when I bound his soul to Aaron's dying essence. But prophecy has a strange way of creating loopholes to ensure the balance. Believe what you will, but I am here to help you, to protect you." Azrael didn't plead, didn't beg, his tone was matter of fact.

"I don't need your protection anymore; can't you feel it?" Energy crackled around her. "I can protect myself. I can rescue Aaron and kill Lilith in the same breath. I'll take the fight to her instead of hiding in Arcadia, end it now. Then my life, all of our lives, can go back to normal. Don't you understand? Aaron would never leave me in hell."

"Your power may have grown, but you still lack control.

Look at yourself, Quinn, so full of hate. This is what she wants, to divide us. Your rash decisions will be the death of you and of all humanity. Don't *you* understand? That's exactly what she wants, to use Aaron as bait to draw you to … what is it you humans say? Home field advantage?"

Quinn lowered the sword and loosed her grip on Azrael but commanded him to stay where she could see him. He slumped against the wall and rubbed the back of his neck. Maybe he was right about one thing. She was a fool to walk right into Lilith's trap and risk everything for one person. Saving him would be selfish, but her heart wanted to do the selfish thing. Going to Arcadia made sense, let the eclipse pass, and then turn the fight back to the Underworld. That's what Aaron wanted her to do. Quinn pinched the bridge of her nose, her head and her heart were in direct conflict with one another, and she paced.

Through the front window, the sun dipped beneath the horizon, the fiery orange and red hues that painted the evening sky reminded her of the molten beauty of Aaron's new wings. Every second away from him felt like eternity. No telling what Lilith would do to him. She couldn't let Aaron sacrifice himself for her again. Sacrifice. She stopped mid-stride.

"The voice of the sacrifice will break the lock, restoring darkness unto the light…" Quinn recited the last sentence of the prophecy, mulling over its meaning. "It never says who the sacrifice is. It never specifies. If Lilith kills Aaron, if he dies sacrificing his life so that I might live, wouldn't that fulfill the prophecy?" she asked Azrael.

Azrael whirled around ruffling his feathers in agitation. He didn't know how to answer. She could sense his confusion and shock as he ran the scenario through his thought process. When he didn't try to reassure her, she was wrong, Quinn's heart slammed against her chest. Wide, burning amber eyes met her own, and his dread scraped across her barrier and intensified her own horror.

"No. That's not possible." Azrael shook his head. His pace quickened; wings thrown wide.

"But it isn't specific, is it? By not rescuing Aaron, couldn't he become the sacrifice? Are you willing to bet the human realm on it?"

Azrael rubbed his temples, his jaw tight. "If she kills him..."

"She *will* kill him if I don't show up. If I hide like a coward, he will die, and the box could be opened anyway." Quinn gripped the handle of Kaemon's sword, the star-blade suddenly heavy in her hand. "You said yourself that prophecy was the way the universe balanced Lilith's defeat in Eden. It's why Kaemon came back as Aaron, why we happened to be at the same school, why he ended up in the Underworld. Everything he's done is to keep me safe. What if hiding in Arcadia is useless? What if she opens the box anyway, using Aaron? If I don't come to her, she'll be angry enough to do it."

"Even with all your powers intact, even if you managed to open a door to the Underworld, you wouldn't know where to start. Your bond to Aaron has been severed; you have no idea where Lilith is keeping him." Azrael got down on one knee in front of her and bowed his head. His wings fell forward, cloaking him like an inky cape. "If you are so stubborn that you would undo a millennium of planning for love, then let me help you. You will need me. I will not leave your side. I have vowed to go where you go and protect you no matter how stupid you are. I swear it."

"And how do you plan to do that, Azrael? Angels can't enter the Underworld, it is forbidden, you said so yourself."

"My essence is tainted enough to enter. In order to gain her trust, I had to prove myself to her ... " he cleared his throat " ... to do a few unsavory things over the years. I have been to her palace, and I know how she thinks; she believes I've betrayed The Light for my own benefit. We can use that against her."

"Haven't you?" Quinn held Kaemon's Qeres blade to Azrael's throat. "Why should I trust you now?" She would make him beg, make him grovel.

Azrael beat his wings and threw his arms wide.

"Use your powers and read me. I will strip my barrier down to nothing. Dig as deep as you want, I will not resist. All I have done has been for you."

"Then why the secrets?" Quinn asked. "Why not tell me everything from the beginning?"

"Understanding only comes through walking your own road, not by walking someone else's. Wisdom and knowledge are two different things. Ask Eve what it was like to gain untold knowledge but not have the wisdom to comprehend what it meant. Would you seek her path? Banished, ashamed, forever changed? Would you let Lilith destroy everything Eve did to build a life for her children here?"

Quinn grabbed his chin with a hand and wrenched his eyes to hers. Azrael didn't resist as she searched his memories, his thoughts, looking for any hint of a lie, of betrayal, but everything Azrael said was true. He was there to protect her, to protect humanity. He truly believed everything he'd done was for the greater good, every sacrifice, every decision.

"Are you really going to trust this guy after what he did to Aaron?" Marcus asked.

"He's telling the truth." Quinn released her hold on Azrael but kept the Qeres blade in her hand.

"How do you know that?" Reese asked.

"I read him. He can't hide from me, not anymore."

"You say walking my own path leads to wisdom. I can see

it now; there is no way to avoid this prophecy. I choose to go to the Underworld, to face my fate."

"And if you are wrong about Aaron being the sacrifice?" Free from her control, Azrael rose gracefully to his feet, squared his shoulders, and clasped his hands behind his back.

"Then we must make sure nobody dies by her hand."

"The way is dangerous."

"Just tell me."

Azrael sighed. "Your blood is the key. It has the power to open doors to new realms."

"So I bleed a little, and the door to the Underworld opens? Sounds simple."

"Simple? No. Your blood is only part of it. You can't just stand in your room and prick your finger. To get to the Underworld, you will need to find a place where the veil is thin, a place touched by darkness. And then there are binding runes to keep demons from coming through the open doorway. And if everything goes according to plan, then you will be able to travel to the Underworld."

Quinn studied Azrael. "A place touched by darkness?"

"Yes, a place where tragedy happened, where the demons have already ripped a hole. There, the seam, the veil, doesn't exist. The human realm and the Underworld will overlap with no resistance."

Quinn chewed on a thumbnail. "Like Jeff's house?"

"You can't go there," Reese said. "It's a crime scene. There's tape all over the house. Our friend died there, Quinn. It's wrong, it's creepy."

Quinn held her hand up to silence her friend. "Is the veil thin enough there?"

Azrael nodded. "But we will need time to prepare, and we must act fast. The eclipse starts in a little more than forty-eight hours."

"Then we better get started." Quinn pulled out her phone and dialed Caleb's number.

"Who are you calling?" Reese asked.

"Reinforcements. We're going to need all the help we can get."

29

Quinn paced in front of her bay window, hands behind her back, shoulders hunched. Her left eye twitched, and the edges of the world blurred in the exhaustion of two sleepless nights. Hours of planning, discussion, and heated disagreements ran through her head in a constant loop of worst-case scenarios. The dawn cast pale fingers of light across the wooden floor of her bedroom, and Quinn wanted to curl up in a ball and let the warmth chase away the constant chill in her bones.

Azrael paced with her, right hand worrying the handle of his golden sword, left hand hovering over the empty scabbard where the poison star-blade usually hung. The Qeres blade lay on the windowsill, its glowing blue runes sparkling like a million stars against the metal.

Caleb had gone downstairs for caffeine. He hadn't slept one wink either, coming over as soon as his shift had finished yesterday morning. Azrael had been putting him through his paces, teaching him how to use Quinn's Qeres dagger while she amplified his innate gift. Now he could see non-human essences as well as she could, which meant he could defend Reese and Marcus in this realm while she and Azrael descended into the Underworld.

Reese and Marcus lay curled against each other on her bed, her head on his chest, his arm draped across her shoulder. If only they could stay that way forever, peaceful and safe in each other's arms.

There will be no peace for them if the box is opened, and if you fail, all of humanity will be consumed by darkness. Azrael spoke to her through their link so as not to wake her sleeping friends.

You don't need to remind me what's at stake.

I still do not think this is the best course of action. We do not know for sure if this sacrifice is the boy or if it is you. So many things could go wrong. It's not too late to change your mind.

His concerns echoed her own. They had been arguing over the same thing all night, but she wouldn't let him see her waver, feel her doubt. Today, she would succeed or die trying.

Are you willing to take that chance, Azrael? If I hide in Arcadia and the box is opened anyway, there is nothing either of us can do. In the Underworld, we at least have a chance. I see no other choice.

There is always another choice.

Hiding like a coward while everything I love is destroyed is not an option. Our plan will work. I will pretend to be your prisoner. You deliver me as you delivered the box. Tell her I was going to run to The Light, and you stopped me, whatever you want. Once she's convinced, do what you do best—stab her in the back.

Azrael stopped at the foot of Quinn's bed. His shoulders sagged while his wings rose and fell with each breath. *Your death is a great possibility. Theirs too.* He nodded at Reese and Marcus. *Even the full force of the heavenly host will not be able to defeat the evil that will pour from that box and into this reality if your plan does not work.*

As if sensing she was being watched, Reese rolled over,

and Marcus snuggled in, spooning her, smiling in his sleep. They fit perfectly together, like two puzzle pieces. The deep aching wound that had been there since losing Aaron oozed open, and Quinn bit back a sob. In a different life, that might have been the two of them in bed, content and safe, but the world was not a safe place, not with the demons bent on enslaving and feeding off the negative energy of humans. Lilith had to be stopped, and maybe Quinn could get her life back, get Aaron's life back, too, if everything went to plan. Of course, when did anything ever go to plan?

You worry about getting the host to the portal, and I'll do the rest. I have to try, she answered.

Yes, Master. Whatever you say, Master, Azrael hissed at her.

You are not my slave.

Then give me back my blade so I can protect you with it.

Kaemon's blade. Quinn narrowed her eyes at Azrael.

Have I not shown you my intentions are true? Have I not given everything I know to succeed today?

Resentment and concern twisted together in Azrael's essence, and she sensed his desire to break free from her control, to take back what he saw as his, but he could not touch it without her permission, and this needled him, putting him even more on edge. He took two steps to the windowsill, hand hovering above the Qeres blade. His jaw worked, frustration and annoyance pulsing from his essence. Yes, he would die to protect her, but he did not like having his choice, his freedom to do so, taken away from him.

Quinn slid the blade from the windowsill away from him and balanced the flat of the curved metal on the palms of her hand. A dull hum of electric current ran up both arms and through her body.

Reveal the deep things of darkness and bring shadows into the light. As she read, the runes on the sword glowed brighter and then dimmed. Quinn caught Azrael's expectant glare and offered the blade back to him. He looked at her, and she pushed the handle into his hand and closed his fist around it.

You are free. But if you cross me, you will regret it.

Azrael bowed low. She felt joy and relief wash over him. Proud though he was, he could not hide his gratefulness from her. He would not fail in protecting her.

And you can return the blade to its rightful owner once this mess is over.

Azrael swallowed his defiant thoughts and nodded.

I will scout Jeff's house one more time before we leave. The eclipse will be upon us in a little over an hour. Timing is everything.

Quinn nodded. *Thank you, Azrael.*

He squared his shoulders, stepped onto the windowsill, and walked straight through the glass, his onyx wings absorbing the sunrise as he flew across the horizon.

"Hey, Blondie, I made you some coffee." Quinn turned and took a large cup from Caleb.

"Thanks, Meathead," she said. "And thanks for helping with this mess." With Caleb, she didn't have to explain anything; he understood in a way Reese and Marcus never could.

"You're welcome." He picked up her favorite fuzzy blanket off the floor and draped it around her shoulders, his hands lingering a little longer than they should. "I always wondered why I had this weird ability. Now I know. Everything I've seen has been to prepare me for this moment. Our meeting wasn't by chance. I feel it with every fiber of my being."

"Aaron said the same thing. Look what happened to him." She watched the curling steam rise from her mug.

"Aaron didn't know what I know." Quinn felt Caleb's desire, a side effect of boosting his ability and becoming so familiar with his essence. She tried to deflect his emotions, but it wasn't so easy. Caleb was an open book. Either he didn't know how to hide, or he didn't want to. Conflict churned within him. Part of him wondered if he would have a chance at something more than friendship if Aaron didn't make it back while another part hated himself for daring to wish such a thing.

He fought the urge to run his fingers through her hair and kiss her in case everything went horribly wrong and he never had another chance. Quinn couldn't blame him. His embrace would be a comfort to her, too, but that's all it would ever be—a comfort and nothing more. She remembered what happened the last time she had turned to easy solace.

"I care about you, Caleb." Quinn shivered and pulled the blanket tighter around her. "But I can't."

"I know. Strictly friend zone." Caleb patted her shoulder and settled in her rocking chair. "We'll get him back, Blondie." The wooden rockers creaked against the floor. "But if you see any hot, single girls trapped down there in Bar Underworld, bring one back for me, okay?"

"Just call me your Underworld wingman." Quinn smiled, glad the tension between them settled back to normal.

"You sure you don't want to grab a cat nap?" Caleb rubbed the stubble on his chin. "I can keep watch."

Quinn shook her head. "I couldn't sleep even if I wanted to."

"What time is it?" Reese yawned and pulled the covers off Marcus and onto herself, leaving his torso bare.

Quinn looked at the clock. "Seven thirty."

Reese groaned. "I feel like I've been punched in the head by a gorilla."

Marcus let out a loud snore, and Reese elbowed him in the chest. "Wake up, sleeping beauty."

Marcus snorted and bolted upright. "Demons? Where? I'm ready."

"No demons." Not inside anyway. Quinn watched as shadows danced beneath the canopy of the big oak outside. She counted at least half a dozen.

"Good, I don't think I can face them without a cup of coffee," Reese said, unaware of the gathering darkness.

"I made a fresh pot." As if sensing her unease, Caleb joined Quinn at the window. His right arm twitched against his side, and he grabbed the Qeres dagger from the nightstand and handed it to Quinn.

"You are a god, Caleb. I think we'll keep you around," Reese said.

"Oh! And don't forget the doughnuts," Marcus added.

"Is food the only thing you think about?" Reese stretched and pulled back her long, black hair and secured it with an elastic band she kept around her wrist.

"Not the only thing." Marcus arched his eyebrow and winked at Reese. "Want to join me for a shower?"

"Maybe another time."

"Your loss."

"Towels are kept in the hallway closet," Quinn said.

"What about your mom?" Marcus asked.

"I don't think she'll want to shower with you either," Quinn said.

"No, I mean won't she wonder why there's a strange man in your shower?"

"She left for work about an hour ago." Quinn wondered if she should have said goodbye, just in case.

"And she didn't even make you pancakes?" Marcus shook his head.

Not pancakes, but waffles with fresh strawberries, and not her mom, but her dad. Before he'd left and everything had changed. Quinn shrugged. "Welcome to my life. It's no big deal, really."

"Well I think it's a big deal. Reese will make you pancakes, won't you?"

"My mom always said a man's place is in the kitchen." Reese crossed her arms over her chest.

"I make a wicked omelet," Caleb offered. "I'm sure I saw some eggs in the fridge."

"Now that's what I'm talking about! If my girlfriend wasn't in the room, I would kiss you." Marcus winked.

"Maybe later." Caleb puckered his lips and made kissing noises. They both laughed.

"Man, it's good to have another guy to joke around with." Marcus clapped Caleb on the back. "You're all right with me, Caleb, and when we get Aaron back, we will finally outnumber team estrogen." Marcus grabbed a towel and sang his way out the doorway and into the shower.

"Four omelets and coffee coming right up." Caleb followed Marcus out of the room.

"You better not be joining my boyfriend in the shower!" Reese called, a grin as wide as the Grand Canyon on her face.

Quinn wanted to remember this moment—Marcus joking, Caleb's grin, Reese full of giggles. It might be the last time they would be together, and she didn't want her last thoughts of her best friends to be gloom and doom.

"Are you sure this plan will work?" Reese pulled her green hoodie over a white tank top and folded her legs under her.

"Absolutely!" Quinn hoped she sounded more confident than she felt. "I'll open the door to the Underworld, and Azrael will take me through it. I'll pretend to be his prisoner. I'll distract Lilith, and Azrael will free Aaron. Then I kill Lilith, and we all come home." Quinn snapped her fingers. "No blood, no screams, no opening the box. Simple."

Guilt pinched at her gut. She shouldn't drag either of them into this, but Azrael insisted they would be safe as long as they stayed within the protective runes. Besides, Caleb would be there to keep watch, Qeres dagger at hand. Azrael made sure to stress how important their role was, their love for Quinn would tether her to the human realm and help her find her way back. Besides, it's not like they could follow her into the Underworld. They needed to stay in the house, inside the protective runes, and wait. She would be through the portal, and they would wait for her to come back through, safe in the human realm.

"I wish we could do more. Where is Azrael anyway?"

At the sound of his name, Azrael shimmered before them.

"Good morning, Az." Reese threw a pillow at him, and he drew his remaining golden blade, cutting it in half, feathers flying everywhere.

"Hey, that was my favorite one." Quinn shook her head.

"We have had this discussion before. My name is Azrael, not Angel Boy, or Az, or anything other than my full name. Please tell your friends to stop calling me by that stupid nickname."

"Okay, as long as you try to be nice."

The light burning beneath Azrael's skin dimmed, and he furrowed his brow. "As you wish." He bowed deeply. "You are awfully cheery for a girl who is about to travel into the Underworld and risk the whole of humanity as well as her life and those of her friends."

"The plan will work." Fake it 'til you make it. That's what Marcus had said, and that's what she did.

"I can get you in and back out again alive, but you have to trust me. Have you practiced blocking? Lilith is powerful. One slip, and she will see the ruse."

"Ruse?" Reese laughed.

"Please tell your friend if she spent less time listening to that horrible screeching you call music and more time reading a book, she wouldn't think 'ruse' to be such a strange word."

"I can hear you now, ya know," Reese said.

Azrael narrowed his eyes. "You promised," he said to Quinn.

Quinn shrugged. "Whatever I did to change their essences made you visible to them all the time now. Nothing I can do about it."

"I don't like it," Azrael said.

"You don't like anything," Quinn replied.

"What did I miss?" Marcus ran a towel over his head and dumped it on the floor.

Quinn cleared her throat and pointed to the laundry basket in the corner.

"Women," he grumbled, wadded the towel, and tossed it like a basketball. "Two points for Marcsexy."

"Does he really have to come with us?" Azrael asked.

"Where she goes, we go, so get used to it," Reese said.

Azrael ignored Reese and turned to Quinn. "I have patrolled the neighborhood around the house. If you go down the back alleyway, you can hop the fence and into the backyard."

"Is it locked? How do we get in?"

"Immortals don't use doors."

"That's comforting," Marcus said.

"Did you get everything we need?" Azrael asked Marcus. "Candles, mirror, salt, permanent marker."

"Yeah, yeah, Caleb and I put it all in the Jeep last night. Speaking of Caleb, where's my omelet?"

Quinn pursed her lips and shivered when the sun disappeared behind the blackest cloud she'd ever seen and turned morning into dusk.

"We've got company, Blondie," Caleb called up the stairs

Quinn ran to the window. Shadows slithered from the

trees and pushed through the grass at the edge of the drive like corpse hands.

"Why now?" Quinn grasped her dagger a little tighter and turned to Azrael.

"A pre-emptive strike to show her strength."

"Hey, what's your mom doing home so early?" Reese asked.

"Crap, what day is today?" Quinn's mother's Mercedes pulled into the circle drive.

"Thursday, the seventh. Why?"

Quinn pinched the bridge of her nose. A car door slammed, and her father stepped from the passenger side and into the middle of a nest of demons.

"Great, just what we don't need. I told her I didn't want him here." Slamming her own car door, her mother stomped over to the trunk and began pulling out his suitcase. Once it was in her hands, her father grabbed it from her and said something nasty. To retaliate, her mother flung the car keys at her father's feet and cursed him. They yelled obscenities back and forth when a baby started screaming from the backseat.

A baby. He had brought her half-brother, Jacob, with him. Jealousy and hurt ate at Quinn's heart, turning it bitter, and she suddenly wanted to rip him from the car seat, put him in a box, and ship him back to his mother in California. Quinn shook her head. That wasn't what she wanted; the demons were getting to her, confusing her.

Your shield, Azrael warned. It was then she realized nothing stood between her and the darkness. Digging deep, she pushed the bubble of light up and around her, making sure to encompass Marcus, Reese, and Caleb. The demons were multiplying exponentially now, spreading up and out from their yard to the next, and the next, and the next, swathing the entire neighborhood in gray.

"Azrael." Before she completed her thought, he was through the window and out in the yard, swords drawn, ready for a fight.

"What's happening?" Reese asked.

"You don't want to know," Caleb answered. "We need to go. Now." He grabbed the Jeep keys from Quinn's desk and tossed them to Marcus.

"Stay close, and they won't be able to get to you." Quinn raced down the stairs and out the front door, Caleb, Marcus, and Reese on her heels.

Caleb ducked as a vase broke through their neighbor's window, sailed past his head, and crashed into a million mosaic pieces against the doorframe. A large, black lab streaked past Quinn and headed for the safety of some bushes. Horns honked, people poured from their houses, neighbors screamed at one another, children clawed at their siblings, drawing blood. Alarms blared, and everywhere she turned, demons fed on the chaos, leeches sucking at pain and anger. The more they fed, the bigger they got, and the more bedlam they created.

"What do we do?" Marcus clamped his hands to his ears.

Quinn's mind raced. There was no way she could protect all these people. Azrael stood at the end of the driveway, slashing and tearing through demons as fast as he could, but for everyone he took down, three more appeared. His voice rang out to the heavenly host, and a flock of at least a hundred angels streaked across the sky, a rainbow of wings shimmering as they joined Azrael in the fight, Qeres blades hungry to find and kill their enemies, but even at that, they were outnumbered at least ten to one. And this was only the beginning. The box wasn't even open.

"Hey, Blondie, I think we need a little help here." Two smoky demons tethered themselves to Quinn's mother, long needle fingers stabbing her through the back, sucking the anger from her like greedy children. Quinn grabbed her mother's arm, working to push her barrier out to encompass her like she had in the kitchen, but her mother was too far gone. Turning back on Quinn with inky eyes, she shoved her hard, knocking her to the ground.

"Don't touch my daughter." Her father took two big steps around the car, grabbed her mother by the wrist, and twisted, ignoring Jacob's increasing screams from the back seat. He couldn't see the dark demon tapping the window, searching for a crack to get to Jacob, too, but Quinn could. She looked at her parents, then at her brother.

"Quinn, do something," Reese begged, her voice quivering.

Do what? There were too many, they were too strong. The angels were engaged on all sides. Azrael fought to hold as many off as possible, but even he was losing ground. She was one girl. She would fail, and they would all die. Sweat beaded on the back of her neck as an overwhelming sense of hopelessness dragged at her limbs. She couldn't do this. The sound of another piercing scream snapped her out of her bleakness. Jacob stared at the demon as it scratched at the glass. He banged his little fist on the window. She could feel his fear—intense, confused. No. It couldn't be. He could see them too, just like her. Anger pulsed through her essence. Jacob, so small, so innocent. He didn't deserve to grow up as one of Lilith's slaves. She had to try, if not for herself, for him.

Quinn ran forward, Qeres dagger at the ready, and slashed the poison blade through the demon tormenting her sibling through the window. Then she wrenched the door open and grabbed her brother from his seat, surrounding him in her protective barrier. She bounced him on her hip, whispering softly in his ear, and he clung to her, small hands digging into her shirt, tear-soaked cheeks buried in her neck.

"Shhhhh, Jake. You're safe," she cooed until he quieted.

On the other side of the car, her mother now had her hands around her father's throat, squeezing as hard as she could, his face turning blue. Quinn handed Jake into Marcus's waiting arms and took off running.

"There, there, little man. It'll be okay. Your sister's going to kick some demon butt, and she'll be right back." Marcus tickled Jake's chin, and he laughed.

Taking a chance, Caleb grabbed Quinn's mother from behind. Mrs. Taylor kicked and screamed as he pried her off Quinn's father, who fell to his knees and crawled away, coughing and dragging in ragged breaths. Mrs. Taylor bit Caleb on the arm to try to get away, but he gritted his teeth and held tight.

"She's too strong." Caleb moved his arms down and away from her mouth, pinning her arms to her sides. "You better do something fast. I don't think I can hold her."

Quinn rubbed her hands together, letting the heat of her power build inside her. She needed to focus and force this beast to reveal its name, but there were so many demons around, it was hard to get a fix on any individual identity. As she approached, her mother thrashed against Caleb, butting her head backward, trying to smash his face. Caleb's muscles rippled as he wrestled her to the ground and pinned her against the concrete.

"Hurry," Caleb urged.

Behind Quinn, something growled, soft and low. She spun to see inky eyes staring up from her father's face.

"Dad. It's me." She took a step back, palms up. "It's Quinn."

Then he pounced, quick as a jaguar, fierce as a lion. Quinn was crushed beneath his weight as he slammed into her. They went down, a tangle of arms and legs, onto the lawn. Her head snapped back, skull hitting the grass with a dull thud. Her father grunted and scratched at her skin as they rolled. She tried to gain the upper hand, but fueled by hate and demon energy, he was much stronger than she was. Quinn's heart raced, a stampede of horses in her chest, as he pinned her to the ground, his tall frame looming above her. This monster was not her father, not anymore. A hand clenched like a vise around her throat. He was going to kill her.

Before he could squeeze, Reese launched onto his back, wrapping around his neck. Just the distraction she needed. Quinn's muscles tensed, and she turned to run, but she wasn't fast enough. As if Reese weighed nothing, he threw her to the ground, caught Quinn by the ankle, and dragged her through the grass. Mud and dirt lodged beneath her fingernails as she scrambled to get away from him, but his iron grip held her tight. Quinn screamed as he shoved a knee in her back, lifted her head up by the hair, and pressed her face into a pile of ants. A thousand tiny legs crawled across her cheek, up her neck, around her ears, her skin on fire with their venom.

"Azrael, do something!" Quinn heard Reese yell.

And then the pressure was gone, and she was free. Quinn leapt to her feet and ripped the black hoodie from her body, throwing it to the ground and slapping at the ants crawling on her skin and in her hair until each one was dead. Tears streamed down her face, breaths coming in big gulps, heart kicking her ribcage. Azrael held her father, clothes ripped, mud streaking his face, in a vise grip. Beside them, her mother stood, blue eyes glassy and unfocused.

"Do it," Quinn snarled, and Azrael nodded. He flourished his sword, separating the demons' essence from her father's as he'd already done for her mother. *Slash, slash, slash*, the demons dissipated in a whiff of gray mist, their immortal souls no match for the Qeres poison blade.

"Are you okay?" Reese wrapped her trembling arms around Quinn, and Quinn hugged her close.

"Thank you," she whispered. "For trying to get him off me." She could feel Reese nod against her shoulder. "Did he hurt you?"

Reese shook her head. "I know how to fall. Is it over?"

"The Elites have managed to scatter Lilith's forces to buy us time, but we need to hurry." Azrael looked to the sky where the moon inched closer to the sun. "I don't know how long they can hold them back."

"Okay, just let me say goodbye first." Quinn took her brother from Marcus and patted the baby's back. "Hi, Jake. I'm your sister."

"Q-Quinn?" Her mother blinked and looked around. "Aren't you supposed to be at school?" She blinked again, free from demon influence, brow furrowed in confusion.

Her father dropped his hand and rubbed his neck, taking a step back. "What happened to your face?" he asked, concern knitting his forehead. He reached to touch her cheek, swollen and red with welts, and although she understood it hadn't really been her father who shoved her face into the dirt, she flinched. He cocked his head and blinked, still not fully aware of what had happened.

She forced a smile. "It's nothing, I tripped." Quinn looked at her watch and tentatively handed her brother to her dad. His chubby hands reached for her, grabbing the air, a pout growing on his face. He didn't want to leave her, and the truth was, she didn't want to leave him either. "Don't worry, Jake, I'll be back." She gave him a big raspberry on his cheek, and he giggled at her.

"You should go inside," Quinn told her parents, and they both nodded but didn't move, still only ghosts of their former selves. "Really, take Jake inside, I think he's hungry." Quinn gently guided them into the house.

"Wait," her mother said. "Where are you going?"

"School. Remember?" she said as cheerily as she could. "I'll be back soon."

They nodded, still dazed and confused by the ordeal.

"What about the cake I'm going to bake you? A late birthday treat," her dad said.

"Cake, after school?" she asked.

"Okay, sweetheart." He smiled, and she cringed at the memory of inky eyes and strong arms pushing her down. "Sorry I couldn't make it for the real day, but happy belated birthday."

She swallowed. "Thanks, Dad," she forced herself to say, and then closed the door in his face.

"Will they be all right?" Quinn asked Azrael.

"They won't remember, but the empty darkness inside left by the demons will take a while to dissipate." Azrael examined her wounds and sent a wave of healing into her body, pushing the ant venom from her pores, healing the bruises, eradicating the swelling.

"Will Jake be safe with them?" Quinn was surprised by how much she cared. Looking into his perfect blue eyes and feeling his warm cheek against hers, she had fallen for him. Her brother, and she wanted to protect him no matter the cost to herself.

"Safe enough." Azrael's expression darkened. "With those two," he added.

"Can you post a guard?"

Azrael nodded and two angels landed at the front door.

"Thank you."

"They will do their best to keep them safe, but the attack isn't confined. Demons are pushing forward across every tear in the veil at once. We've never seen such an organized attack."

"What does that mean?" Reese asked.

"Yeah, why now? I thought she had to open the box or something," Marcus said, entwining his fingers with Reese's.

Quinn's heart pinched. "Is Aaron dead? Did she open the box?"

Azrael shook his head. "No. The veil is still intact, but thin. The box has not been opened. Lilith assumes you are the sacrifice. She might be right, Quinn. We do not know anything for sure. This plan is risky."

"If we don't go and she kills Aaron, the box might open. If I go as sacrifice, the box could open. Either way, there doesn't seem to be a way to stop it."

Aaron was right; this was bigger than either of them.

30

Westland had always been a beautiful place to live, with its manicured lawns, big trees, and friendly people. Now it looked like it was hit by a zombie apocalypse. Neighbors in bloodied nightgowns and ripped business suits wandered the streets in a daze. Broken glass littered the asphalt, wrecked cars steamed and wailed, and in the distance, the sound of sirens approaching.

Quinn stared out the Jeep window as Marcus maneuvered through block after block of devastation, dodging broken fire hydrants, busted mailboxes, and people alike. Her home was a battleground. Shadows clung to the city like smog, choking out the sun and infusing the air with the smell of sulfur. The heavenly Elite forces engaged demons on the ground, in the air, on every corner, pushing them back one by one. For now, they were winning, but what would happen if Lilith opened that box?

Marcus pulled the Jeep into a narrow back alley, gravel popping beneath the tires. Thankfully, it looked empty, almost serene compared to the rest of the streets. He rolled to a stop in back of Jeff's house. Marcus opened the door for

Quinn, and she stepped out into the chilled air and looked up at the large two-story Spanish Colonial that was her sanctuary during her parents' divorce. A chain-link fence separated the perfect backyard, complete with pool and covered patio, from the alley. How many times had she and Jeff swum in that pool? How many dinners had she eaten there? How many movies had she watched snuggled up with Jeff on the couch? Now he was gone, and so was Kerstin.

In her heart, she once wished them both dead at least a million times; now she wished Kerstin stood in front of her with some snide remark. Dark shapes moved in the arched windows, and Quinn shivered.

She startled when Caleb clapped her on the shoulder. "You okay?" he asked. Deep scratches lined his skin—nail marks from Quinn's mother.

She nodded, grabbing the black duffle bag from him and throwing it over the fence. If she didn't get Aaron back and keep Lilith from crossing the veil, their deaths would be the first in a long line of people she cared about.

"Guess we should go." Quinn looked at Reese and grabbed her hand.

"Yeah, let's get this over with before I change my mind."

"Ladies first." Caleb boosted Reese over the top of the chain-link fence, followed by Quinn. Marcus scrambled over, along with Caleb. Azrael waited on the back porch, screen door cracked open, concern written on his hardened face.

"Is it just us?" Quinn asked.

Azrael nodded. "We are on our own. This attack has every spare Elite engaged. As, I suspect, was Lilith's plan."

"Can't we do it here, near the door?" Reese asked, shying away from the gloomy doorway. "I don't think I can go in there. What if his blood is still on the floor or something? Jeff's blood, Quinn."

"Quinn's best chance of entering the Underworld is where the veil is thinnest. Where the boy's blood was spilled, she must spill her own. Dark magic to light, the balance will open the door," Azrael insisted.

"Blood, demons … this is some dark stuff," Marcus muttered.

"The taint in this house is beyond anything I have seen before. I've cleared it twice since I got here, but for every demon I kill, three more cross the veil. Darkness has taken root, and even I cannot weed it out. If you want to do this, I will go with you, but the humans should go home. They will be a liability."

"Who are you calling a liability?" Marcus puffed out his chest in challenge.

"Where would we go?" Reese said. "You've seen what those demons are doing to Westland. Azrael's right. There is no safe place. We're coming with you."

"And then what?" Quinn ran a hand across the back of her neck. "Will the protective runes be enough?" She turned to Azrael.

"They will help, but there is no safe place," Azrael answered. "Not for anyone anymore. We must not fail."

Reese tightened her grip on Quinn. "I'm not leaving you, not now, and neither is Marcus or Caleb. Right?"

"It's dangerous, Reese," Quinn said.

"You're stuck with us, Blondie. Whether you like it or not," Caleb said.

Marcus nodded. "It's settled. We're all in."

Quinn looked at her watch, and then to the sky. "Fifteen minutes until the eclipse starts." She handed Marcus the duffle bag, and he slung it over his shoulder. "You will all need to do exactly as I say and watch your back until we get the runes drawn, and you're safe in the circle." She drew the Qeres dagger from its sheath and handed it to Caleb. "You'll have to be their eyes once I enter the portal. Once I'm on the other side, they won't be in my bubble of protection anymore, which means Reese and Marcus will no longer be able to see the demons coming. I'll be leaving them blind and vulnerable. It will be up to you to warn them, protect them."

"You can count on me." Caleb ran a thumb along the edge of the blade. It glowed in response to his gift.

"Don't wander off. My barrier can only reach so far." Quinn closed her eyes and pictured a bubble of light around her. She expanded the bubble until Caleb, Reese, and Marcus's essences were encased in light as well.

Azrael drew both blades, one golden as the sun, the other cold as moonlight, and handed one to Quinn. "If anything, so much as threatens you, don't hesitate." A rare smile of encouragement lit his face.

Kaemon's Qeres star-blade hummed in her hand, its blue runes crackled like lightning, casting an otherworldly light on the floor. She stared at it pulsing in her fist. Azrael would be vulnerable without it—his golden sword did not hold the poison that could kill, the reason he coveted Kaemon's blade, part of the reason he took it.

Azrael stiffened as she wrapped her arms around him in a hug. *I'm sorry I doubted you.* She spoke her forgiveness through their link and felt him soften.

I'm sorry, too. He let the tips of his wings enfold her, then smiled, and let her go.

"Okay, let's do this." Quinn held out her hand, and Reese took it. Marcus took hers in turn, making a chain with Reese in the middle and Caleb at the rear. "Don't let go of my hand unless I tell you it's okay." They all nodded.

"Do not fear. I will be right behind you," Azrael said.

The door squeaked open on its hinges. Quinn peeked inside. The windows were boarded up, and shadows grew like dark, twisted vines across the floors and up the wall of the kitchen.

"Holy mother of God," Marcus said under his breath. "Is this what you were dealing with all on your own? No wonder you were afraid nobody would believe you."

Quinn nodded and stepped into the kitchen, and the shadows parted like a curtain, shrinking back from her barrier and the light of the blade. Whispers upon whispers overlapped one another, and Quinn sensed anger and disquiet in the air. It was like walking into a pile of fire ants. The darkness was agitated, upset at her presence. This was their feeding ground; she had no right to it.

"Something's not right, Quinn." Reese's nails dug into the back of her hand, and she could feel her friend's rapid heartbeat through her fingertips. "I feel so sad, like there's no point to anything. Can't we stop here? I want to sit down, to sleep or something."

"It's the demons, Reese. They're trying to get to you, to feed off any negative feelings you're having. Think about something happy, something good."

Quinn felt it, too; the dark power was strong here, an oppressive weight on her chest dragging her down. Guilt and regret sucked at her heart. Her barrier winked around them as she fought to keep it from bursting under the heavy melancholy pressing against her essence. What was the point of all of this? She should give up, let them in.

Azrael touched her on the shoulder, and some of his strength poured into her. Her shield became stronger than before. The light inside him flickered and pulsed as her shield brightened, snapping her out of despondence.

Quinn straightened. Squeezing Reese's hand as tight as she could, she led the way down a deserted corridor, the blue light of her sword reflecting rows of glass frames filled with Jeff's smiling face. A face soon buried six feet under, skin brittle and cold, eyes worm eaten, flesh decayed. She shook her head to erase the morbid thoughts.

A short hallway ended at the bottom of an enclosed staircase so narrow that Marcus's wide shoulders almost touched both walls at the same time. Dark walls enclosed the steep wooden steps that led to the second floor. Quinn stopped on the first step and stared up the dim narrow stairway. They would have to go one at a time, Reese behind her, Marcus behind Reese, and Caleb at the rear.

"Hold tight," she whispered. "Don't break our connection."

She couldn't see two feet in front of her. Even the glowing blue of the star-blade couldn't penetrate the darkness. She swallowed and took a step. The floorboards creaked, and something stirred above her. Hundreds of bat-like demons hung from the ceiling above them, wings folded against their furry bodies, talons digging into the oak beams. She turned to Reese and Marcus and pressed her finger to her lips. Five more steps until they reached the top.

Four steps. Three. Quinn stiffened when the next step squeaked and groaned beneath her weight. Two demons opened their red, glowing eyes, and Reese screamed. Letting go of Quinn's hand, she pushed at Marcus to get past him, and he stumbled backward and down.

Quinn's barrier trembled as they stepped outside her protection. Exposed, a demon wrapped its leathery tail around Reese's neck. Reese whimpered as Marcus swiped at it, but it blinked out in a puff of smoke and reappeared, hovering above Caleb. Quinn grabbed Reese's hand and pulled her back up the stairs, expanding the bubble of light around them again.

"You can't let go," Quinn stressed. "It's taking all my focus to keep us safe. *All of it*. Holding hands makes it easier, but it still takes a lot of energy."

"S-Sorry," Reese stammered and nodded.

A deep breath calmed her hammering heart. The demon hissed and rubbed against her bubble, looking for a vulnerable spot. Quinn sagged against the wall, exhaustion creeping up from her toes into her legs, but she fought against it. There was too much at stake to quit now. The light on the Qeres star-blade burned hot, and Quinn slashed out at the demon. It roared in hate, twirling out of her reach and waking its brothers with a loud screech.

A whirlwind of wings, and fur encircled them. Reese and Marcus pushed close to her, until there was no space between them. She could feel Reese's trembling and Marcus's rapid breathing. Caleb stood with his back against Marcus, dagger at the ready. Rows of sharp teeth snapped at the air around their faces, talons reaching for them, but they were unable to penetrate Quinn's defenses.

If Quinn could access her power, she might be able to banish one, or maybe even two, but that would mean letting go of the protective bubble. She didn't have enough energy to do both at the same time. Sweat dripped from her forehead, salt stinging her eyes. Demons poked and prodded her shield on all sides, and she was afraid one of them would find a weak spot. She held firm, concentrating all her thoughts on keeping them out, unable to move forward and unwilling to go back.

From the bottom of the stairs, Azrael taunted the demons, brandishing his sword, trying to draw their attention, but the demons had no interest in him. They wanted Quinn, wanted to feed on the fear growing inside their little bubble.

Caleb turned to Quinn. "They'll follow me, right? As soon as I leave your protection?"

"Yes, but—"

"That's all I needed to know, Blondie." Before she could

stop him, Caleb let go of Marcus's hand, and jumped down three steps and out of her barrier. Smelling his vulnerability, the demons howled and charged him.

"Go. We'll hold them off as best we can." Azrael and Caleb stood back to back. Azrael's golden blade flashed as it cut through the first beast that came at them. It dissipated in a puff of smoke and reappeared as the sword passed through it, but Caleb caught a wing with the point of the dagger and the demon howled in pain. The dagger's poison would slow them down, but the only thing that could kill the demons would be the Qeres blade, and Azrael had given it to Quinn for her own protection. Of all the things she thought about Azrael before, selfless was never one of them. Maybe she had been wrong; maybe Aaron had too.

"Go while they're distracted!" Caleb called to her.

The handle of the Qeres star-blade burned against her palm. One slice, two, she slashed out at the demons that pushed against her from above. Inch by inch, she cut their way up the stairs, the poison from the metal blade finding its mark every time and turning them to dust before her eyes.

Reaching the landing, she let herself take a deep breath. A long hallway ran along the second floor. Inky webs crisscrossed the entire hall, each strand as thick as a finger. From behind, Quinn listened to the beating of leathery wings, more demons gathering in the narrow stairway behind them, cutting her off from Azrael and Caleb. No way out. They were trapped now.

Quinn used Kaemon's sword to cut through the strands of webbing. Something skittered in the shadows, the vibration on the giant web disturbing whatever had made it. Quinn swallowed, and she heard Marcus gasp.

"Please don't tell me those are giant spiders," he whispered.

"Don't even dare," Reese spat.

"Through there." Quinn pointed toward a doorway where a large shadow moved back into Jeff's bedroom. She kicked the cracked door all the way open and jumped back, waving the sword in front of her. When nothing attacked, she tiptoed forward, Reese and Marcus pressed firmly against her back. This room made the rest of the house look radiant and cheery. Shadows, so dark not even a sliver of light could penetrate, clung to the windows. It was as if they entered a black box, a coffin.

Using the light from the star-blade like a torch, they inched their way to the middle of the room. The air was so cold, like a tomb, that she couldn't stop shivering. Blood stained the hardwood floor, and she heard Reese suck in a breath.

"It's not fresh."

"And that's supposed to make me feel better?" Reese asked.

Something scuttled in the corner, and Quinn whirled the blade around to illuminate the gloom, but its light reveled nothing.

"What was that?" Marcus asked.

"Nothing." Quinn wiped a sweaty palm on her jeans. "Let's get this over with and get out of here." She looked at her watch. Seven minutes to go.

Reese fished a page from the pocket of her jeans, the protection runes drawn in prefect detail, and Quinn held the blade over it to illuminate the writing.

"I don't see how a few symbols are going to keep us safe. Not in here." Reese held out her hand, and Marcus passed her a white candle from the duffle bag

"You don't need to understand it. You just need to do it exactly as I told you." The atmosphere of the room shifted as Azrael entered the room, his light penetrating the murk, and Quinn's hope swelled.

Caleb followed. Demon ash covered his hair and his clothes, but he smiled at Quinn, and she shook her head. "I can't decide if you're stupid or brave, Meathead. You could have been killed."

"It will take more than a few demons to get rid of me, Blondie." Caleb winked and took a black Sharpie from the duffle bag.

A low hiss came from beneath the large four-poster bed.

"Um, Quinn…" Reese pointed a trembling finger as a hairy leg disappeared back into the underbelly of the mattress.

"We must act quickly." Azrael snatched the marker from Caleb and drew a giant hexagram, in perfect proportions, across the floor. "The candles go here." Azrael pointed to each of the six tips of the hexagram. Caleb and Marcus placed a candle on each tip and stood back.

In the center of the hex, Jeff's blood spilled dark red across the wooden floor. With his sword, Azrael etched a triple spiral in the dried blood, symbolizing Quinn's essence. West of Quinn's symbol and between two of the points, he used the marker to draw a rising crescent moon, and on the east, a setting sun.

"But doesn't the sun set in the west?" Reese pointed out.

"In your realm, yes." Azrael didn't add more, and Reese seemed to take that as a sign to be quiet and let him work.

For the next step, Azrael raised his golden sword and brought the tip down hard, the boards shuddering with the impact. He then scraped a wide circle around Caleb, Reese, and Marcus, digging a deep groove into the floor with the tip, connecting each tip of the six-pointed star. When the circle was complete, it flashed with orange flame, and then winked out, leaving a scorched outline; then he nodded to Quinn.

Using the star-blade, she carved four curling shapes into

each corner of the circle. Harmony, love, faith, and protect—the four opposites to chaos, fear, doubt and forsake. Each curl glowed blue before fading. Around them, Caleb traced the outer markings of the circle with thick lines of salt, reinforcing the protective barrier.

"Reese, you sit at the moon; Marcus, at the sun."

Reese eyed the four-poster bed and shook her head. "I'm not putting my back to that. There's something under there."

"You wanted to come—insisted, in fact. You must find the courage now to continue. If you stay in the circle, it will not hurt you." Azrael took Reese's hand. Once she nodded, he guided her to her spot.

And they will be safe? Quinn asked Azrael privately.

Safer in this circle than they would be out on the street right now. You should say your goodbyes. Make it quick.

Quinn put her arm around Reese and leaned her head on her shoulder. "I love you."

"Don't even say it that way, like this is goodbye or something. Don't you dare say that, Quinn." Reese grabbed her and held on tight. "I love you too. I can't finish senior year without you, ya know. This will work; this has to work."

"No, of course it will work, but I needed, wanted, to tell you." Quinn swallowed and forced a smile, pushing the last of her doubts back into the depths of her heart. "I'll be gone for a blink of an eye. You won't even have time to miss me."

Reese gave Azrael a pointed look. "You better take care of her."

"It is my duty." He bowed low, wings expanding up and out until they touched the ceiling.

Quinn felt the weight of Marcus's muscled arms join her best friend's as he squished them into a bear hug. "You better bring my bro back with you. I'm tired of all this girl talk and chick flicks." Quinn and Reese laughed.

"Yeah, I need to meet this Aaron guy, see if he's worth all the trouble." Caleb stood before her; brown eyes bright.

"I think the two of you are going to get along just great," Quinn assured him.

"Let's just get this over with, okay?" Reese squared her shoulders, took a deep breath, and sat cross-legged on top of the moon symbol.

"Agreed," Caleb said.

Marcus knelt in front of Reese and kissed her forehead. "Caleb and I will be with you the whole time. Nothing to be afraid of; we can do this." He smiled at her, and she hugged his neck.

Marcus winked and settled himself across from Reese, leaving enough room from the edge of the center of the hexagram so they wouldn't be sucked into the portal or whatever might happen when it opened. Azrael passed Caleb a lighter. The lighter clicked and ignited. Caleb held the flame to each wick until it caught. Orange light flickered and danced across the walls, deepening the contrast between shadow and glow.

"Caleb, you stand at the southern pinnacle, and Quinn will stand here." Azrael pointed to the empty spot next to him.

"Well, Blondie, I guess this is it." Caleb stared at the Qeres dagger in his hand. "You sure you don't want to take this with you?" He offered it to her.

"You'll need it more than I will." Quinn wrapped her hand around his. Warmth spread from his skin to hers, and she smiled. "Promise you'll take care of them?"

"I promise." Caleb cupped her cheek and looked into her eyes. She let his lips say goodbye. A soft, lingering peck, bittersweet. "Good luck, Blondie." A quick hug, and he took a step back and into his place.

"Thanks, all of you, for believing in me." Quinn swiped at

a tear. "I couldn't do this without you." Quinn looked at her friends, selfishly wishing they could come with her. Her knees wobbled, and sandpaper coated her tongue. Would she ever see them again?

"No time for crying. You've got demon butt to kick." Marcus winked. "We'll be right here when you get back."

"It is time," Azrael said.

Quinn stepped within the circle, legs vibrating with excitement and fear, and stood at the northernmost tip of the hexagram. She looked down at the dark stain of blood beneath her purple sneakers.

"How long will the portal stay open?" Quinn asked.

"Until your blood dries. Fifteen minutes, twenty maybe," Azrael answered. "And then it will close behind us. Time moves differently in the Underworld than it does here, slower. What may seem like hours or days would be only minutes here," Azrael said. "If everything goes to plan, you will not even have a moment to miss us."

Quinn checked her watch. Eight fifty-nine, the eclipse would start in one minute. Holding her breath, she waited for the second hand to tick the last few seconds, not sure what to expect. Exposing her palm, she dragged the Qeres blade across her lifeline and winced at the cold sting as metal bit into her flesh, and then handed the sword back to Azrael. He slid it into the scabbard at his left hip, and then they waited.

The candles burned brighter as the air stilled around them. Blood pooled dark and red in the creases of her skin, and she tipped her hand up, letting her vital fluid spill down, a waterfall cascading from her hand onto the floor. Fresh blood collided with the dead, and the wood crackled as her blood ate away at the floor like acid, turning the edges black.

As the door to the Underworld opened, something thrummed beneath them, buzzing. Quinn stepped back from the expanding hole and glanced at Azrael beside her. His wings trembled, every muscle tense as he crouched, fists tight, swords poised over his head, ready to strike. Reese covered her ears and closed her eyes, Marcus inched a little farther away from the edge, and Caleb raised his dagger, ready for a fight.

When the air exploded up and out, Quinn ducked. A swarm of giant wasps, each the size of a fist, erupted from the depths of the Underworld. Azrael didn't waste any time, he twisted and flourished his swords, movements flowing like liquid, one into the other, as he cut them down one by one before they had a chance to attack.

Demon dust rained down upon them, and Reese coughed, waving a hand to fan away the smell of rotten eggs.

"That was dramatic," Caleb wheezed.

"Yeah, remind me never to get on your bad side, Azrael," Marcus said.

"Was that all of them?" Reese stammered.

Azrael cocked his head and listened. "It is quiet. Almost too quiet."

Quinn chewed on her thumbnail. "She must not see me as a threat."

"She doesn't know you as well as we do, Blondie," Caleb joked.

"Thanks for the vote of confidence. I'm going to need it." Quinn wondered what going through a portal to the Underworld would feel like. By the looks of it, it would be a short journey. She'd expected an endless pit yawning below, but it wasn't a hole at all: the ground itself had changed. Volcanic rock replaced the wood floor, revealing a piece of the realm that existed alongside her own. More like walking from carpet to tile, or stepping from one room into another, than falling down the rabbit hole.

"We have to go. Now, Quinn." Azrael held out his hand,

but before Quinn could take it, a gust of wind snuffed out the candles, immersing the room in night.

Reese gasped. Scurrying. Claws on wood. A faint *click-thump-click-thump* behind them. A shadow slithered from under the bed. Not a shadow, a person, on its stomach, arms bent at odd angles, but not really a person. Azrael drew his blades once again, their light illuminating a monstrosity. All loose tendons and muscles, it looked like a man stripped of his skin. Empty sockets stared out of an angled face as veins pulsed up its fleshless neck. It stared at Reese, its target, and licked blood from its lips. Its breath rasped through a half-decayed throat. Spit bubbled and gurgled at the corner of its mouth.

"Don't move," Azrael warned, but it was too late. In fear, Reese had stumbled outside the protective circle. She let out a scream as the thing grabbed her ankle. Marcus reached for her, wrapping his hand around her arm as Caleb slashed with his dagger, but the thing started dragging Reese under the bed. Marcus grunted, using all his weight to pull her back.

Quinn lunged forward to help, but Azrael stepped in front of her, blocking her path.

"Let me go!" Quinn screamed and pounded her fists on his chest.

"There is no time. The portal will close soon, and all will be lost. Go. I will get her back."

"Screw the portal. Azrael, I command..." But before she could direct him, he lifted her up and pushed her through the open portal.

31

Quinn landed hard on her side, elbow scraping against the sharp black terrain of the Underworld. Rage jolted her to her feet, and she ran for the shrinking doorway, but it was too late. Her blood was almost dry, and the edges of the portal narrowed so only a small six-inch crack remained.

Ragged breaths escaped from her mouth, and she pressed an eye to the crack. On the other side, she could make out Azrael fighting with all his might against the zombie creature stalking the room, but she didn't see any signs of her friends. They had gone quiet, and Quinn feared the worst. Azrael said he would take care of them, and she needed to trust him. Trust, the thing she struggled with most, the reason her life was such a mess in the first place. Maybe she could squeeze through the shrinking crack or use her blood to open a new doorway home.

"If something happens to them, I'll never forgive you!" she screamed at Azrael seconds before the portal snapped shut, cutting her off from the human realm.

If they were dead, knowing would tip her over the edge;

destroy the thin wall keeping the grief and fear at bay. There was nothing she could do to change it. Hope was what she needed, not doubt, and without a true answer, she could choose which one to hold onto. One answer would destroy her, the other give her strength. The best thing she could do was put them from her mind, focus on the grim task ahead, and deal with the truth later.

Cool fingers of moonlight kissed the barren landscape. Nothing moved, not an animal, not a speck of dust. It was the most lifeless place she had ever seen. Even the air felt dead, stagnant. Tortured pockmarked rocks, like the surface of the moon, stretched desolate and empty in every direction.

Quinn paced, curling a short strand of hair around her finger. The plan hinged on Azrael bringing her to Lilith as his prisoner. Without him, she wasn't sure where to go or what to do next. She was alone and lost in a foreign place.

Quinn. She turned to the whisper of her name.

On the distant horizon, the unblinking eyes of an ominous castle tower watched her every move. Lilith.

Quinn. The voice whispered again. *We are waiting. Aaron is waiting.*

An iron chain pulled tight around her heart. One girl against the Silver Queen and all her minions. A laugh bubbled from her lips. All of this was absurd, and yet it wasn't.

Don't lose it now, Quinn said to herself. *The whole world is counting on you.* She was Eol Ananael, essence of Eve. She'd opened a portal into the Underworld, and she could banish demons with a thought. Wish it and it will be. Believe you can do it and you will. She couldn't go back, only forward. If she didn't go forward, there would be nothing to go back to. Drawing in a deep breath, Quinn balled her fists and began walking.

Stay strong. Believe. I am the essence of Eve. I have the power to stop this. Me.

Quinn.

Quinn.

Quinn.

Quinn.

Whisper overlapping whisper, name overlapping name, a drumbeat, a death march as she strode onward, the shadow of Lilith's palace reaching out like a hand. Sorrow and agony crushed her lungs, and she struggled to breathe. She wanted nothing more than to fall to her knees, curl into a ball, and release the aching wail growing in the very depths of her soul.

Her shield pulsed, flickered, and then faded like a flashlight with a dead battery. Panic gripped her as she searched for the spark of power that kept her protected, but it was suffocated. Doubt and darkness were too strong here; they ate away at her defenses until there was nothing left.

She walked for hours, days, minutes—time held no meaning. Hopelessness filled the empty spaces inside her, weighing her down. She stumbled, got back up, and stumbled again, grim determination the only thing keeping her moving forward. Her sneakers scraped across the rock, shoulders ached, eyes burned. This was torture, worse than fighting a horde of rabid demons. Endless trudging, endless thinking, an eternity to ponder every mistake and bad decision and the realization that no matter what she chose, the odds of getting out of this alive were slim to none. She couldn't imagine a truer hell.

Turning eighteen was supposed to be a stepping-stone to adulthood, to independence, but Quinn never felt more like a scared little girl. For all her supposed power, she had no idea how to use it to stop Lilith. She didn't have a clue about what to do. Plan after plan was considered and thrown out. All she could do was move forward, to her fate, to her destiny, whatever that might be. Quinn lifted her chin and carried on, Lilith's palace looming ever closer.

Finally, she came to a set of onyx steps that led to an arched doorway at least twelve feet wide and three stories tall. Seven serpents were carved into the polished granite, twisting and writhing against one another. So lifelike she thought she heard them hiss her name. At her approach, the doors swung open with a sigh, revealing a black and white checkered floor like a chessboard and the soaring black granite columns of an entrance hall. Not two steps in, the doors banged closed behind her, the lock clicking into place with another hiss.

Desperate, Quinn dug deep within, looking for an ember of light to bring up her barrier, but her gift forsook her. The darkness in this palace was too absolute for her powers to penetrate, leaving her completely vulnerable.

Quinn straightened her shoulders and suppressed the tremors that grew in her knees and traveled to her hands. The squeak of her rubber soles echoed from the arches in the ceiling, so loud it masked the roar of the blood in her ears. Threads of cold snaked across her skin, and goose bumps prickled as she passed through the deserted hall. Torches set in human skulls burned with a cold blue fire, the glow of the empty eye sockets leading her through the darkness.

At the end of the hall, another set of doors swung inward, opening into a large round room. At the back of the rotunda, three steps ascended to a dark throne. A woman with raven-black hair stood in front of it, a floor-length cloak shifting like smoke around her. Over a dozen demons with eagle heads on human bodies stood in a semi-circle around her. More lined the walls, too many to count, bone armor against ebony skin and thick muscles. Each carried a spear, their sharp serrated tips reminding her of a giant shark tooth she'd seen at the aquarium once. Quinn met the glare of Lilith's inhuman silver eyes and held them, chin up, heart knocking against her chest.

Show no fear. Show no fear.

Two wraith-like guards broke formation and seized Quinn. Wrenching her arms behind her back, they dragged her across the floor and pushed her to kneel in front of their master.

"Is that any way to treat our honored guest?" Lilith tutted. "She has come to set your brethren free. Isn't that right?" Quinn jerked her arms free as the guards took a step back, their avian eyes constantly shifting and turning in their sockets and stood tall in front of her enemy.

Lilith descended her throne and paced in a circle around Quinn, scrutinizing every inch of her body. "I don't see what's so special about you. An insignificant girl, no more than a child." She laughed. "Eve was not all she seemed either. I will not make the mistake of underestimating you as I did her. Let's not waste time. Today is a special day, and I have a very special gift for you."

Lilith clapped twice, and Quinn's breath caught in her throat as Aaron stepped from behind a column to stand next to Lilith's throne. His face looked gaunt and drawn. Dark circles swallowed his eyes. They had taken him, but not without a fight. Blood coated his left wing and matted his sunset feathers into dark red clumps. Scratches covered every inch of him, welts, and bruises too. An armored collar pulsed around his neck. His green eyes stared at her, unfocused, unseeing, and in his hands, he held a mahogany box.

"Aaron?"

He didn't even blink. She reached out with her essence to touch his, but instead of the familiar warmth, she was greeted with a cold, hard edge. Quinn bit her lip as hard as she could and swallowed the guilt that threatened to drown her.

"He can't hear you," Lilith said. "Unless I allow him to. Which I won't."

Quinn's throat constricted, muscles tensed, calculating how many seconds it would take to wrap her hands around Lilith's neck, and took a step forward.

"Make one more move, and I promise I will make him suffer." Lilith draped an arm across Aaron's shoulders and narrowed her eyes, stopping Quinn in her tracks.

"See, if you're reasonable, I'm reasonable." Lilith flipped her shadowed cape and lounged back on her onyx throne. A goblet sat on a table beside it. She swirled the cup and took a drink. This was her show, and she wanted Quinn to know it.

Setting the cup back on the table, she said, "I wasn't sure you would come, Quinn. For one brief second, I thought you would listen to that Sentinel of yours and run to Arcadia to hide while everyone you loved died. Better if you had, but I was certain you wouldn't let the boy languish in my keeping. Seems I was right. Where is that traitor, Azrael, anyway?" A wry smile played across her lips. "I didn't think he would want to miss this."

"Sorry I'm late to the party, Lilith." Azrael strode through the doors, fingers caressing the pommels of his swords. Blood smeared his face, splattered his bare chest. Human blood, or demon? Cold dread crept up Quinn's spine, and it took all her resolve to keep from grabbing Azrael's sword and stabbing him with it.

Not now. Azrael's thought was a sharp arrow straight to her mind, but when she tried to reply, she hit a powerful wall. If something happened to Reese, Marcus, or Caleb, she would never forgive him, or herself.

"Ah, Azrael. What a surprise. I hoped you were otherwise

engaged." Lilith sighed and took another sip from her cup, unfazed by his sudden appearance.

"Your distraction was but a trifle," Azrael said.

Lilith shrugged. "You can hardly blame me for trying, old friend. I'm not sure where your loyalties lie. I couldn't risk your interference now, could I? I do hope there wasn't too much bloodshed." Her words dripped with sarcasm.

"The casualties are none of my concern. I did what was required. I am here for a greater purpose, or did you forget our deal?" He looked at Quinn, golden eyes burning bright, and Lilith's followed.

Show no weakness. Focus. Lilith wouldn't hesitate to seize on any little negative thought. Quinn shifted her emotions like Azrael taught her, keeping her mind fluid, never settling on one particular feeling or thought for more than a millisecond. Lilith frowned as if disappointed and turned back to Azrael.

"I already ensured your place as her Sentinel and promised you a seat on my council. What more do you want?" Lilith asked.

"I want the kingdom of Arcadia for myself, and I want Kaemon. He has been a thorn in my side for far too long. Release him to me, and I will help you kill the girl myself." Azrael shifted slightly, positioning himself beside and a little in front of Quinn.

"No. It can't be," Quinn growled, her hands balling into fists at her sides. "I read you. You swore your loyalty. I felt the truth in your essence."

"Oh, Quinn, you little fool. I've been at this game far longer than you." He patted her cheek. "Did you really think I would settle for whatever scraps The Light throws at me? I am sick of being a pawn, and sick of your whining. Arcadia has always been my end game."

Quinn spat in his face, and he wiped saliva from his chin, grinning.

"Very ambitious." Lilith leaned forward and drummed her fingers on the armrest, silver nails clacking against stone. "King of Arcadia and Kaemon as your slave? I'm sure we can come to some kind of arrangement."

"No. You can't!" Quinn took two steps up before Lilith's guards restrained her, dragging her away from their mistress. She jerked and pulled against them, straining to break free, but they had the strength of ten men, and Quinn was powerless, devoid of magic, a normal girl facing powers beyond her imagination. "Please. You promised. My life for Aaron's." Quinn's voice echoed against the arched ceiling. "I don't care what happens to Arcadia, or to me, but he is to leave this place unharmed."

"Ah, and so the sacrifice speaks." Lilith rose from her seat and descended the stairs until she was eye to eye with Quinn. "I've been watching you, Quinn. You don't seem that surprised by Azrael's betrayal." She grabbed Quinn's jaw and squeezed. "It all seems a little too convenient."

Fighting the urge to wrench her face away, Quinn took a deep breath and steadied her voice as best she could. "I had my suspicions. Too bad your distraction left him intact," Quinn spat. "Azrael is a liar and no friend of mine. I hope he rots here." Her thoughts shifted like the wind, never still. Lilith had to believe that she believed Azrael's betrayal. Thoughts were wind, were water, were smoke.

Glare to glare, Lilith studied Quinn, then laughed a full belly laugh. "Oh, I like you, Quinn. If only you didn't have to die. We might have been good friends, you and I, if the circumstances were different. Well, Azrael, looks like your little ward is all grown up and thinking for herself. A convincing little actress indeed, but a master liar can always smell deceit, and her breath reeks of it."

"She is nothing to me. A spoiled, selfish child." Azrael spread his wings, chest puffing up in defiance. One hand reached for the Qeres blade, muscles tense as he shifted his weight forward ever so slightly, circling to block Quinn from Lilith's view.

"I'm sorry, Azrael, but I can't have you suddenly overcome by your Sentinel duty, now can I? I've seen how strong that bond can be. Lack of trust is one of my flaws, you understand, and you are a wild card." Before Azrael could pull his blade fully from his scabbard, a demon, four feet long with an armored body and a million legs scurried up his leg and over his shoulder to fasten around his neck. Azrael's shoulders slumped, eyes glazed, just like Aaron.

Lilith grabbed Azrael's leather sword belt and pulled him close. He didn't even flinch as she undid the knotted buckle and slid his weapons from his hips and handed them to her guard. "A gift for you, Ikkatat."

The guard nodded and fastened the belt to his own waist then bowed before his master.

"And feel free to use them if he moves." She patted Azrael on the shoulder, and Quinn thought she saw his jaw tighten. "Part of me does hope you'll move, though," she whispered in his ear, "I do love watching angels' wings wither and fall, like leaves from a tree, when struck with Qeres."

"You have what you wanted." Hate writhed in Quinn, and she struggled to remain calm. "I am here of my own free will, not because of his tricks or yours. My life for Aaron's. That's what was promised."

Lilith raised her hands to the ceiling and cried, "And the voice of the sacrifice will break the lock! Let it be heard that the voice of the sacrifice has spoken!" The demons pounded their spears against the tile. "Selflessness becomes you, Quinn. My children thank you." With a wave of Lilith's hand, ropes of fog wound around Quinn's ankles and looped around her wrists, binding them in front of her. She didn't fight it.

"The deal is sealed. You have me, now let Aaron go." Quinn's voice boomed, powerful, commanding.

Lilith raised an eyebrow. "Let him go? There is no other place for him, this half-angel, half-human hybrid. His essences are not fit for any other realm. Would you have me toss him out into the seam to wander the void for eternity? And they call me cruel."

"For the box to open, I have to sacrifice myself for him. That's how it works." Sweat trickled down Quinn's back, her mouth dry as a bone.

"You have to be willing to sacrifice yourself, which you are. That is all." Lilith ran a finger across Aaron's cheek. "Besides, you don't want to leave me, do you, Kaemon?" A pained expression skirted Aaron's face as Lilith pressed her lips to his. He pulled her close, hands caressing her spine, fingers entwined in her hair, mouth hungry on hers. Quinn looked away, a tear forming in the corner of her eye. That wasn't Aaron; neither was he Kaemon, the fierce angel who stole Eve's heart. They were nothing more than a puppet, a toy Lilith used to hurt Quinn, to rip apart her heart.

"That's enough now, my love." Lilith pulled away and patted Aaron's bare chest. "We have eternity to spend together. No need to be greedy."

Aaron bowed, awkward and halting, the thing around his neck pulsing at Lilith's command.

"Let's get started, shall we? No need to wait any longer." She took the box from Aaron and placed it next to the cup on the table. From her belt, she drew a long knife, metal singing as it came loose from the scabbard, and placed it in Aaron's open palm. "You do the honors, my love."

Aaron's hands trembled; his face flickered from placid to pained as he descended the three steps of the platform, each step a little more hesitant than the last. He wouldn't do it, couldn't, not Aaron. Quinn stood still as the cold tip pressed against her neck. She tried to meet his eyes, to connect, but his gaze edged hers. The blade dug deeper yet didn't cut. Warm breath, in, out, in, out, unsteady on her cheek.

Trembling, she cupped his chin, and he blinked. A spark ignited between them, and she felt his essence fight to gain control. *Hold onto him, hold tight,* she reminded herself, and hope surged pure and true.

Aaron. His essence called to her like a beacon. She wasn't alone. Aaron was in there somewhere, she just had to reach him. He needed her; she needed him. Together they could get out of this. Lilith watched intently, so Quinn kept her expression calm.

Aaron, her essence whispered to his. *I love you. Don't let her do this.* Aaron's hand shook, his jaw tight. The collar around his neck pulsed, and he dragged the blade down until it rested above her hammering heart. A tear slid from his eye and down his cheek, and that's when Quinn felt the knife enter her flesh.

32

*A*aron couldn't bear the sick, sucking sound the knife made when he pulled it from Quinn's body, the way his hand gripped the handle, the way his flesh reacted to Lilith's every command. Blood bloomed like a wild rose across Quinn's chest, staining her white T-shirt pink, red. Wide, violet-blue eyes stared into his, and he couldn't look away. Lilith wanted him to be still and watch, a sentient statue as Quinn's warm, red life force oozed out onto the tiled floor and pooled around his bare feet.

Crushing weight squeezed Aaron's lungs, and he wanted to cry, to rip his gaze away from the light dimming in Quinn's eyes as she stumbled forward, reaching for him. Instinct screamed to catch her, to pull her into his arms and comfort her, but Lilith's power still constrained him.

"What a fitting end to such a tragic love story." Lilith descended from her throne, box in hand, and knelt next to Quinn. Pressing one palm into the blood, she coated her skin in crimson gore then smeared the red upon the wooden casket that held her children. Moans and screams rose and fell from within the demons' prison, the ancient runes blazing to life, gold and blue. A lock appeared where none was before, and with a click, a sliver of smoke slithered from a crack in the lid. Placing the quivering box in the center of the room, Lilith took a step back as Quinn's sacrifice birthed her children, dark and writhing, into the world.

Quinn swayed against Aaron, lips parted, breath ragged. Her head sagged to her chest as her heart slowed. He could feel it through their bond, its beat counting down the seconds until she lost consciousness. No pain, nothing but a cold numbness spreading outward from her breast, to her torso, her legs.

Inside, Aaron's essence beat against his useless body, yelled at his feet to move, pleaded with his arms to catch her before she fell, begged his fist to ram the blade into Lilith's back as she watched the demons emerge from that cursed box, anything but this passive spectating. But the more he squirmed, the tighter Lilith grasped him. Even the tears building up behind his eyes, she denied him.

Fingers caressed Aaron's cheek, slid down his neck, and came to rest on the armored control demon wrapped around his throat. It pulsed and squirmed, pumping an unending flow of venom into his system that made it impossible for him to act on his own initiative.

"Hadavar," Quinn rasped the demon's name while Lilith was distracted with her brood. A current of light leapt from her hand straight into the demon's body, and it fell from Aaron's neck, turning to ash at his feet. Aaron willed his fist to open, and the knife clattered across the hard floor.

He was free.

Quinn smiled at him. The most intense feeling of love he'd ever felt emanated from her essence to his, and then her eyes closed, knees buckling, the last of her energy spent on him. He pressed her limp body to his and lowered her to the floor.

A PART of Quinn understood as she crumpled to the floor, her life pouring from a gaping wound in her chest, that Lilith used her blood to fulfil the prophecy. No escape from destiny, from fate. Many paths led to the same end. She understood that now as her essence ebbed and faded, the light within winking out, but Quinn didn't regret her path, her choice. Aaron, Quinn, it didn't matter whose blood spilled today. Lilith would have opened the box no matter what. A willing sacrifice was all she needed.

Aaron's anger, white-hot and blinding, reeled against her. His green eyes, wide and frightened, held hers, and she wanted to tell him it would be all right, that she wouldn't have it any other way. But she couldn't force the words from her mouth. Freeing him made her happy, and this wasn't the end, she could see that now. Loopholes within loopholes. Aaron was the key, the linchpin to restoring balance. Eyes, heavy with lead weights, slammed shut. Her legs wouldn't hold her weight anymore, and she sensed she was falling, powerless to stop herself. Darkness, absolute and unending, spread out before her, and she embraced it as she drifted into unconsciousness.

"I TOLD YOU TO STAY AWAY," Aaron whispered in Quinn's ear as he rocked her, brushing a blond hair from her pale face. "Damn you, Quinn. Why didn't you listen to me?" Tears coursed down his cheeks, dripped from his nose, all the emotions he'd been forced to hold in racing to the surface. "You're so stupid, and stubborn, and selfish sometimes. Do you know that?"

Aaron pressed his body against hers, willed her to open

her eyes, something, anything, but she didn't respond. So much blood. Everywhere he looked. Warm and sticky against his chest. It covered his arms, soaked his hands. Clenching his fist his red-stained nails dug into his palms. Quinn's blood on his hands.

Sulfur choked the air. Aaron covered his nose with the tip of a golden wing and looked up. A mushroom cloud, gray and billowing, shot upward from the opened box. It spread across the domed ceiling, rolled down the walls and across the floor. From within the gathering smoke, demons materialized and formed a circle around them.

Restless from a lifetime of imprisonment, the demons snarled and hissed at one another, all seeking the attention of their dark mother. Lilith stood in the center of the rotunda, arms outstretched, face turned to the sky as she chanted. A crack opened above her, the seam between the Underworld and the human realm ripped open, revealing the sun being eaten by the moon, the eclipse well underway.

"Behold, my loves, a feast awaits you!" Lilith cried.

Fights broke out between brethren as they surged forward. A cloven hoof clomped against the side of Quinn's head, scratching the side of her face. Another clipped her hip as the demons jockeyed for position. Spear butts pounded the ground around them, too close for Aaron's comfort. Creating a canopy with his wings, Aaron hunched over Quinn and dragged her backward through the stampede of talons and paws, hiding her behind a large pillar and away from the crowd gathering around the open portal. One last look at Quinn's pale face, and he folded her arms over her chest and kissed her forehead.

"I'll make them pay. I swear." Trading grief for anger, he let Kaemon's full power rise to the surface and consume him in vengeful wildfire. Fireworks of rage exploded in him, and he sprang into a crouch, chest heaving, wings spread wide.

They would all pay, each of them torn to pieces, with his bare hands if he had to, for what they'd done to Quinn, to Marcus, to his home.

A murderous battle cry clawed its way from the pit of his stomach and ripped from his lungs as he raced forward, scooped up the discarded knife, and launched himself into the air.

Like a bullet, he flew straight and true. Nothing would keep him from his target. Demons lunged for him, only to meet a swift swipe of a muscled wing. Some took to the air in chase, but none had the power of anger behind him.

Lilith turned at the commotion too late. Aaron slammed into her, and they tumbled head over feet in a tangle of wings and shadow. Pure hate gave him the advantage, and he forced Lilith to the ground, grabbing her wrists in one swift motion and pinning them above her head. Anger pulsed against his chest. Cold steel flashed in the torchlight as he raised the knife, still wet with Quinn's blood, and plunged it straight into her chest.

A laugh, cruel and mocking, bubbled from her lips. Aaron sat back on his knees, chest heaving, jaw clenched. Clutching the blade in both hands, he raised his arms over his head once more and channeled all his loathing into the blow. Stabbing her chest was like driving a nail through vapor. Silver eyes, calm as frozen lakes, stared up at him. Her full lips turned up in a maddening, sly grin. Again, he raised the knife, and again he stabbed down with no effect, over and over until his muscles ached and sweat ran down his forehead.

"Are you finished now?" Lilith's body disappeared from beneath him in a puff of smoke and reappeared to his left. She placed a calm hand on his shoulder and pried the knife from his clenched fist. Lilith's army encircled them, a wall of shifting shadows and raised weapons.

"Did you really think I would be so stupid as to put a Qeres blade in your hand? Human steel can do nothing to one such as me." She twirled the blade between her palms and returned it to the sheath strapped to her thigh. "Prophecy has been fulfilled. The girl is gone, and soon my children will feast on your precious humans. Even you can't ruin this beautiful moment for me."

Aaron's muscles rippled and tensed. His wings itched, and he shifted into a low crouch keeping his eye on Lilith as she paced around him.

"I grow weary of this game, Kaemon." Lilith smoothed a strand of raven hair from her eyes and held out her palm. Dark energy pulsed outward, hitting him with the force of a train. Pain exploded between his shoulder blades as he slammed against the granite throne, the air rushing from his lungs. He gulped and fought to regain his breath. Tendrils shot upward, tethering his ankles and wrists in tight knots to the seat.

Lilith nodded to Ikkatat, the captain of her silver guard, and Kaemon's own Qeres blade came loose from its scabbard. It sang to him, called to him like an old friend. He worked at his bonds, praying the small movement of his wrists unnoticed by Lilith. Getting to that blade meant his life.

"How much more Qeres poison do you think your immortal essence can take, Kaemon? How much can Aaron's human spirit absorb before it succumbs as well?"

Ikkatat approached, blue runes glowing through the smoke-filled room, and settled the tip of the blade right above Aaron's left wing. Ikkatat flourished the blade, separating a single golden feather from his wing. Aaron gritted his teeth against the pain and watched the golden feather turn gray, then black, then fall to ash at his feet. Another twist of pain, another feather gone.

"I would love to experiment myself, but as you can see, I have my hands full. I'll leave it to Ikkatat to take you apart, one feather at a time to test the boundaries." With a wave of her hand, the surrounding mist morphed into a set of foggy steps leading through the crack in the ceiling. Lilith led the ascent, followed by her silver guard, each beating their spears against bone armor, calling their brethren to follow. One by one, the shadows pushed their way through the ever-widening fracture and disappeared into the human realm.

33

A hand pressed against Quinn, hot, urgent, and frantic. She wanted to tell the hand to leave her alone, to let her sleep, but it wouldn't stop touching her. If she could, she would have slapped the thing away. *Leave me to my destiny*, she thought, sinking back into oblivion, but the thing wouldn't let her go. An ache pinched her chest. It poked her consciousness as it spread through her body and filled all the hollow places. Intense pain, blinding, burning, lanced through her, and all her muscles tensed at once. Arching her back, she sucked searing air back into her lungs and screamed. A hand clamped over her mouth, and she kicked and writhed beneath strength greater than her own.

For The Light's sake, Quinn, stop struggling, and let me heal you. Black wings came into focus, hovering like an inky umbrella above her. *Do you know how hard it is to replicate your blood? That was only the beginning. Your heartbeat is still erratic, and the knife grazed your heart. I still have that to fix.* Concentration knitted Azrael's forehead. Molten eyes glowed through the gray and ominous smoke that swirled around him. The box, she remembered. Demons unleashed from their prison. She had to stop them. A cacophony of bone-chilling shrieks and cries rose and fell amidst the ever-shifting fog. She moved to sit up, but Azrael had her pinned to the floor.

There is nothing you can do to stop it now, Quinn. Lilith's army is already pushing through the veil. The Elite forces of the heavenly host have been called to war, ready to meet them. Westland has already fallen.

My friends. My mom. Jake. Panic stabbed her heart, its beat pounding her chest like a sledgehammer. Numbness spread from her left arm and squeezed tight around her lungs. Black devoured the edges of her vision.

Quinn. Calm down! Your heart is not strong enough yet. Azrael's harsh tone scared her. His fingers stroked her hair, his thoughts a mad rush of calming visions leapt into her mind—oceans, kittens playing with a ball of string, palm trees. From his left arm, he untied a leather cuff, part of his armor, and forced it into her mouth.

Try to hold as still as you can. Azrael rubbed his palms together and placed them on top of her breastbone. *Deep breath now. It's going to sting.* Warm fuzzy blankets, rain on the roof, a field of wildflowers—anything to distract her from the incoming strike. Lightning fried her insides, and she bit down. All her muscles convulsed, and her eyes rolled back in her head. She couldn't stop herself.

Please, I can't take anymore, please, Azrael, please, she begged.

Every muscle violently convulsed with the burning agony of Azrael's healing touch to her heart. Her back arched in defiance, fists opened and closed, stomach rolled. Death was easier than this fight for life.

The best thing you can do for your friends, for your family, is let me heal you so that you can use your powers to turn the tide. Caleb and the others are waiting. They're still alive. They need you,

Quinn. Now, take one more deep breath. Another rush of current seared through her, and the pain eased.

Energy flowed through her now, her power intact, and she felt better than she ever had before. Euphoric even. *I-I feel different,* Quinn stammered as she sat up

Hyperaware, she could sense them, all of them, pinpricks of darkness against a background of white light when she closed her eyes. Using her own blood to release Lilith's dark children from their prison ensured they were now linked, each of them, to Quinn. The voice of the sacrifice will break the lock, restoring darkness unto the light: that was the loophole in the prophecy.

Quinn couldn't help the grin spreading across her face. She—Eol Ananael, the essence of Eve, power made of the secret wisdom—was a black widow spider at the center of a shifting web. The demons couldn't move without alerting her to their presence, to their names. Fear and excitement thrummed through her essence. She sprang into a crouch, lithe as a jaguar. *Bring it on, Lilith.* The demons, nothing, could stop her; she was invincible.

Tread carefully, Quinn. We do not yet understand the full meaning of this. It could be nothing more than a side effect of the healing. Azrael sat back on his knees, his eyebrows drawn into a deep V. *Either way, you are still made of flesh that bleeds and bones that break. I caution against rash action.* He looked haggard, his usual olive complexion pale as ash, his inner light diminished. Wrinkles gathered around his dim eyes; his usual casual exterior replaced by something else. Fear. Real fear. And then she noticed a pile of black feathers around her like fallen leaves. Azrael folded his wings to hide the bald spots and looked away. *Never mind that now.* He met her eyes with a grim smile and stood.

Looks like your boyfriend's distraction may have worked a little too well. Azrael steadied himself against the column. She'd never seen him so frail, so dazed. *He's as foolish as he is hotheaded, but I guess I should thank him for keeping Lilith occupied while I made my escape. We must put our differences aside for the greater good.*

Aaron? Quinn cocked her head. The dense mist obscured her vision, but she didn't need to see him. She could sense him, their bond flaring to life the moment she wished it. *Don't worry about Aaron.* One thought, and her power seared through the ropes that bound him. This was going to be fun.

A swift kick to Ikkatat's knee, a cuff to the ear, and the Qeres blade found its way back into Aaron's hand. Quinn turned in the direction of a terrible hawk-like scream and smiled. *He's taking care of himself.*

She rubbed her hands together and opened her palms. A ball of golden light grew from the center of each, two tiny suns illuminating the darkness. Even the air around her crackled and sizzled from the voltage she emitted. The gray fog parted before her, twisting away from the light as fast as it could. Within seconds, the fog cleared completely to reveal an almost empty room.

Every demon followed Lilith up the smoky stairwell and into the human realm, leaving only Ikkatat to tie up any loose ends—and not very well, it seemed. Azrael took a step toward Aaron to help him, but Quinn shook her head. Aaron wanted this kill, needed it.

She folded her arms to watch a true warrior at work. With Kaemon's skills, he was magnificent, fluid as water, smooth as cream, as if he'd been born with a sword in his hand. Kaemon, she had to remind herself. Qeres blade shining bright blue in one hand, Azrael's golden soul blade in the other, Aaron parried each of Ikkatat's spear jabs.

Left, right, head, knee, Ikkatat advanced, the spear's reach longer than that of the sword. But it was heavier, too. The next strike pulled Ikkatat off balance, leaving his left flank open. Quick as a tornado, Aaron used his wings to launch into the air, spun the Qeres star-blade in a wide arc, and slashed down. Before he could bring up his spear to block Aaron's blow, Ikkatat's eagle head fell at his feet and exploded in a cloud of ash.

Chest heaving, Aaron dropped the sword and looked at Quinn with intense green eyes. Closing the ten-foot distance between them in a rush of steps, he scooped her up in a tight embrace. Fingers grasped her shirt, dug into her flesh. She, in turn, wrapped her arms around his neck, the protective dam she'd built around her heart splintering at his touch, and she let it all out, the fear, the shame, the joy. Every kiss an apology, every heartbeat a promise.

He pressed her against him, his wings beating the air in giant swoops. Tears streaked through the blood and dirt that smeared his face, and he buried his head in her hair, murmuring her name over and over. One thought flowed into the next as their essences converged. Their souls stood naked in front of each other, vulnerable, more intimate than anything she'd ever felt before. Each past mistake melted away in the wake of his warm lips on hers. Hungry and rough, it lit her skin on fire, a burning so bright and so beautiful that she never wanted it to end.

Her hands found his bare chest, the heat rising between them so hot she thought she might combust. No place to hide, no secrets left to bury, no words needed. This is what it was like to know and be known, to love and be loved, to see another's soul so completely that even the ugly parts radiated as perfection. No darkness could stand between them, not anymore.

I hate to interrupt your reunion, but there's still the small matter of Lilith and the demon horde.

Quinn literally wanted to kill Azrael for throwing water on her perfect moment. One moment of happiness, one moment not to think about the insurmountable task ahead of them, was that too much to ask? Damn Azrael.

Ignoring him, she let Aaron pull her hips to his as she drew out their kiss just a little longer. Azrael's annoyance beat against her essence like a fist on a door. He cleared his throat and coughed, this time gaining all of Aaron's attention and his ire. Narrowed green eyes turned on Azrael. If looks could kill, Azrael would be dead.

"He saved my life," Quinn reminded Aaron. She laced her fingers with his and sent him calming thoughts until his muscles relaxed and his grip on her hand eased. Not exactly forgiveness, but at least tolerance. She could work with tolerance.

Azrael, still a bit pale and unsteady, kicked at the pile of dust that was once Lilith's fiercest guard and retrieved his leather sword belt. Fastening it around his hips, he picked up his own golden soul sword, wiped it with the end of the red sash tied around his waist, and returned it to the scabbard. Now, only the Qeres blade still lay next to Ikkatat's remains. Aaron's jaw worked, eyes blazing, as Azrael's palm hovered over the carved hilt.

Reverently, Azrael recovered the sword, blowing ash from its curved surface. The edge of his lips twitched and his shoulders heaved. Placing the flat of the blade across his palms, he knelt before Aaron and extended the sword up until it was parallel with his face.

"Know that everything I did was for the greater good, done at The Light's bidding." Though Azrael's attempt at an apology rang true, it still held a hint of distain.

Contrition doesn't come easily to this fierce creature, Quinn thought, *but it will have to do*. She would need both of her Sentinels watching her back to set things right.

Aaron rubbed the back of his neck, looked at Quinn, and grinned. That's when she realized just how much she'd missed that easy smile. With one hand, Aaron took the blade, its blue runes blazing with his touch. The other hand, he offered to Azrael.

This was the boy she loved. Kaemon might be quick to righteous anger, but Aaron's compassion tempered the warrior's spirit. Everything they had both been through brought them to this moment, changed them. They were steel made stronger in the heat of the fire, and together they would strike.

"Now what?" Aaron asked.

"Lilith was counting on Quinn being taken out of the game," Azrael said.

"Then she must continue to believe Quinn's gone," Aaron added.

"Arcadia." Azrael nodded. "We will take her there. Regroup with The Light's battalions."

"Buy us time to come up with a strategy," Aaron agreed.

Absorbed in her own thoughts, Quinn looked up through the crack in the ceiling. Angels crossed the sky in great golden arcs, meteorites falling to earth to meet their enemy. The moon, its path frozen when the veil fell, masked the sun. Only a faint white halo remained.

"No, we're not going to Arcadia. We're going to Eden."

"Eden? Quinn, are you crazy? There's nothing there." Aaron shook his head.

"Let Lilith focus on The Light, let Arcadia believe I'm gone. Let all of them believe I'm out of the equation." Quinn's voice rang out across the empty rotunda.

Darkness called to her, demons, thousands upon thousands, hungry, so hungry. Saliva dripped from the corner of Quinn's mouth, and her stomach growled with the thought. Humans by the millions waited, their secret shames ready to feast upon—a never-ending supply of misery to harvest and enslave. To the demons, humans were nothing but food to soothe their insatiable appetites, but she was hungry, too, and they had no idea what was coming.

"Trust me, while they fight for control, we'll take the demons out, one by one." She took Aaron's hand, and turned to Azrael. "Together." She smiled. Quinn was the predator, and they were her prey. Nowhere to hide, she would track down every last one of them and send them back to hell where they belonged.

And then I'm coming for you, Lilith, Quinn thought. *Oh, yes, I'm coming for you.*

ACKNOWLEDGMENTS

As always, OF DARKNESS DROWNING would not be possible with my amazing editor, Courtney Koshel, who believed in Quinn and Aaron's story, and my ability to tell it, even when I didn't.

Thank you to my family, both American and Scottish. I am so blessed to have such an amazing support system. Your love and encouragement help get me through the dark days. I love each of you more than I can express.
Thank you to my wonderful critique partner in crime, Sarah Johnson, who took the time to give me feedback and talk me off ledge after ledge. I've learned so much form sharing my work with you.

Thank you to the support of my new publishing home, Snowy Wings publishing and to Cammie Larson for the stunning cover design.

And, last but not least, a special thanks to my loving husband,

ACKNOWLEDGMENTS

who works hard so that I can purse my dreams. David, you are my strength and calling in a storm. I love and appreciate you more than word can say.

ABOUT THE AUTHOR

Heather L. Reid is both American and British and has called six different cities in three different countries home. Her strong sense of wanderlust and craving for a new adventure mean you might find her wandering the moors of her beloved Scotland, exploring haunted castles, or hiking through a magical forest in search of fairies and sprites. When she's not venturing into the unknown in her real life, she loves getting lost in the worlds of video games or curling up by the fire with a good story. For now, this native Texan is back in the Lone Star State, settling down with her Scottish husband and dreaming up new novels to write.

Website: www.heatherlreid.com
IG: @heatherreidbooks

Lightning Source UK Ltd.
Milton Keynes UK
UKHW010625081020
371236UK00002B/65